FEEDING MRS. MOSKOWITZ

AND

THE CAREGIVER

Library of Modern Jewish Literature

FEEDING MRS. MOSKOWITZ
• Barbara Pokras •

AND

THE CAREGIVER
• Fran Pokras Yariv •

Two Stories

SYRACUSE UNIVERSITY PRESS

First Edition 2010

10 11 12 13 14 15   6 5 4 3 2 1

Disclaimer: The characters in these novellas are fictitious.
Any resemblance to actual individuals is purely coincidental.

∞ The paper used in this publication meets the minimum requirements
of the American National Standard for Information Sciences—Permanence
of Paper for Printed Library Materials, ANSI Z39.48-1992.

For a listing of books published and distributed by Syracuse University Press.
visit our Web site at SyracuseUniversityPress.syr.edu

ISBN: 978-0-8156-0978-0

Library of Congress Cataloging-in-Publication Data

[CIP copy to come]

Manufactured in the United States of America

CONTENTS

FEEDING MRS. MOSKOWITZ
* Barbara Pokras *

THE CAREGIVER
* Fran Pokras Yariv *

FEEDING MRS. MOSKOWITZ

• Barbara Pokras •

To Bob Malkin, my husband and my "angle," love forever, and to Mildred, "unique in every way."

Barbara Pokras is an Emmy award–winning film editor and a member of American Cinema Editors, Inc., Motion Picture Editors Guild, and New York Women in Film and Television. She was an adjunct professor in the Cinema Department of the University of Southern California (1995–97) and is a graduate of that university.

Barbara and husband, Bob Malkin, live in Upstate New York, where she writes for the Woodstock Film Festival, grows organic vegetables, and always keeps a pot of soup on the stove in winter.

Acknowledgments

To friends old and new who have read and commented on this work, especially Dolly Fendell Gordon and Emily Adelsohn Corngold. Rabbi Ted Falcon provided inspiration and connected me to my spiritual roots. Dr. Anne Anzel Lawrence helped in many ways. Los Angeles friends Andrea Scharf, Ron Raley and Patricia E. Raley, and Janet Oberman Takeyama are dear to me still. I value the friendship of Mark Swed.

Roberta Allen deserves special mention. Her classes and workshops provided much needed motivation. There is no more generous or loyal a friend than Phyllis Prinz. My gifted writing group, Robin Kramer, Charlotte Scherer, Bennett Neiman, Mercedes Miranda, and Tom Cherwin gave useful feedback. Rei Fraas and Harriet Livanthinos provide friendship, humor, and support. Nancy Jainchill, Ph.D, enriches my life. Nancy Malkin Doall and Margie Juszczak give love, encouragement, and family. Golde acquired some of the characteristics of Jennie Baer, my grandmother. Hers was a soft bosom to embrace, and I don't think she ever yelled at me, even when I wet the bed. Louie Baer was the gentlest man I ever knew.

As a film editor, I have spent many years in the dark. I am all the more appreciative of the constant encouragement of my sister, Fran Yariv. Fran, you are truly a force! Our mother would be proud!

I am indebted to Mona Hamlin, Annelise Finegan, D. J. Whyte, and Lynn Hoppel of S.U. Press for their enthusiasm and attention to detail. Jeanne Rebillard, your insightful comments and expertise helped move this project along.

And most of all, to Bob. You love everything I write, and for that and much, much more, you have won my heart forever.

The Accident

It shouldn't be so terrible, just a few things I need." Golde Moskowitz knew if she didn't take the empty cans with her, she wouldn't remember. So many things to remember, achh! And so hot! You wouldn't think the heat would be so bad; you'd think the heat could warm the bones, make the arthritis feel better. But no, can you believe it? The heat was as bad as the cold!

Golde rinsed the little empty can from the peas and scrubbed the tin from the sardines so it shouldn't smell like fish. She cut off the label from the empty wax-paper box, and threw the rest in the trash. And the little jar of Alka-Seltzer with only one tablet left, that, too, she stuffed in her pocketbook along with the old *TV Guide*, so she wouldn't forget to get the new one.

"Okay," she thought, as she looked around the apartment and wrapped the strap of the pocketbook three times around her wrist so no one on the street could grab it from her. "I think I got it all." And with that Golde left, early in the morning, to do a little shopping. She locked the door from the inside and the outside, and then she checked it twice, and went back to check it again when she got to the sidewalk just to be sure. What would happen next, you wouldn't believe!

Mornings were tough for Natalie. Was it the angle of the sun? The private and terrifying knowledge of living in a city built on sand? Of desert shifting beneath her feet? A certain malaise seemed always a part of Los Angeles, where time passed like vapors, seeming to leave nothing behind. It was especially disquieting after therapy. Everything seemed to hint at a kind of relentless cheeriness. It filled her with an irritation impossible

6

to shake, all the more so for the guilt it produced—guilt at feeling bad in such a wonderland, palm trees and swimming pools, movie stars and limousines, a land of other people's dreams.

Wasn't therapy supposed to help? Why did it have to bring up feelings she wished she could ignore, especially about Rose, the mother she never understood, the mother who had the audacity to die before she could be known? Even though nearly a year had passed since the death, the grief was still fresh, like a raw spot inside that wouldn't heal.

Traffic ground to a halt. The route along the Wilshire corridor was even more congested than usual. She rolled down the car window, peering out to see what was causing the delay. A whoosh of hot, sultry air invaded the cocoon of her car. She heard the drone of construction up ahead, jackhammers and dirt scoopers. Monstrous machines, frightening mechanical dinosaurs, insatiable, ripping streets, devouring buildings, spewing black smoke and bits of concrete.

Rolling the window back up, she surrendered to the helplessness of living in a boom town. The constancy of building and rebuilding, tearing things down and digging things up, made her feel uncomfortable, unsettled.

She felt, rather than saw, the eyes of the man in the next car staring at her. Turning to the right, she saw him. Fiftyish, balding, stocky build. Invasive, arrogant eyes of a man nesting in his Mercedes sports car, top down. For a brief moment, she thought she might know him. A dentist she once used? A neighbor in her condominium? She knew she was mistaken the instant their eyes met. He smirked and grabbed his crotch. She looked away, angry at the assault, angry that she allowed herself to be complicit in this little rape. And then he was gone, turning right with a piece of her, a piece she might have needed.

Should she have challenged him? What would Rose have done? Quickly look away, she imagined. Pretend it never happened. To Rose, men simply did not exist. Natalie couldn't recall hearing Rose talk about men, especially after the divorce.

It was hard to remember what he looked like. Funny, she remembered the bristly tweed of his herringbone jacket rubbing against her cheek when she was a little girl when he would swing her in the air. Harold died years after he left Rose, after he married a woman from another state, a stranger, a woman he married much too quickly after the divorce. Who could blame Rose for closing the door on any possibility of sex or intimacy with men? If she hadn't shut down, it might have made a difference. It might have created a bond between mother and daughter, a safe, pleasurable area for intimacy.

Thank God for Artie! Artie was a gift. But gifts are seldom free. The price for having Artie in her life was simply to forego expectations. A small price, it seemed, to reap the rewards of this extraordinary man, to savor the wit, the intelligence. To be devoured in bed, to taste the salt of his skin. Artie resisted commitment. He needed to be won. His tenderness toward her must certainly be the road leading to love. Would Rose have approved? Probably not.

What a loss, she thought, imagining Artie's arms sliding around her waist, feeling the contradiction of the warmth of his breath causing chills to run down her spine, a scary and exciting anticipation of what would soon occur. If only Rose had had a man she cared about the way Natalie cared about Artie.

Now it was too late. Too late to fix things. Too late for brunches and shopping trips, spontaneous meetings for coffee, the sort of things other daughters did with their mothers, the things she had postponed while waiting to feel strong and confident, waiting to become the daughter she sensed her mother really wanted. It seemed so crazy to be an orphan. Orphans were skinny little girls with dirty knees and kinky red hair and hand-me-down clothes, not thirty-six-year-old women with diaphragms and respectable jobs!

So easy to distract, to fiddle with the radio dial ". . . President Reagan met today with Middle East envoys . . ." Soon the sounds became voices streaming from a void, well modulated, anonymous, abstract. The rhythm of the radio became a river, and it pushed her along. Traffic eased. Passing the Beverly Hilton Hotel, its boxy white exterior sparkling, offering shelter to the rich, she turned onto Santa Monica Boulevard. The delay had been costly, and now all the traffic lights conspired against her. Impossible not to be late for work.

The red light at the intersection of Santa Monica and Fairfax was particularly long. An old lady wearing a plastic rain hat and carrying at least two purses and a shopping bag crossed in front of her. A couple of kids skateboarded behind her, disreputable little Fred Astaires doing a complicated dance twist that gave them the momentum to scale the bump of the curb. Natalie watched the plastic-headed lady cross safely to the sidewalk. Did eccentricity belong mostly to the old?

Was it easier when the inevitable invisibility of age set in? When the severing of human ties, the deaths of those held dear, created the splendid and terrifying isolation in which the bizarre becomes normal?

Natalie had so many thoughts in such a short time, she surmised that the light had turned green, so as she turned her head toward the stoplight she started to accelerate. Her foot barely pressed the pedal when she realized something was terribly wrong. There was resistance, a flash of something falling beneath the hood of the car. Then she heard the scream.

"My God, you hit an old lady! Are you crazy?"

Sure enough, Golde Moskowitz lay sprawled beneath Natalie Holtzman's dusty red Toyota.

All those years, the journey across continents, eyes that witnessed the reign of czars, Stalin and Roosevelt, revolutions, a child stillborn in the middle of an alien ocean, tossed over the side, sliding under strange waves, part of her, in the ocean still, straining, looking for the lost child, coming to America, coming to the land where streets were paved with gold. All those years, all that struggle, and for what? To lie on hot pavement, to lie in pain in a land still foreign, not really her own! And it all seemed more than she could bear.

So she bellowed, "Why? Why you do this to me? *Why?* I do everything right! *Everything!!!*"

Natalie had no answer. It was all happening too fast. Golde was struggling to get up, and Natalie was trying to keep her from moving, faint memories of lessons learned in high school first aid—or was it Girl Scouts?—just beyond her reach.

Golde, though short, was stocky and strong with rage. She pulled herself up and sat on the bumper of the Toyota.

"Somebody! Call the paramedics! Call the police!"

Natalie skimmed the edges of panic.

"You! Zooommmmm, zooommmmm, so fast!!! Why?"

Nothing was happening the way it should. Didn't this woman know that Natalie hadn't done it on purpose? Shouldn't she appreciate Natalie's efforts? Why didn't anyone help?

Golde sat baking on the bumper while Natalie tried to keep her calm. But Golde would not be placated.

"I'm sorry," begged Natalie, "It was an accident." The tremor in her voice was strange, unfamiliar, like a little creature living deep within, finally let out of its cage.

Bystanders hung around the perimeter for a while, curious, maybe even empathetic, but not getting involved. Involvement meant commitment, and commitment could be costly. Golde continued to groan. Someone yelled at Natalie.

"You're blocking traffic, lady. Pull over to the side."

Who would take pictures? What about witnesses? Where were the police? She spotted a bench under the canopy of a bus stop. Could she leave the old woman sitting there and then take off? Impossible! Too late to change this horrible dream.

Golde slid from rage to pain as she pulled up a grayish polyester pant leg to reveal a knee visibly swelling, unquestionably wounded.

"Look! Look what you did to me!" she moaned.

"I'm sorry! I didn't mean to hurt you . . ." But it wasn't enough. She knew Golde didn't believe her.

And as Golde bent to examine the wound, pain shot through her back and she writhed in agony, wailing against the assault, against Natalie, against a God who would do this to an old lady.

Natalie tried to quell the panic that came in waves. What if nobody came? What if no one had called the paramedics? She made a decision.

"I'll take you to the hospital," Natalie told the old woman. "It's only a few blocks to Cedars. Here, let me help you."

Golde, though, was not eager to be helped by this frail girl, the monster who had caused all the trouble. She was about to pull away when a young Hispanic man came over and helped Natalie get Golde into the car. Instinctively, Golde felt safer. Even if the girl hadn't done such an awful thing, Golde trusted men. They were the doctors, the educated ones. Even when they weren't so smart, they knew how to fix things. They were stronger, more capable. They were the ones who *davened* in shul while the women sat upstairs and kept quiet. Women stayed at home. They shopped, played canasta, cooked big meals, watched *Jeopardy.*

The man put the seat back up straight and though they placed Golde into the car very carefully, she yelped with pain. Natalie felt a peculiar familiarity with the damp weight of Golde's body. Golde's face contorted in pain as Natalie struggled to help with the seat belt. For an instant, their eyes connected. Golde's eyes were remarkably gray, like concrete, the same shade as her short, coarse hair.

Officer Davis took the report. He was a big-boned, lean hunk of a man with honest brown eyes and a gentle, knowing manner. He didn't seem to belong in the ill-fitting blue serge suit with sleeves just a tad short, and as he bent down to write, Natalie could see the thinning hair, the inevitability of baldness he didn't try to hide.

Was he forty? Forty-five?

She wondered what it would be like to be with him. She would learn to like football, and he'd take her to Italian restaurants with red vinyl booths. He wouldn't be complicated like Artie. They would get married. She'd fix big breakfasts and they'd meet after work for martinis. Later, they'd watch some TV and then tumble into bed, making easy, uncomplicated love.

Maybe they'd have a baby.

"We send one copy to your insurance company, and the other goes to Sacramento . . ."

His voice, so reassuring, made her feel this sort of thing happened every day. She felt her muscles start to relax. When he held out the clipboard with papers for her to sign, she noticed his wedding ring.

She erased the baby in her head.

The shot they gave Golde was starting to take effect. So much hustle-bustle! Everybody doing something, so busy! Like the market, or the shops on Fairfax. She knew they were working on a man who had a heart attack, and somebody who had been stabbed in a fight. Still, she wished they'd pay more attention to her. She liked it when the doctor came in. She could tell him about the crazy lady, the crazy lady who ran her over. And even though it hurt when he touched her, she could tell that he was a good doctor because he listened to her. But then he left and she didn't know how long they would leave her there, and she started to feel frightened. That's when they gave her the shot. And now she could drift, she could watch them move around, the young girls in white. She knew they wanted to take x-rays, that's why they wanted to keep her there. And anyway, how would she get home? Somebody had taken her purse, even though she didn't want them to. She knew she had change for the bus, and a five-dollar bill, and her glasses.

She had the medicine for her high blood pressure and the drops for her glaucoma. And some coupons for Ralph's and Thrifty Drug Store and the empty cans and the *TV Guide*.

Maybe they would keep her overnight. That would be okay. They could help her go to the bathroom. Anyway, the air conditioner in the apartment wasn't working, and when it did, it was too expensive to use. Golde hated the hot weather. It made her thighs stick together and she sweated under her breasts. It was hard to sleep in such heat.

When Joseph was alive he would drive them to the beach, and Golde would bring a thermos of iced tea and the glasses she saved from the jelly they used on their toast. They would pull their canvas backrests near the water and sit until it was almost dark and starting to get chilly. He would buy them ice cream, always the same flavors, strawberry for Golde and butter pecan for himself. They didn't need to talk the way people think you need to talk these days. Golde couldn't understand these Americans, always thinking what they had to say was so important!

Her eyes filled with tears thinking about Joseph, even though it was so hard toward the end, when he was so sick. Not that it was always so wonderful! There was plenty of struggle, it was no picnic. Still, to bury a husband in a strange land! She never thought it would happen to her.

"Mrs. Moskowitz?"

For a second Golde thought maybe someone would tell her they had found Joseph, he had come back to help her because he knew she was in trouble. She always suspected he wasn't really dead, that somebody else got put in the ground.

"Mrs. Moskowitz? Are you feeling well enough to tell me what happened?"

The voice was coming from the outside, not from inside of her as she had thought. She looked up.

"Mrs. Moskowitz? I'm Officer Davis."

She liked his voice. She could tell he would listen to her. She showed him what happened to her knee and told him about Joseph and how terrible it was to bury a husband. He brought her juice because the medicine was making her thirsty and the nurses weren't around. Then he asked her plenty of questions, you bet, and she got angry again and cried. Finally she got tired of crying, and Officer Davis said something kind and funny and she smiled at him.

Then the nurse came in and said, "Okay, Mrs. Moskowitz, it's time to go to x-ray," and she was sorry to leave such a nice man, but maybe he would come to visit her in her apartment on Hayworth. After all, it was right around the corner, and she could make tea and the little cookies Joseph liked.

The next thing she knew they were pushing her down the corridor, and she felt like she should be sitting up, she felt like a movie star.

The x-ray wasn't so bad, really, not so terrible. She fell asleep for a few minutes, just dozing, then she woke up and started to hurt again, not a lot like before, so they gave her some aspirin and told her she didn't break anything, thank God, she just got banged up real good, and could somebody come and sign her out so she could go home.

That's when she started to cry again, because she remembered there wasn't anybody she could call.

Natalie hung around after Officer Davis left. She was worried about Golde, and she knew she wouldn't be able to get any work done. She called her office. Christie answered.

"Brewer and Associates . . ."

"Christie, it's Natalie. There's been an accident . . ."

"Oh God! Are you okay?"

"Yes, but I'll be late . . ."

Christie would handle anything that came up. Natalie didn't want to talk about the accident, and luckily, Christie didn't pry. Christie was one of those young California blondes ad agencies use to decorate their reception areas. She was also truly sweet and competent in a non threatening way. She had been at the agency since before Natalie started her job in the art department. Natalie always felt Christie's good looks kept her from being taken seriously by the male executives. Christie didn't seem to mind, though. She wasn't very ambitious.

Once, she let Christie talk her into going for a drink after work. Christie chose "happy hour" at a Mexican restaurant. For Natalie it was neither. Christie was oblivious to Natalie's discomfort as she sipped an enormous margarita and picked the salt away with her impossibly long, bright red acrylic nails. Natalie asked her how she could work with them—they seemed to make her hands incapable of normal function.

"You learn to use your knuckles," Christie said.

Sure enough, Natalie began noticing Christie and other women with artificial nails doing exactly that—grasping, picking things up, gesturing not with fingers but with skillfully rehabilitated knuckles. It seemed a little like training an amputee to walk on prosthetic limbs.

The stale smell of the hospital reminded her of the "happy hour" night, and she knew she'd have to shower to get rid of the odor. Even then it would linger in her lungs and the lining of her nose, a reminder of the accident.

And what about the personal consequences, the practical matters of insurance and liability? Even more troubling were the barely discernible issues, the little inklings having to do with the ghost of Rose. Strange! She had never knowingly injured anyone, and then in a second, all that had changed. It seemed to her that in some crucial way her identity had changed with the accident. She had become someone else, someone with a shameful secret.

A chill ran through her and she thought about the heat, how oppressive it was outside. She thought about how uncomfortable it would be for Golde. Would she be able to walk? How would she sleep with the pain in her back? She suddenly felt a more personal responsibility. She couldn't just leave.

She walked over to the nursing station.

"Pardon me," she said to the nurse who seemed to be in charge. "How's Mrs. Moskowitz?"

"Are you a relative?"

It hadn't occurred to Natalie that she wouldn't have access to Golde. She simply had to know what was going on. She had to be able to help, so she lied.

"Yes," said Natalie calmly. "I'm her daughter."

Golde stopped crying and was about to tell Nurse Hernandez that she had no one to call when the strangest thing happened. Another nurse, Mrs. Taylor, a big, plum-black woman with pretty, oversized pearl-color glasses, came in and said, "You can get Mrs. Moskowitz ready for discharge. Her daughter is here."

Golde felt pretty certain she didn't have a daughter, but she thought maybe since Joseph couldn't come, he'd sent someone else, just so he could be sure she'd be taken care of. Anyway, she could use the five dollars for herself instead of spending it on the cab. She could buy some strawberry ice cream for the freezer, or get her hair set at the Paris Beauty Salon. She liked it when they wrapped her hair around the little plastic tubes with the holes in them. Then they would cover the rollers with a big, triangular net and stuff cotton around the sides so her face wouldn't burn.

"Okay Mrs. Moskowitz," the girl would say. "You can sit under the dryer."

They would give her magazines to look at and check her once in a while, like a turkey in the oven. The heat of the dryer would make her sleepy, and she'd doze off and imagine she was nineteen again and her waist was twenty-one inches around, and her hair was practically down to her knees.

Thinking about the beauty salon made her feel calmer. Maybe she'd get a rinse, too. She would tell them to be careful with her knee, the one that got hurt today, and they would roll a little plastic manicure stool over to the shampoo chair so she could use it for a footrest. She knew they'd watch out for her back.

So while they were wheeling her down the hall she thought maybe they were taking her to get her hair done. Maybe it didn't turn out so bad after all. When they got to the front desk, they gave her her purse and showed her that they didn't take anything, not even a single coupon, and they asked her to sign her name on some papers. They gave her some medicine for the pain and told her to come back in a week, they wanted to check her, and she figured that would be okay, she didn't have much to do these days. She looked around for the daughter Joseph had sent. She didn't see anyone.

But then she heard somebody say, "I'll take you home now," and she looked around and it was the crazy girl, the one who hit her with the car.

Golde didn't know what to say, because now she was feeling confused. Maybe Joseph sent this one because the daughter's car wasn't working. Anyway, all the nurses seemed so sad that she was leaving, she could tell they really liked her, that's why they wanted her to come back.

"Now, rest that knee, you hear Mrs. Moskowitz?"

"You take care, we'll see you next week!"

So she was busy saying 'good-bye' to them, and she figured okay, she'd let this girl take her home.

Though Golde whimpered when they put her in the car, she was nonetheless subdued from all the medication, and she mostly ignored Natalie.

"I'm going to take you home," Natalie said as they pulled away from the hospital. "Where do you live?"

Golde shot her a funny look, like she was trying to understand what was going on but couldn't quite grasp it. She was sweating, the heat was thick, like jelly. She knew now she wasn't going to the beauty parlor, but she thought Joseph made a big mistake sending the crazy girl to drive her around.

"Hayworth," she said. "3115 Hayworth. Downstairs. In the back."

The bandage on her knee felt too tight, it was cutting into the calf of her leg, making the veins stand out, and her back was beginning to radiate pain. She moaned.

Natalie wished she'd be quiet. Golde's sounds made her nervous. It was nearly noon, and she was feeling disoriented. She wanted to go home, take a cold shower and change her clothes. First, though, she'd get Golde settled and make sure there was someone to care for her. She turned left on Hayworth and scanned the numbers.

"There," Golde said, pointing to one of those deteriorating pale-pink stucco boxes done cheaply in the fifties. The little bit of lawn in the front was matted and brown with thirst. Natalie parked and went around to help Golde.

"Here, put your arm around my shoulder," Natalie offered.

She bent down, and Golde wrapped a damp, stocky arm around Natalie's neck. Golde groaned as Natalie pulled her along, step by step, till they reached the door to the apartment.

She dug through Golde's purse and found her keys and struggled with the unfamiliar lock as Golde leaned her full weight against Natalie.

Natalie opened the door and switched on the light. The apartment, a small, dank one-bedroom with a kitchenette built into the corner, was half painted, as though someone had started with good intentions and then given up. It smelled of medicine and sour food. Natalie felt ill, but she thought she'd better make the best of it for Golde's sake.

"We'll get you settled and I'll tidy up," she said, leading Golde over to a threadbare couch. She fluffed some pillows and helped her sit back. She propped Golde's leg up on a chair.

"Is there anyone you'd like me to call? Do you need someone to stay with you?"

Golde didn't answer. Natalie thought she might be sulking. Actually, Golde was thinking about her friend Minnie from the building. If Minnie were here, she could help. They could sit together and talk, maybe they could figure out why God would do such a thing.

They used to shop and play canasta together, and on hot nights they'd walk around the block. They talked about their husbands, how it was before they were widowed. Then Minnie got strange. She would forget things and cry for no reason. One day, she took off all her clothes and walked outside, right out to the street. That's when her son, Martin, put her in a home. He cried and he said he felt terrible about it, but it would be the best thing for Minnie. Golde knew it would be the end—they put you in those places so you could die.

Then there was Mrs. Abraham from the Senior Center, but Golde thought she was mad at her because Golde didn't go there anymore, not since the time she had the fight with Mr. Jacobson because she thought he took her wallet.

What a big ta-doo, and everybody taking his side, saying, "Poor Mr. Jacobson, he would never do such a thing!" Imagine how Golde felt when she went home and found the wallet right where she'd left it, right on top of the toilet! So she stopped going, because she was certain nobody liked her anymore.

Natalie wished Golde would answer, would give her some direction, tell her what to do so she wouldn't feel so helpless. Instead, Golde ignored her.

"Let's get some fresh air in here."

Natalie silently commended herself for the cheerful performance she was staging, while Golde was trying to figure out why Joseph would send such a crazy person to help her. She felt betrayed.

Golde watched the girl go to the air conditioner and try to turn it on, but it just blasted warm air. Natalie turned it off and opened a window instead. Then she started straightening up, moving things into different piles. That made Golde very nervous. She wanted to be sure Natalie didn't steal anything.

Golde followed with her eyes as Natalie stood by the sink, rinsing the few dishes that Golde had left from her breakfast. Then she opened the refrigerator and poked around inside. There was some cottage cheese and sour cream, half a package of Swiss cheese growing hard around the edges, jars of mayonnaise and horseradish, and a bowl of cold boiled potatoes. On the bottom shelf she found some vegetables, an old-looking grapefruit, a couple of apricots and some pears, and a bottle of club soda. A loaf of bread sat on the counter.

"Do you want something to eat?" Natalie offered. "How about a cold drink?"

Golde thought for a moment. "I wouldn't mind."

Natalie felt relieved. She fixed a small salad with cottage cheese and fruit and a glass of club soda. She pulled a TV tray over to the sofa and arranged Golde's lunch on it. While Golde ate, Natalie went to the bathroom, splashed her face with cold water, and fixed her makeup. It surprised her that she still looked the same, that she seemed to be the same person. She soaked a washcloth in cold water so she could wipe Golde's face.

Golde finished eating and let out a big yawn. Natalie did the dishes, prepared a cheese sandwich for Golde's dinner, and put it in the refrigerator. There was comfort in helping a stranger.

"Isn't there anyone I can call for you?" she asked as she helped Golde lie down. But she didn't get an answer, and she thought maybe the medicine was making Golde too confused to remember.

She opened Golde's purse and nearly cut herself on the sharp edge of an empty tin can. She pulled out the pain pills. Golde would need another one at four o'clock. Natalie left a big note with a glass of water and a pill on the TV tray.

She looked around the apartment and found an old black rotary-style telephone. She jotted down Golde's number and then put the phone on the TV tray, along with the remote control for the television set across the room. Golde had drifted into a light, pleasant-seeming sleep, a gentle, whistling sleep, like a breeze.

Natalie left, quietly closing the door behind her. None of Golde's neighbors were around, not even the manager. She thought about leaving a note for someone to check on Golde, but then she changed her mind. Better to let her rest. Anyway, Golde had the phone right next to her, so she could use it if she needed to make a call.

It was a little before two o'clock by the time Natalie got home. Her cool, clean condo felt like a sanctuary after Golde's dreary little cubicle. It was Monday, and she was glad she had straightened up and cleaned over the weekend. There were some messages on her answering machine. She listened to them as she undressed. Caroline wanted to know if they could get together for dinner next week, her dentist's office reminded her she was due for a checkup, and Artie called to tell her he was back in town, he'd like to see her, he had a lot to tell her.

She smiled and replayed Artie's message. She loved his voice. Whenever he said he had a lot to tell her, it meant they would make love.

She would ask him, "What? What did you need to tell me?" and he would slip an arm around her waist and pull her close.

"This," he would say, kissing her, "I needed to tell you this."

His hands, so intuitive, found all the right spots. He knew her rhythms, he added his own. He took her beyond her boundaries, past any possible, silly resistance, into a place of sheer sensation, like infancy, a universe devoid of reason.

How could she not know he saw other women? Even if he hadn't told her, she would know—she could tell by his lovemaking, the little bits of newness, always surprising, troubling, and delightful. Certainly it bothered her, but she assumed it was when he was out of town and that the others really didn't matter. When they talked about it, he would tell her he just couldn't deal with commitment, it frightened him, and that if that's what she needed, he understood. That meant she'd have to stop seeing him, and she simply couldn't do it, the cost was too great.

But the compromise, too, had its cost. She no longer asked him about the others, and she gave up the idea of being the special one, the only one he wanted to be with. And she let him think she was just fine, that the spaces between his visits were full, that she didn't need him as much as she really did while feeling the pain of knowing how little he needed her.

She knelt on the floor and pulled the phone over and tapped out his number. She loved being naked when they talked.

"Hello Artie," she murmured. "It's me. What did you need to tell me?"

Golde slept for most of the afternoon. She had strange dreams, with colors like she hadn't seen since she was a child and pale, swirling shapes and voices calling her, some of them from trees. Joseph was in the dreams, and he was young, like when she first met him. Her father was there, too, and he was holding the baby she lost in the ocean, and he was laughing and the baby was happy. Even though Golde was sad and missed the baby, she was glad her father had found it. While she was dreaming she thought she had to remember the baby was safe; when she woke up she needed to remember she didn't need to keep looking for the baby.

But then, slowly, something started to build up, something not so nice, like she was caught in something, she was being pulled. She felt waves of heat, and then she hurt, and all the colors, all the nice colors went away, and she wanted to scream, only she was sleeping so she couldn't, but then there was a noise, maybe it was her. But it was from the outside, and gradually she realized it was the telephone, the telephone was ringing, it was waking her up.

She couldn't remember how the phone got next to her, but she was glad, it made it easier. She pulled herself up so she was sitting, and it hurt but she could do it, thank God, because now she had to go to the bathroom, at least she could move around a little by herself.

She picked up the phone.

"Hello?" she said, and before anyone could answer, she added, "Who is it?"

"It's Natalie Holtzman, Mrs. Moskowitz. The lady who took you home."

Natalie was pleased she had found a way to tell Golde who she was without referring to the accident.

"Who?"

Golde was trying to put a picture on the voice at the other end of the phone, but it wasn't coming out right, she had to keep changing it. Golde remembered the black nurse, Mrs. Taylor, and the girl who shampooed her hair, but she couldn't remember Natalie. She figured she better be friendly, just in case.

"What a nice surprise," she said.

Natalie felt relieved. Golde seemed to have forgiven her.

"I wanted to remind you to take your pain pill," she offered. "It's on the tray next to the phone. And I left some water with it."

Golde found the pill and stuffed it in her mouth.

"Just a minute," she said to the friendly stranger, "I gotta wash it down."

She put the phone down and swallowed the pill. She picked up the receiver.

"There."

"Are you feeling better?" the voice inquired.

"I can't complain," she replied. "At least I'm not dead."

"I left a sandwich for your dinner. It's in the refrigerator."

"Thank you." Golde offered. "But to tell you the truth, I could really use some coffee cake from the Diamond Bakery, and maybe a little coleslaw from the place next to the butcher shop."

"I'll bring you some groceries in the morning," Natalie said. "Are you all right till then?"

Golde figured she'd be okay. She'd watch a little TV and lie on the couch.

"Take another pill before you go to bed," the voice on the phone said. "It'll help you sleep." Then she said "good night" to Golde and hung up.

Golde sat with the phone in her hand. Then she began to remember. She remembered what happened, how she got knocked down by the car.

That's why she went to the hospital.

That's why she needed the pills.

Relieved that Golde sounded better, Natalie decided to work for a few more hours and then meet Artie. And though everyone at work seemed concerned about her accident, she didn't tell anyone about Golde.

It was clear to her now that what she had done constituted a shameful taboo, like incest or child abuse. Even though it was an accident, it was also something more. It was testimony to her personal inner chaos, it was Rose, it was a manifestation of all she feared most, of being out of control, of unbounded, undifferentiated rage.

Was that why she had chosen a career in graphics? Were words too civilized? Limited in ways that brushstrokes were not? When she and Artie argued, she found it hard to articulate her feelings. She was no match for him. He used words to discredit her feelings, to make tight little boxes of reason around them. Her arguments shriveled, deflated like little balloons pierced by his logic, proving again how little leverage she had with him.

She held up the sketch she was working on. Not bad. She made a few revisions. The client would be in on Monday, so she knew she could make up for the time she lost by finishing up on Saturday.

It was so much easier to relax on those weekends when she worked. The privacy, the feeling of being alone in the office, was comforting. The space really seemed to belong to her. Sometimes she'd come straight from the gym in cutoffs and a T-shirt, her hair still wet from the shower. She'd make coffee and wander around. After a while she'd slip into work effortlessly. Others might come in, usually later in the day. Sometimes they brought their kids. No one felt they had to work late, but lots got done because the phones were quiet.

Natalie put the sketch aside and checked her watch. It was six-thirty, too late to call the insurance company. Thank God! She dreaded having to make the call. She knew they would ask her a lot of questions and she feared it would be like it was with Artie, she wouldn't be able to trust her words, they could sabotage her. She imagined the worst.

"We know you're guilty," they would say. "You did it on purpose. Besides, we know you're in therapy, so you're probably crazy, too."

Yes, she knew it was silly, but nonetheless a wave of anxiety started in her stomach and rippled out.

The heat had subsided, giving way to a gentle Santa Ana wind. She let herself get absorbed in the transparency of the early evening light.

"It's ending," she thought. "Thank God this day is ending!"

Artie was padding around the apartment in his wrinkly boxer shorts looking for something to play for her. His place was always a mess, but the clutter was good. It was books open to special pages and papers worth reading and records resting in their plastic sleeves, ready to be enjoyed. Because he traveled a lot he never seemed to put away his suitcase, and she truly never knew if he was coming or going. She guessed crumpled shirts meant returning and newly laundered ones meant going away.

Natalie poured more red wine from the bottle on the floor. They were waiting for the pizza to be delivered.

"Here it is!" Artie was triumphant. "I want you to hear this, I found it at The Music Exchange."

He turned the volume up on a soulful version of "Blue Moon" by the Marcells. It was wonderful.

Artie knew what was worth hearing or reading. It was a gift. And it freed her of the responsibility of keeping current. Was she lazy? Perhaps. She could simply enjoy an effortless kind of appreciation of a splendid day, good coffee, colors and aromas. That was the balance—she chose the sensate, a universe of form and texture. Artie's world was mental. He lived in intellect.

By the time the pizza arrived she had almost forgotten about Golde. He was telling her about a book he was reading, something to do with the debunking of a scientific theory everyone had taken very seriously. And in the middle of his story, in the middle of the pizza and wine, Golde started to rise up in Natalie, and she couldn't contain it. She needed to tell him.

"Something terrible happened," she said, and she blurted out the story of the accident, of her guilt, of Rose and Officer Davis and of feeling afraid. She started to cry even though she didn't want to, and he put down his food and held her lovingly, like a child, soothing her, telling her not to worry.

She began to feel safe, and Golde started to fade away and she didn't want to think. She wanted to concentrate on all the little ways their bodies fit together. It seemed important to remember the curve between neck and shoulder, back and rib. And just when she thought she knew it, it would change, he pulled her closer, a whole new set of parameters to learn, a new geometry, each change a shift, an escalation, a pull toward some central place, familiar but unexpected, till slowly, miraculously, they were making love.

Then they took a bath together and finished the bottle of wine, and he told her it wasn't a good idea for her to see Golde, she should talk to a lawyer or just let the insurance people deal with it. She knew he was right but it was too late. She had already made a commitment.

The next morning was even hotter than the day before. Natalie was grateful that the shops along Fairfax opened early. She'd be able to shop for

Golde and still be at work on time. She hadn't walked along Fairfax in years, and she was struck by its quaint, European ambiance. Prices were good, too, at the little open-air fruit shops and specialty markets. Everyone competed for business, and if you shopped carefully, you could pick up some terrific bargains. She'd have to remember to do some of her own shopping here. How much better than supermarkets! Their cavernous, fluorescent-fake cheeriness depressed her, and she suspected the food they sold was tainted, leached of nutrients by virtue of the impersonality of the surroundings.

She picked up a big head of lettuce and some cherries and oranges. She considered the peaches—too ripe, but the bananas looked good, and so did the tomatoes. Corn could be hard to digest, so she chose cucumbers and carrots and yellow squash. Then she went next door to the Diamond Bakery and waited in line until they called her number, and even though the saleslady was rude to her because she wasn't a "regular," Natalie didn't take offense. She bought a beautiful coffee cake and a fresh, plump, corn rye without the seeds just in case Golde wore dentures. She found the delicatessen that had the coleslaw that Golde liked, and she also bought a beautiful half chicken, still warm from the rotisserie, and some cream cheese and baked sturgeon and black, greasy olives, and a quart of low fat milk.

Pleased with her purchases and satisfied that she was comfortably ahead of schedule, she found a little café where she could have a quick coffee. She wanted to think about Artie, about how delicious it was to wake up together, usually she first, burrowing closer, studying his face. He always slept on his back, she on her side.

Once she said to him, authoritatively, "Most men sleep on their backs," and he laughed and said, "Have you slept with most men?"

He would like it if she had. How could they fit so well together and yet have such separate agendas?

But nothing could diminish the pleasure of those mornings. He woke up slowly, happily, wanting to make love. She felt the pull, the irresistible pressure of hands sliding down her back, the scent of skin, the eroticism of the mundane, of traffic on the street below, radios and barking dogs and car alarms, the miracle of perfectly ordinary life around her and then *in* her.

A touch would sync up with a sound, creating the most surprising moments, inexplicably delicate. The outer sounds would fade away, and other sounds took over, deep, internal ageless sounds. When it was over they'd laugh and hug for a few minutes, then he'd hop out of bed, put on a record and take a shower.

Once she heard the water running she knew he was gone, on to the next thing. In the beginning she wanted to shower with him, and his resistance surprised her. She soon realized that was how he disconnected. Though she felt excluded, she respected his boundaries.

She would make the bed and wait her turn for the bathroom, and when she came out, they would leave together.

"I'm history," he would say, giving her a final hug. "I'll call you from the road."

The sound of animated Yiddish distracted her. A couple of Orthodox Jews walked by, deep in discussion, on their way to shul. Even on a day like this, so hot, they wore dark serge suits and felt hats. Some even wore long wool coats. They would go and thank God for making them men, and their wives wore wigs or scarves on their heads and couldn't be touched when they had their periods.

In some strange way, these women had an advantage. Their world had shape and definition. She wondered what it would be like to be one of these women. She wouldn't have to think so much, she wouldn't have to worry.

She'd have a place; she'd belong.

Golde had been up for a long time, since an hour before dawn. She'd slept on the couch, in her clothes, because it made her feel more secure even though it was uncomfortable. She woke up a few times during the night. One time she was cold, so she got the knit afghan that hung over the chair and used it for a blanket. And then she had to go to the bathroom and then she was thirsty. And she hurt, but it wasn't like before, thank God.

She didn't like her bed so much, the mattress sagged in the middle from where she slept alone, and there was never enough air in the bedroom because the window was stuck and she couldn't open it. She always had bad dreams when she slept in the bed. It was better to sleep on the sofa so she could go to sleep by accident, like a mistake, and she fooled the dreams, they had a harder time finding her.

Not that they didn't! But it was easier to control because she was closer to the front door so they knew she could leave if she had to. That's why she slept in her clothes.

When she woke up for good, even though it was still dark outside, she went to the bathroom and took off her clothes very carefully and slowly, and then filled the sink with warm water and took a sponge bath. She cried a little because it hurt when she dried herself and then she wished Joseph would come back, she *really* needed him. She put dusting powder on wherever she could reach so that she wouldn't sweat so much and she would smell nicer.

It took her a long time to figure out what she should wear, but she didn't want to put on underwear, it made it too hard to go to the bathroom, so she put on a pink cotton house dress she got from Mode 'O Day a long time ago. It had snaps in the front and little embroidered flowers on the pocket.

She left her old clothes in a pile on the bathroom floor. She figured she'd pick them up later when she felt better, and put them in the hamper. Then she made tea, and then she remembered something about coffee cake, did she have some? She looked around and couldn't find any and was disappointed. She ate a piece of toast with jelly. Then she sat down on the chair, very carefully, and waited.

She must have started to doze, just a little, lightly, because she heard a "tap-tap-tap" on the door and it woke her. It was light out, and it felt better than it did in the dark. She couldn't imagine who could be coming to see her.

When Minnie lived in the building they would visit each other, but she was pretty sure Minnie wasn't coming back. She remembered Officer Davis, who asked her all the questions. Did she invite him to visit? She hoped it was him, so she shouted out, "Just a minute, please, I'll be right there," and she was glad she had washed and changed her clothes. But she was sorry she didn't have some coffee cake to give him.

Maybe he would help her put her clothes in the hamper, even though she might feel a little embarrassed because of her underwear being on the floor.

By the time she got to the door, she decided she would make him boiled eggs and toast, but she couldn't remember if she had any eggs left in the refrigerator. She knew she had bread for toast, but maybe he would want some coffee, too. Way up on the top shelf she had a can of Maxwell House left over from when Joseph died and the rabbi came over to tell her it would be okay to have the minyan in the shul, that way he could get ten men to do it, because Joseph didn't know so many people.

So she had a can of coffee, and probably a percolator, but she seemed to recall something about the little glass part that fits in the top. Did she lose it? Did it break? She began to feel very anxious. She hoped he liked tea.

She opened the door, but it wasn't the right person on the other side. It was the crazy girl Joseph sent, the one who caused all the trouble. She was going to say something to keep her out, but then the crazy girl said, "Look, I brought you a coffee cake from the Diamond Bakery, I hope it's the kind you like."

And Golde figured, what did she have to lose?

Golde smiled her best smile.

"Won't you come in, please?" she said, very polite, very civilized.

Natalie was delighted by the friendly greeting. She was relieved to see that Golde had changed her clothes and looked refreshed. She almost laughed when she saw the housecoat. They were uniforms for her mother's generation. Rose had a couple of them and once tried to give her one. She refused, but when she went through Rose's things last year she decided to keep the housecoats, along with Rose's favorite flannel robe and the bright orange floral muumuu she'd picked up in Hawaii on the Club Universe Tour.

Golde followed Natalie over to the kitchenette and watched her unpack the groceries, and once in a while she would make a comment, or simply cluck her approval.

"My goodness! What beautiful cherries, they must have cost a pretty penny!"

Natalie washed the fruit and arranged it in a little imitation crystal bowl she found in the cupboard. She put it on the TV tray by the sofa so Golde could help herself without having to get up.

Golde figured it was a good idea, because when Officer Davis came over she could offer him some cherries with his coffee. She'd have to remember to ask the crazy girl to pull down the coffee from the top shelf, and the percolator, too.

But right now Golde was looking at the beautiful chicken, and the sturgeon, and how did she know Golde loved those shiny black olives, and, my goodness, the *good* kind of coleslaw, the creamy kind, not the kind with vinegar! Golde started thinking maybe she would have a party with all this food.

While Natalie was unpacking the food, Golde was figuring out who she could invite, besides Officer Davis, who she knew was coming anyway. Let's see, how about the nurses from the hospital, the ones who liked her, the ones who wanted her to come back. And maybe the rabbi who buried Joseph, and she couldn't forget Minnie, only she hoped she was still alive. Martin would know, but she wasn't sure she had his number.

But then she started to worry because maybe she didn't have enough plates, and what if she forgot to invite somebody, and did she have any clean underwear? What about the clothes on the bathroom floor? What if she ran out of food? She started to get very nervous and upset, and then her back started to hurt, and she got confused and started to cry.

The crazy girl got very concerned and put her arms around Golde, and said, "There, there."

Golde knew she really liked her, maybe the crazy girl really *was* the daughter Joseph sent, look at all the food she brought!

Natalie took Golde over to the sofa and fluffed up the pillows that had gotten matted down and made a nice comfortable place for her to sit. She wondered if Golde had forgotten to take her pills. She counted them, and sure enough, Golde had forgotten, so Natalie brought her some water and gave her the pill. Perhaps Golde took other medications, too.

"Mrs. Moskowitz, do you take any other medication?"

Golde stopped crying, and thought for a minute.

"Yes, come to think of it, I got those pills for my high blood pressure, and the drops for my glaucoma."

Natalie looked around the apartment, but she couldn't find anything. Then she looked in Golde's purse and found them. She read the labels and saw that Golde needed to take one every morning, and she needed the drops, too.

Golde was starting to trust Natalie, she was just like a nurse, she brought water and asked her polite questions about her medicine. She liked the way Natalie helped her get the drops in her eyes, it was so much easier than doing it herself. And really, it was very nice of the crazy girl to come over and help her.

Yes, Joseph really knew what he was doing!

Natalie went over to the kitchen and cut Golde a big slice of coffee cake and put it on a plate, with a napkin, and fixed her some tea. Golde ate the coffee cake and washed it down with tea and thought about how delicious it was. Maybe she didn't need to have a party, she could eat it all herself, maybe just save a little piece for Officer Davis. Meanwhile, Natalie was fixing a plate for Golde's lunch and another one for dinner.

Now it started to make sense. This girl must have made the sandwich she found in the refrigerator because it wasn't the kind Golde made for herself, she never put lettuce on hers.

It was nice having somebody in the apartment, especially somebody who liked her. This girl looked pretty strong, too, so Golde thought maybe she could help her out a little bit more.

"Honey," she said, "you wouldn't mind maybe picking up in the bathroom, huh?"

That way she wouldn't have to ask Officer Davis, he wouldn't have to handle her underwear because she would be embarrassed and also Joseph wouldn't like it.

The girl seemed happy to do it, she even figured out to put everything in the hamper, and then, can you believe it? The crazy girl said to Golde, "Would you like me to do your laundry?"

For a minute Golde worried that she might steal something, but then she changed her mind. Joseph would never send a thief, so she said, "Please, if it's not any trouble."

Then she remembered the coffee and the coffee pot and Natalie climbed up on a chair and pulled it down and left it on the counter, and the little glass part was okay, thank God. She thought, wouldn't it be nice to have the radio right next to the sofa so she could listen to the talk shows, so Natalie brought it over and plugged it in the wall. Natalie checked Golde's knee and made the bandage looser and said it looked better, the swelling was going down.

Natalie looked at her watch and said, "Look at the time! I really must leave."

Golde felt very sad. She liked this girl, she was just like the nurses.

Natalie kissed her cheek, and said, "I'll call you later."

Then she thought for a minute. Maybe Golde should have her number just in case she needed her.

THE HONEYMOON

Natalie got to work right on time. Being with Artie combined with helping Golde made her feel purposeful and pleasantly fulfilled. She made a couple of sketches—quick ones, but they were good, and had a short production meeting with Jason Burke, the head of her department. She was about to start another sketch when she sensed a feeling in her stomach she couldn't identify. She looked at her watch and saw that it was lunch time and the feeling was hunger.

She hadn't even thought about the heat until she stepped out of the air-conditioned office. It was like a sauna. She worried about Golde and decided to call her right after lunch.

But after grabbing a quick salad across the street she came back to a stack of messages. A rush job had just come in, and she had her graphics workshop that night. She would have to race to get out early enough to make it. No time to call Golde. Anyway, Golde had her number if she needed her.

The next time she looked at her watch it was six-fifteen and she suddenly remembered about the insurance. Secretly, she was glad she had forgotten to call. The accident seemed further away now. She realized she'd barely have time for a sandwich before class, and then she remembered Golde's laundry. She'd do it when she got home and take it over in the morning. The thought of another early morning visit to Golde brought an unexpected wave of anticipatory pleasure.

It was ten-thirty when Natalie got home. She checked her messages. Artie called, he said he knew she wouldn't be home but he wanted her to know he was thinking about her—lustfully—and he was going to bed early. He'd call her later in the week. She played his message three times and savored it, like a lollipop, and then moved on to the others. She played Artie's message one more time because she loved hearing his voice and thinking about him.

Then she sorted through Golde's laundry. There were a few pairs of peach-colored rayon underpants, the kind that old ladies wear, and some big, baggy, worn-out bras with thick straps and big cups like elephant ears. And a corset like thing with elastic at the waist, and the polyester pants Golde was wearing when the accident happened. Natalie felt sad fingering the elastic waistband. Then there was the grayish-white jersey top that Golde had worn that same day. And another pair of polyester pants, the same kind, only in navy blue, and a couple of towels, and a cotton sundress, sleeveless, with stripes going the wrong way, horizontally, so that unless you were very skinny it would make you look fat. Natalie put everything in one load in the machine and while the wash was going, she pulled down the big box in the closet where she kept Rose's things.

She carefully lifted the lid and laid everything out on the bed. How elegant Rose must have felt in that silly orange floral muumuu with the little bits of purple accenting the dark green of the leaves. She was sorry she had never complimented Rose on it, but truthfully, she remembered feeling embarrassed by her mother's terrible taste. How could she have known then that it held special meaning for Rose? That it took courage for her mother to spend the money on the trip to Hawaii?

She held up the housecoat and saw that it looked about the right size for Golde, and there were a couple of blouses she hadn't remembered keeping. One was lavender rayon with a linen collar. The other was an ivory polyester with a scarf attached to the neck, and pearl buttons.

While Golde's clothes tumbled in the dryer Natalie poured a glass of wine and sat out on the balcony in her underwear. She thought about Rose and Golde and everything that seemed to be happening. Was it only yesterday? She yawned. Sleepiness washed over her, and it was peaceful, calm.

She folded Golde's clothes and piled them on the dining-room table, and then she took Rose's things and put them next to Golde's. Because she was very relaxed from the wine, everything seemed to blend and belong together. She could see Rose wearing Golde's sundress and Golde wearing the lavender blouse with her polyester pants. She imagined them together, the three of them walking down Fairfax laughing and talking and enjoying the colors and the smells of ripe fruit and fresh bread.

As she slid into bed she added Artie, and she and he coupled off, arms around each others waists, involved in one another, letting Golde and Rose go on ahead. Then she gave them a baby, a beautiful, smiling baby, and she made it look like the Gerber baby, only with Artie's curly hair.

Soon things became surreal, and Golde's face got very big, filling up the space.

"Her face is as big as the moon," Natalie thought, and then she fell asleep.

Golde waited for Officer Davis, but he never came, and she worried that maybe she gave him the wrong address, after all, it was so confusing in the hospital with everybody running around like nobody's business. She hoped at least he would call so she could tell him she found the Maxwell House coffee and the coffee pot, and that the little glass part wasn't broken, so he could have coffee with his cake and cherries.

It was like an oven in the apartment, and she thought Minnie had the right idea, so she took off her clothes. She didn't go outside, though, that wouldn't be good, they might put her in one of those places, God forbid, and she didn't want to die. Besides, she saw purple bruises all over her from where she fell, and they made her feel embarrassed and ashamed.

She kept the radio on all morning, glad for the company, but she didn't really listen to the words. It was more like she heard the sounds as if it were a song, first one voice and then another voice. And then once in a while some music and then shouting when they were trying to sell you something. Around eleven o'clock she started hurting again. She remembered the pain pills, so she took one, and then she looked at all the food in the refrigerator and ate some.

She took another little piece of coffee cake and sat down and started to doze a little bit when she heard a "plip-plop" and she looked down and saw a couple of pieces of mail lying on the floor. She worried that the mailman had looked through the slot and had seen her naked. She wanted to go look at the mail, but she was too sleepy to get up, and she knew even if she did she couldn't bend down. So she drifted off for a while, just snoozing, and the voices from the talk show went inside her, so she had people visiting, only they were inside the radio and the radio was inside her. It didn't make any sense but she didn't care because she knew it was a dream.

But when she woke up she was hot from sweating, and she was scared because she couldn't remember how she got naked, and she hurt and she needed to go to the bathroom. She didn't like the way she smelled, at first she thought it was someone else, someone who didn't bathe. But when she went to the bathroom to wash she looked in the hamper, everything was missing, and she remembered the crazy girl took her clothes, and she worried maybe she wouldn't bring them back.

The phone rang, only it was a wrong number. Golde saw the piece of paper Natalie had left with her number on it and she wondered, should she call her? Maybe she should ask about her clothes, very politely, just to be sure she got them back, but it felt like she hadn't talked to anybody in a long time and she wasn't sure her voice would work right. Then she worried about the mail on the floor because she pushed the letters around with her foot and she saw her social security check, and she knew she couldn't walk to the bank yet, her knee still hurt, and who would deposit it for her?

She knew she could trust Officer Davis and maybe the nurses, but nobody called her. She worried about one thing and another, and she stayed up nearly the whole night feeling frightened and anxious because she knew if she slept the dreams would be horrible, she wouldn't be able to wake up if she needed to. It got cold, so she went into the bedroom to get something to put on, only when she flicked the switch the light didn't go on. How could she change the light bulb? It was way up on the ceiling! Without the light she was afraid of tripping on something, so she couldn't get dressed and her nakedness made her feel like an animal.

She wrapped herself in the afghan and sat down in the chair because she couldn't trust the sofa. She cried herself to sleep and slept an ugly sleep, all gray and brown and thick. She woke up crying, hurting everywhere, inside and out.

She wasn't prepared for the tapping at the door, and because she was naked and frightened she didn't want to open it. Even if it was Officer

Davis or the nurses, she was afraid they'd put her away somewhere like they did with Minnie. She heard someone calling her name and she recognized the voice. But she no longer felt confident about Natalie. Why would Joseph send a daughter who would hurt her and then take away her clothes so she would have to be naked all night?

"Mrs. Moskowitz? It's Natalie Holtzman. Please open the door."

Golde started to whimper. She wrapped the afghan around her even tighter. Maybe Natalie would go away.

"Mrs. Moskowitz. Are you okay?"

Golde squeezed her eyes shut very tight and felt hot burning tears roll through the cracks and trickle down her cheeks. She shivered and moaned. She felt like she was inside out.

Natalie jiggled the doorknob. It was locked. Panic rose inside her, spreading, taking over. She knocked again. Her hand trembled. She put down the laundry and walked around to the side, but the curtain obscured her view through the window.

Then she heard the whimper, soft, like a kitten. And even in the heat she felt a chill, a kind of foreboding, a shift in time so that it was like walking through molasses. She felt like she stepped outside of herself and watched herself knock on the manager's door.

Myra Goldberg didn't like to interfere in her tenants' lives. Most of them were old people, and they always had a million complaints—the weather, their health, their no-good children, the noise from the street, you name it! But that didn't mean she didn't keep an eye out. You *had* to. After all, you wouldn't believe how the neighborhood had changed in the thirty-six years she'd lived there!

So when Natalie told her she needed to see Golde, it was natural for Myra to be suspicious. She really didn't know too much about Golde except that she was a little bit crazy and stayed by herself. But the girl seemed concerned and very sincere, so she finally agreed to open the door.

Myra felt a little better when she saw the laundry sitting by Golde's door—it gave Natalie's story credibility—and she knocked.

"Mrs. Moskowitz? It's Mrs. Goldberg. Are you all right?"

They waited a minute and then she knocked again.

"She's probably sleeping," Natalie offered as calmly as possible. "I'll just slip in and leave the laundry for her."

Myra shot her a look.

"I can't be late for work," Natalie said. "Please."

Myra opened the door and Natalie slid past her, pushing her out of the way.

"Thank you," she said, closing the door on Myra.

Myra stood outside the door and felt a little cheated that she got pushed out, after all, Golde Moskowitz was her tenant. Even though she craned her neck to try to see inside, she couldn't really see anything. She decided to open her window shade so she could see Natalie leave.

Natalie stood inside Golde's apartment for a long, breathless moment. She felt like she was looking through a fish-eye lens. Everything shifted dangerously. She heard Golde whimper.

Natalie slowly moved toward the chair where Golde sat wrapped in the afghan. She knelt down beside her.

"Mrs. Moskowitz? It's me, Natalie. I'm here to help you."

Golde didn't respond. Natalie took her hand. It was cold and dry. She stroked the pudgy fingers. They sat that way for a while, until slowly, Golde looked up at her.

Natalie felt her heart pounding, making "wooosh-click" noises, crazy rhythms. Golde's eyes locked onto hers. They were the gray of thunderclouds, thick as rain.

Golde pulled her hand away

"You!" Golde hissed, like a gunshot.

"What?" Natalie was startled.

"You! *You!! You!!!*" Golde chanted.

Natalie froze.

"You!!! You!!! You!!!" Golde spun a wall of words around Natalie. They stung like bees. "Why? *Why??"*

It couldn't be happening! What about the food she brought, or the places she planned to take Golde?

"I'm an old lady! Why?? *Why???*"

Natalie backed away from the chair.

"Shame on you! *Shame on you!!!*" Golde's voice took on a menacing, whining quality. "You should feel *ashamed* to hurt an old lady!!!"

Natalie was stunned. She wanted to defend herself, fend off the attack, but it was as though her bones turned to dust. It took all of her strength to keep from disintegrating.

And then Golde shuddered, and a long, deep, anguished sigh poured out of her. For a long moment nothing happened, time seemed suspended. Natalie perched at the edge of the earth. And then, finally, Golde started to cry, and it built into torrents of wet, hot tears.

Even though Natalie wanted to run away, she couldn't. She couldn't do to Golde what she had done to Rose, and she stood her ground. Then she felt her own anguish rise, and tears poured out of her, and she went over to Golde and sat next to her and embraced her and begged Golde to forgive her.

The two women sobbed into each others hearts and they seemed to become one person, as though the exchange of tears created a marriage between them.

Golde seemed to forget her rage, and after a while a calm spread over the two of them like a cool sheet, like a sweet breeze, and Natalie stroked Golde's hair and Golde held Natalie gently, and they stayed that way until it was okay to speak.

"Do you hear the birds?"

Golde nodded.

The song of the birds filled them with peace.

Natalie wiped Golde's face with her hand. Slowly, she got up and brought some water and helped Golde take her pills.

As she fixed Golde's breakfast and did all the other things that needed to be done, she knew Golde belonged with her.

She knew what she needed to do. She would take her home.

Myra Goldberg was sitting by her window drinking coffee when she saw the girl come out of Golde Moskowitz's apartment carrying a couple of bags and a big, bulging, nylon plaid suitcase. She put down her cup and craned her neck to see what she was going to do, and sure enough, the girl put the stuff in her car. Then she went inside the Moskowitz apartment again. After a few minutes she came out with more shopping bags, put them in the car, and went back into the apartment.

The next time, when Natalie came out with Mrs. Moskowitz, Myra Goldberg was waiting for them. Golde was limping.

"Why hello, Mrs. Moskowitz," Myra offered in a friendly tone. "What a lovely muumuu."

Golde looked up at Myra, then down at the orange muumuu. She was feeling better now. Natalie had washed her and helped her dress, and not only did she remember to bring the clothes from the hamper, but she brought other clothes, too. Nice ones, and just the right size.

"Thank you, Mrs. Goldberg," replied Golde. "To tell you the truth, it's brand new."

Actually, Golde remembered that Natalie said it belonged to somebody else, but it felt brand new, and you could smell the detergent from the washing machine.

"Mrs. Moskowitz will be staying with me for a couple of days," said Natalie. "I have an extra bedroom and it's much cooler at my place."

At first when Natalie suggested it, Golde got scared. She thought about Minnie. But Natalie assured her that everything would be fine, and that she'd bring her back whenever she wanted. And besides, Natalie told her the air conditioner worked and she'd have a big beautiful room. And she shouldn't worry, there was lots of food, and a good TV set, and a radio for the talk shows. She even had a little patio with some potted plants so Golde could sit outside and get a nice breeze. So she figured she'd try it, maybe just for a day.

And besides, she knew if she couldn't trust the sofa then soon she wouldn't be able to trust the chair, and pretty soon she'd be sleeping right out on the street! At least in a new place, the dreams wouldn't know where to find her.

"Maybe you should leave me a number, Mrs. Moskowitz, just in case I need to get ahold of you." Myra couldn't quite put it together. Who was this girl? Where were they going? It didn't make sense.

"Of course," said Natalie. She scribbled something on a piece of paper from her purse and handed it to Myra.

"We really must go," Natalie said. "Thank you for your help."

"Mrs. Moskowitz, are you sure you should be leaving?" Myra knew she was interfering, but she wanted to make sure Golde knew what she was doing.

Golde wasn't really sure of anything, she was floating. After all that crying, it was like a curtain came down and made her feel more peaceful again, more like herself. She couldn't remember why she was so upset with the daughter Joseph had sent. After all, she was such a nice girl, and she did so many kind things. Why, look at the clothes she brought! Besides the muumuu, she gave her *two* housecoats, both from Mode 'O Day, you couldn't get those anymore. And beautiful blouses—and all of her own clothes, so clean! Not to mention the food, and promising to take her to the bank to deposit her social security check.

Why, this girl really liked her, maybe even loved her. She couldn't disappoint her by not going with her.

Golde realized Myra was waiting for her to say something. She wasn't sure she remembered the question, so she simply said, "So nice to see you again."

Natalie led her away.

Myra stood watching as the two of them drove off. She jotted the license plate number down on the paper as Natalie pulled away, and stuffed it into her pocket.

Golde couldn't believe it when she saw the new place. It was like "The Price Is Right," so beautiful! It really *was* cool, and, my goodness, so much room! Now Golde was certain she had done the right thing by leaving the other place. Yes, it had to be that Joseph had arranged it with the girl, he really *was* watching out for her.

"Do you like it?" Natalie opened the Levolors and dappled light streamed in across the Berber carpet.

Golde beamed. "It's like a magazine."

"Would you like to see your room?" Natalie wanted to get her settled so she could leave for work.

"If you don't mind," said Golde. "I could use a little nap."

Golde's room had a big, beautiful daybed with ruffles on the bottom and lots of pillows. She could tell the mattress didn't sag—why, it looked brand new, like no one had ever slept on it! There was a bathroom off to the side so you wouldn't have to go far to go to the toilet. And can you believe it? It had a TV set, a nice one, even though there was one in the living room, too. And a nice big dresser with a mirror, and a radio on a nightstand next to the day bed. And lamps, so that if the ceiling light went out, you wouldn't have to worry about changing the bulb. Best of all, there was a window that looked out onto a tree, just like the trees in Russia when she was a girl!

Natalie showed Golde the closet and hung some of her clothes. Then she pulled out the mattress and folded back the quilted bed cover, smoothing the clean, lavender sheets. She fluffed the pillows.

"There," she said to Golde. "You'll be comfortable here."

Golde smiled. "It's like a dream." And then she added, "A *good* one."

"There's lots of food in the refrigerator. Just help yourself. You don't need to answer the phone. The machine will do it."

Golde took off the muumuu. She wore a cream-colored rayon slip underneath. Natalie hung the muumuu in the closet.

"I'll make us a good dinner when I get home."

Golde climbed into bed.

Natalie fixed the blinds so the light was filtered. She put a glass of water on the nightstand along with Golde's pill. Then she sat on the bed next to Golde. She stroked her forehead.

"I hope you like it here," she said. "Sweet dreams."

She kissed Golde gently, lovingly, and quietly got up and left.

Golde's dreams were sweet as ginger ale, light as a hummingbird's wings. They were filled with songs from her childhood, sung by angels. Everyone was in them, the living danced with the dead. Joseph and Minnie, and both her parents, and cousins she hadn't seen since she was a child, Myra Goldberg and the nurses, and even people she didn't know.

Her dream became a poem that went something like this:

The river sings to me
of moonbeams braided in my hair
I toss my head
and sprinkle stars across the trees.

When Golde finally woke, even though she was in a new place, she wasn't frightened, she was at peace. She lay in bed for a long time holding onto the feeling of her dreams.

Natalie felt more settled knowing Golde was safe and comfortable. She looked forward to fixing a wonderful dinner for the two of them. Artie and her therapist would never approve, but that didn't matter. She and Artie spent most of their time together at his place, and if she had to choose between Golde and Dr. Reynolds—well, Golde truly needed her. Therapy was uncomfortable and expensive.

At lunchtime she did a little grocery shopping and picked up some beautiful salmon and a good bottle of wine. She grabbed a sandwich and headed back to the office. At about four o'clock she realized she needed to stretch. She got up and walked over to the main reception area just as Jason was coming out of his office.

"Are you coming tonight?"

"What?" Natalie realized he was talking to her.

"The dinner meeting to review the McClary account. I thought you signed up for it."

"Oh my God, I can't! I've got a relative staying with me." Natalie usually looked forward to these meetings.

"Too bad." Jason turned to take a phone call.

Natalie made a mental note to check her calendar more closely. She couldn't let Golde take over. She needed to make sure she continued to participate in all of her usual activities. In fact, it would be good for Golde to learn to be self-reliant. She might even make friends with some of the older people in the building.

She imagined a life in which she and Golde lived independently, both enjoying their separate activities while maintaining a close relationship. She could help Golde expand, take on new interests. She had always wanted Rose to be more active and have more friends.

As she drove home that evening she imagined Golde spending afternoons at the museum, or playing bridge with friends, or learning folk dancing at the Senior Center. Golde would cook dinner sometimes; she probably knew how to prepare some great Russian dishes. They could entertain their friends together, young and old, sharing, learning from one another.

It would be just the way she wished it had been with Rose.

"Hello, Mrs. Moskowitz. How are you feeling?" Natalie looked pleased to see Golde sitting in the living room watching TV.

"Not bad. I had a little snooze."

"Do you like salmon?"

"What's not to like?"

Golde loved salmon, but it was much too expensive except once or twice a year when the price went way down. She knew it was expensive now, so Natalie would have to be crazy and very rich to buy it.

Natalie fixed a beautiful dinner, salmon and fresh asparagus, hot buttered rolls and salad. Golde even drank a little wine, and it made her feel very relaxed, like the pills, only happier. She was starting to like the way the pills made her feel. She would have to ask Natalie to get her more. While she was busy eating, Natalie talked a lot, about this and that, and Golde didn't really listen, except once in a while, just to be polite. She was too busy enjoying the food. They drank tea and ate fruit, and Golde thought, wouldn't it be nice to have strawberry ice cream?

She said, "Honey, you wouldn't happen to have a little strawberry ice cream, would you?"

Natalie felt terrible that she didn't, but she said she'd get some tomorrow, was there anything else Golde needed?

"To tell you the truth, I could use more of these pills for the pain, I'm almost out."

Natalie looked at the label and said she'd call the pharmacy.

And then, because of the wine and the pills and everything that had happened to her, Golde got very sleepy, a deep kind of sleepiness. Natalie did the dishes, and Golde leaned back on the sofa and fell asleep to the sound of the water running in the kitchen sink.

She didn't know how she got back in the bed, but for a second she woke up, just a little, and saw Natalie turn out the light. She fell asleep again, quickly. She slept a sleep without dreams, an indigo velvet sleep.

Natalie poured another glass of wine after she got Golde back into bed. She realized she hadn't even had a chance to check her messages, but when she did there was nothing from Artie and she was disappointed. Although dinner was pleasant, she felt an underlying discomfort, a vague anxiety. She remembered Dr. Reynolds. Tomorrow was her appointment. She'd have to leave very early, possibly before Golde got up. Would Golde feel disoriented? It annoyed her that they wouldn't have breakfast together.

But it would be inconsiderate to Dr. Reynolds if she canceled on such short notice, and he would charge her for the visit anyway. She decided to keep the appointment, just for the sake of courtesy, so that she could tell him quite calmly that she wanted to terminate the therapy.

Natalie woke early, before the alarm went off, to the sounds of kitchen pots and pans and smells of something baking in the oven. As she walked into the kitchen still rubbing sleep from her eyes, Golde turned to her and said, "I thought I'd fix a little something."

Boxes and canisters littered the counter, milk cartons and butter wrappers and spilled flour.

"What are you making?"

Golde opened the oven door and pulled out the rack. "Look, the cookies Joseph likes."

Golde had made dozens of cookies, dozens of misshapen, strange little cookies, cookies missing vital ingredients, baking nonetheless, baking crisp and brown and sad as little orphans.

"They look wonderful," Natalie said. "Shall I make tea?"

"That would be nice." Golde suddenly looked exhausted.

Natalie put a kettle of water on the burner and cleaned the counter and wondered who this Joseph was. Better to let Golde tell her in her own time.

As the first rays of morning sun spread through the trees and across the dining-room table, the two women sat drinking tea and eating odd little cookies—cookies from another time.

"Are you sure that's wise?" Dr. Reynold's expression revealed deep concern. His question was a warning. It told her he already knew she knew the answer.

Natalie hadn't meant to tell him anything about Golde or the accident. She really just wanted to let him know she wouldn't be coming anymore. But whether from habit or something deeper, she heard herself telling him everything. As she spoke, she stepped out of herself and felt angry, deeply manipulated by some betrayal within herself, a Pavlovian response.

Tears burned her eyes. She squeezed them shut. Why did he have to ruin everything? She was just trying to be polite, she was really coming in for his sake, as a courtesy. And here he was, making her question acting in a way that felt absolutely right.

"Where are you?"

The voice probed, not letting her alone, chasing her away, making her run from her thoughts. Why didn't he just say he thought she was wrong to get involved with Golde? Her anger and frustration built.

"Why don't you leave me alone?" She wanted to hurt him. "She's helping me more than you are." She fought to hold back hot, angry tears.

He seemed impervious to her attack.

"Natalie, please consider what you're doing. There are other options."

Why wouldn't the hour end? Finally the little red light on his desk lit up. She stood up, averting his look.

"You know you can call me if you need to talk more about this," he said.

His voice trailed off behind her as she quickly left the office, firmly shutting the door on his words.

She really needed to talk to Artie. And though she usually waited for him to call her, when she got to the office she closed her door and dialed his number. The machine picked up. He changed his message often, always something quick and witty, words he rolled off effortlessly, a message that she would have struggled to create.

"You've reached the unreachable Artie Hamlin . . ." She suddenly felt foolish, and she hung up. After all, what could she say? "Unreachable" meant he was out of town. She'd just have to wait. By the time he got back she'd be feeling less needy.

Dr. Reynolds implied that Natalie's intervention might prevent Golde from exercising her legal rights, might even be harmful. Should she talk to Golde? Offer her alternatives?

Yes, that seemed fair.

Let Golde decide.

Golde tried to figure out what went wrong with the cookies. There was butter and flour and she thought she put in the vanilla and the sugar. Were the proportions wrong? It might have been the salt. Yes, they tasted too salty. But there was something else, something she needed to remember.

When she had awakened that morning, way before dawn, she had known that she had to make the cookies. Things were beginning to become clear. An inner direction was starting to take hold and it had something to do with Joseph.

The apartment on Hayworth was all wrong, she knew it now. Why, Joseph hadn't even finished painting it. Imagine, being a house painter by profession, a good one, and getting so sick in the middle of painting his own apartment! She wasn't supposed to stay there, not without Joseph. The girl came to take her away because this place was better, here she could sleep and feel rested. Here she was safe. And here she could act on the impulses to do important things, like making Joseph's cookies.

This first batch of cookies must have been a rehearsal, a test. She would keep trying until she remembered, until all the ingredients were right, until they tasted like the cookies Joseph liked. She put all the wrong little leftover cookies on a plate.

Golde was still thinking about the cookies as she carefully sponged herself off, especially under her arms and around her private places. Maybe it was almonds. No, it had to be walnuts, crushed walnuts and cinnamon. The girl could take her to one of those shops where they had things in bins, like sugar and pistachios and big chunks of dried papaya. She might remember if she saw it.

Her back still hurt, so she couldn't wash her hair. It felt sticky and damp. Maybe she could get Natalie to shampoo it for her, or better yet, Natalie could take her to the beauty parlor. She could use some of the social security money to have her hair done. Now that she wasn't living on Hayworth, she wouldn't have to worry about rent. That meant she could spend it on other things, good things for herself, little presents like the things Joseph used to bring her, bags of cherries and cotton stockings and flowered scarves in bright colors and maybe even a new dress.

She could almost hear him, he would say, "*Maideleh,* I got a little something you might like . . ." and he would tell her they gave him a little extra on the job, a tip because he had done such a good job painting and he left things so neat.

She put fresh, clean underwear on under the sundress with the stripes going across and pulled the sheets up on the bed. The girl was going to come back at noon and take her to the bank. She was certain they would stop for lunch. Golde didn't eat out very often, it was so expensive. Since the girl had lots of money, she could probably order anything she wanted, even cream cheese and lox.

She found herself smiling thinking about a good lunch, and she sat down in the living room and waited for Natalie to come home.

Yes, it was just like having a daughter, a *good* one, maybe not a crazy one after all.

Golde was dressed and ready when Natalie got home.

"How pretty you look!" Natalie sincerely meant it, for Golde seemed refreshed and the pastel stripes she wore lent color to her face.

Golde beamed. "Thank you. But to tell you the truth, I need to go to the beauty parlor, the one on Fairfax, for a wash and set. You could take me, huh?"

"Oh, uhh . . . sure, but maybe not today."

Golde's smile faded. Natalie felt stricken. After all, Golde had suffered so much. Natalie felt selfish putting her own needs first.

"Well, maybe I could take you there and pick you up later. Would that be okay?"

Golde smiled. "Sure. But first you take me to the bank, okay?"

Natalie and Golde waited in line patiently, until Golde's knee started to hurt. She went and sat down and Natalie waited alone until the red arrow blinked, pointing to the next teller and Natalie helped Golde do her transaction.

"Are you hungry?" Natalie asked as they left the bank.

"I could eat." Then Golde added, "How about the place next to the beauty parlor."

Natalie glanced at her watch. She hadn't planned on driving to the other side of town.

"Okay, but we'll have to make it fast."

The ride over the canyon to Fairfax was pleasant. It always seemed like being in the country, and Natalie loved the way the trees made shifting textured patterns of light dance across the dashboard. It felt especially pleasant today.

She was about to turn on the radio when she heard a little sound, a sound she couldn't place. Then she realized it was humming, and she looked over and saw that it was Golde, and it was as though it was coming from the inside of her, very deep, from long ago.

"*Di di di . . . di di di di di . . .*" Golde's song carried them across the canyon, and when it ended, it was as though it had never been and yet it left a faint trace in the air, like the scent of honey.

"That was lovely." Natalie wasn't sure she should comment; words seemed so indelicate.

Golde looked at her and smiled politely.

"Why, Mrs. Moskowitz, it's been such a long time!"

The hairdresser at the beauty parlor recognized Golde. She looked at her like she was examining a Rembrandt.

"You really do need a cut. And a rinse." She ran her fingers through Golde's stringy hair. "Come back in half an hour. We'll fit you in."

The attention pleased Golde. She would tell them about everything that happened to her.

Natalie rushed them through lunch. Though she had planned to talk to Golde about the accident and her options, it was noisy in the restaurant and it just didn't seem appropriate to bring it up, especially when Golde seemed so happy. She ate with such relish, such pleasure.

"Mmmmm. You want some?" Golde offered a forkful of lox.

Natalie declined. "I won't be able to pick you up until later this afternoon. Will you be all right?"

Golde nodded. Natalie couldn't tell whether she was really listening, she seemed so engrossed in finishing the last bits of her lunch.

"You could take a cab back to my place. Or you could wait for me at your apartment on Hayworth."

Golde looked up. Her smile faded.

"Okay, call me when you're ready to leave. I'll come and get you." Natalie wrote her work number down for Golde. She would have to make some sort of excuse to leave work early. A dental appointment? Some personal business? She couldn't just let Golde wonder around.

Natalie took care of the check and walked Golde next door.

"I've got to go. Will you call me when you're ready to leave?"

"Okay, honey," said Golde. "Maybe I'll do a little shopping, pick up a little something to put in the cookies, huh?"

Natalie checked to make sure Golde had her pills. And she made sure Golde knew which piece of paper had Natalie's work number on it.

Then she felt she could leave.

It was the best afternoon Golde had had in a very long time. Everyone at the beauty salon was happy to see her, even the people she couldn't remember.

When she told the shampoo girl to be careful because of her back and knee, the girl clucked in sympathy and said, "Don't worry, Mrs. Moskowitz, I'll be very careful."

Just to be safe, Golde asked for some water so she could take another pill, and the girl was happy to get it for her. She laid her back in the chair very carefully—why it hardly hurt at all, just a little at first, and she felt a warm stream of water rushing through her hair, massaging her scalp. It felt like a thousand butterflies or all the bubbles from a bottle of seltzer water, and she smiled because the feeling made so many nice pictures in her head.

"I'm gonna leave this rinse on for just a few minutes, so you just relax, okay?"

Golde felt the thick, cool cream land on her scalp. The girl rubbed it in. Her hands made colors, soft pastels behind Golde's eyes. She started feeling dreamy.

She hardly remembered the haircut, except that she felt like Queen Esther. The rollers pulled up her scalp, each one tightened like a little bolt, squeezing her head, lifting up all the loose skin.

"Tell me if they feel too tight, okay, Mrs. Moskowitz?"

Golde smiled.

The girl covered Golde's head with a big pink hairnet and stuffed cotton around it so her ears wouldn't burn and led her over to the dryer and gave her some magazines, just in case she wanted to look through them.

But Golde wanted to drift, and the heat of the dryer took her back through time, back to her childhood, back to meadows and rivers and long, warm afternoons with smells like green apples. Then she felt something like a breath, and it wasn't the dryer, it was from the inside. She strained to focus in on it, and she had to clear away the sounds of the dryer and the *whoosh* of the heat.

Was it a message? It wasn't so much words, it was the *feeling* of words. It seemed to be telling her that she wasn't alone. Then the feeling of words was gone and she fell asleep, and the next thing she knew the girl was gently waking her up.

"Mrs. Moskowitz? Wake up now, it's time to comb you out."

One by one the girl slipped the curlers out of Golde's hair, and each curl bounced like a stiff little soldier. The girl combed and teased and sprayed, and Golde marveled at her skill. The next thing she knew, her hair looked beautiful, just like a wig or a picture in a magazine, all curly and shiny and blue-gray.

Golde paid and gave the girl a pretty good tip now that she didn't have to pay rent. The girl smiled and thanked her and told her to come back soon.

"You know, Mrs. Moskowitz, you should really have your hair done every week."

It was just like at the hospital, Golde could tell they really liked her here, that's why they wanted her to come back. She figured she should come more often. After all, Natalie could drop her off and pick her up. Things were really a lot better now.

Golde felt like a movie star. Everyone was looking at her because she was so beautiful and her hair looked so nice,

but when she went out the door she felt the heat, and she hoped she wouldn't sweat because it might ruin her nice hairdo. Because of the pill, and maybe because of the salty food at lunch, her throat felt dry, very dry, and it seemed to her that the best thing to fix it would be some strawberry ice cream.

She walked over to the place where she used to go with Joseph. There were only a few people in the store. When it was her turn to order, she didn't waste a moment, she knew exactly what she wanted.

"I'll have a strawberry cone please, one scoop, okay?"

The fellow fixed it for her, and just as she took it, as she was about to pay she felt the breath again, from the inside, like before. She stiffened for a moment.

"Are you okay?"

She needed to concentrate on the breath, on what it was trying to tell her. It seemed important.

"Lady . . ."

And then from the side, like a shadow, it happened so quick, she saw a figure dart by, and she knew she knew it . . .

"That's a dollar . . ."

She dropped the money on the counter and turned toward the
figure, but it was gone. Everything started to settle back down. Could
she have imagined it? She licked the ice cream, picking a piece of strawberry out with her tongue. But as she walked toward the door, toward the
place where she saw the figure dart by, she stopped and she looked all
around, like it was a holy spot, someplace very special. Even the breeze
felt different, clean, like the ocean. There was nothing on either side of her,
nothing, until she looked down, and then she saw it, and then she knew.

On the floor next to her feet were little white drops—fresh, little white
drops of paint!

SOMETIMES THEY EAT THEIR YOUNG

The afternoon could not have been worse for Natalie. When she got back to the office Christie seemed panicked.

"God, Jason's in a real snit," Christie told her. "He's going away for the weekend and he wants to see your sketches right away."

"Oh, my God! They're not finished!" She had counted on doing them over the weekend. She glanced down. Christie's nails had sprouted little paintings, elaborate little panoramas studded with rhinestones. Natalie thought of armies of tiny da Vincis making miniature masterpieces, each new nail a challenge, a *tabula rasa*. She wished she could spend some time studying Christie's hands, but it seemed safer to retreat to her office.

As she started to walk away Christie shouted after her, "Oh, you have a message from Dwight Morgan at Tri-State Insurance . . ."

Natalie felt a pressure build. She stopped but didn't turn around.

" . . . he needs to talk to you about the accident."

"Okay." She started walking again.

"Do you need the number?" Christie was dogged.

Natalie pretended not to hear. She closed the door behind her. She needed to sit quietly, to think, to relax. She wished she still smoked. A cigarette would be good. No, the *idea* of a cigarette would be good. A real one would make her sick. She fingered the sketch pad.

Jason walked into her office. "We need to talk . . ."

Natalie felt like she was going to faint. Waves of panic rippled from her stomach, spreading through her. Could he tell what was going on inside? Probably not. Would her voice shake if she spoke?

"Jason, I'm really sorry about the sketches . . . because of the accident and everything, I got a little behind." Her voice sounded perfectly calm.

53

"We're a team here, kiddo. We have to be able to count on each other."

He walked over to the window. His back was to her. "This is an important deal. You know I need to check for revisions before we present it."

"I'll do it all over the weekend. I'll bring them to your house Sunday night."

"I can't let this happen again."

Why wouldn't he look at her? He must be very angry. What about Golde? How could she leave to pick her up? And what about the weekend? She wanted to work Saturday and spend Sunday with Golde.

"I'll do whatever it takes to get it finished. I promise."

Jason turned toward her. "Don't let me down, Natalie."

He started to leave the office, but then turned and pierced her with his look. "And don't let this happen again. *Ever.*"

Natalie watched him leave. She felt the beginnings of rage, a wave of anger she'd have to control. This job meant a lot to her. Sometimes she thought it meant everything—her identity, her self-esteem, certainly her financial security. It made her furious to imagine that Jason would chastise her after all the time and devotion she had given to the company.

How could this be happening when everything she was trying to do seemed right? It was so unfair.

But she had to admit Golde was taking over her life. She remembered a book she was given for Hannukah when she was a little girl. It was about birds, and most of it was interesting and the drawings were beautiful. But part of it was frightening. It was about a certain bird that sometimes would eat its young. She shivered recalling the book.

Then she remembered the message from Tri-State. She was too upset to deal with the insurance adjuster. She would need to feel very composed in order to talk to him, very confident so that her voice didn't betray the guilt she felt. Her words needed to come out right.

She started sketching. Earlier in the day she had known what she needed to do with this drawing, but now it was gone. It was hard to work when she was upset. The chemistry needed to translate thought to form was delicate and required a sense of well-being and trust. Tension worked against the flow. Jason, of all people, should know that. It seemed especially unjust that he would treat her so badly and then expect her to produce. What if she finished the drawings and Jason didn't like them? He could force her to redo them, just out of spite. Could it be that he truly disliked her? That he was looking for an excuse to fire her? Could the pressure be deliberate so that he could get rid of her? What if there was someone else he had in mind for her job?

She wished she had a tranquilizer. She dug through her purse, but there was nothing. She knew she had some Xanax tablets in a little bottle in her medicine cabinet at home. She wished they were here.

She looked at the sketch. It was all wrong. She tore the page off the pad and started over again. She needed a cup of tea. Rose always made tea when things got rough. She remembered when her mother told her Harold had left. Natalie was ten years old.

She had just come home from school and thought it was a

day like any other, but when she went into her mother's bedroom she knew something was wrong. Rose was making the bed, pulling the top sheet up, making it tight. Her face was pale, and Natalie could tell she'd been crying.

"What's wrong?" Natalie asked.

Rose looked at her. Natalie suddenly felt scared.

"Sit down, honey."

Natalie sat on the edge of the bed. Rose sat next to her. She put her arm around Natalie's shoulder.

"Daddy's gone, sweetheart." Rose's voice broke. "He's not coming back." Her voice sounded different, like a stranger's.

Natalie tried to figure out what the words meant, but she couldn't quite grasp it. Though she didn't want to cry, she couldn't help it.

"Who's going to take care of us?"

Natalie couldn't have known then that Rose must have been even more frightened than she. She remembered how they cried together, and how Rose tried to assure her that they would be fine.

After the crying, in the space filled with pain, in that new place of emptiness they'd have to get used to, Rose told her to go into the kitchen and put a kettle of water on the stove. Rose made tea and they drank together, silently, knowingly. Natalie felt grown up. For the very first time Rose was treating her like an equal.

It was never the same after the day of the tea. And yet that memory had a calming effect. A cup of tea had become a way of taking time out, of gathering strength.

She sipped tea and started to sketch, this time with assurance, this time like a grown up.

Golde wanted to hold onto the moment at the special spot by the door of the ice cream shop where she found the paint, but the boy was shooting her funny looks, and she knew it wasn't because of how nice she looked with her new hairdo. He looked mean, like he could have her sent away, so she left.

She looked up and down the street, just in case she could see who dropped the paint, and then she thought she'd better look around the alley in the back. She went around the back but all she saw were big trash bins and a few skinny cats and some kids playing on bicycles.

But the special feeling was gone, and now she figured she'd better sit for a while because she was feeling tired, like a flat balloon. So she sat on the bench at the bus stop and the sun felt good, not too hot, just right. After she rested for a while she felt better and then she remembered the shop that had things in bins, so she went there to find what she needed for the cookies.

She got walnuts and almonds and powdered sugar and two kinds of raisins. Was there anything else? She looked around, but enough was enough. It was time to go back to the new place so she could sit on the balcony with the potted plants and look at the paper.

Natalie's phone number was on the crumply piece of paper stuffed in her pocket book. She found a pay phone and dialed the number.

"Brewer and Associates . . . please hold . . ." and just like that, they made her wait. What if it was the wrong number? Golde had expected Natalie to answer. Should she hang up and dial again? But then she might not have enough change. She started feeling agitated. A man stood behind her and kept looking at his watch, and it made her nervous, he might want to steal her purse, maybe he knew she had her social security money and because her hair looked so nice, he figured she was rich.

She hung up the phone and walked away, quickly, so that he wouldn't follow her, but when she looked back he was making a call. Then she saw her shopping bag on the ground by the phone, so she had to go back and get it and excuse herself to the man she thought was a thief.

She needed a cup of tea and a little something, a piece of coffee cake, and then she would try to call the girl again. She went over to the bakery that had the little tables inside and got something, and sat and relaxed. Little by little she started feeling better, and she remembered the remarkable things that had happened to her today. And she let out a big sigh because she felt like she had been to so many places today, inside and outside, real places and places in her mind.

She looked up at the clock and it was four o'clock already. She figured Natalie would be worried about her, this girl really liked her, so she better go find a phone and call her.

Natalie was just getting her rhythm back when Golde's call came through.

"Honey, you wouldn't mind maybe to pick me up now, huh?"

Natalie envisioned the rush-hour traffic, bumper to bumper over the canyon. It would be impossible. She simply couldn't leave now. She'd lose at least an hour and a half, and if Jason found out he'd make it even harder on her.

"Mrs. Moskowitz, do you think you could take a cab back to my place?" She remembered Golde didn't have a key. "I could tell you where I hide the key."

"It's not so nice in the cab." Golde didn't like taking cabs. They were expensive and she always suspected they charged her too much because they could make the meter run faster than it should. She heard they did that with old people.

"What about the bus?" Natalie knew there was a bus that came over the canyon. "You can take the one that says 'Ventura Boulevard.' Tell the driver to let you off at Coldwater. Call me from there and I'll pick you up."

"Okay." Golde didn't mind buses so much. There were lots of people to look at, and she knew the driver wouldn't overcharge her.

Natalie figured it would take Golde at least an hour to get there. By then, she could leave without calling attention to herself. She could take Golde back to the condo, get her settled, and then go back to work.

"Remember, get off at Coldwater."

"Okay, honey." Golde hung up.

Natalie felt relieved. The problem was solved. She started sketching again, picking up where she'd left off, enjoying the shapes and colors. She was on the right track. This one would be good, exceptional perhaps. Jason would recognize her talent, see how indispensable she was to the company. He would apologize for chastising her.

The intercom buzzed. It was Christie. "Natalie, pick up line two."

It was nearly five-thirty. Natalie assumed it was Golde. Perfect timing, she thought as she picked up the phone.

"Hi, are you ready?" she said as she tucked the receiver between her shoulder and cheek, leaving her hands free to sketch.

"Pardon me?" It was the voice of a man, a voice she didn't recognize.

"I'm sorry, who is this?"

"Is this Natalie Holtzman?"

"Uhh, yes . . ." Natalie put down the pad and held the receiver with her hand.

"Miss Holtzman, this is Dwight Morgan from Tri-State. I'm calling about the accident . . ."

Golde got to the bus stop just as the one that said "Ventura Boulevard" pulled away. She didn't mind so much because the bench was empty and she could sit and wait for the next one. She put her purse squarely on her lap and set the shopping bag next to her, making sure to twist the handle around her wrist so she wouldn't forget it and no one could steal it.

Another bus came, but it said "Downtown" and she knew it was the wrong bus. Then a few minutes later another one came, and this one said "Beach-Cities–Ocean Avenue," and she felt something inside of her, an urging, a little excitement. And she thought, "ocean," and then she thought, "Coldwater—*cold water*" and it made sense, it was a message. She was *supposed* to take this bus, this bus would take her to the ocean, to the cold water where she and Joseph used to sit on hot days.

She got on the bus, and the driver got annoyed with her because she had to count out the change. But then the special feeling started coming back, so she knew she was doing the right thing. She found the only empty seat on the whole bus—it was toward the back—and the most amazing thing happened! There, on the seat, was a little brown paper bag, just waiting for her. She waited a few minutes, just to be sure no one came back for it. When she was sure it was left there for her, she opened it, and what do you think she found?

Cherries! Beautiful big, fat shiny cherries, just like the ones Joseph used to bring her. She put one in her hand and felt how cool and smooth it was, and it made her smile, and then she cried a little, out of happiness, because finally, things were beginning to make sense.

The bus stopped and started, letting people on and off, and Golde was content to watch and drift and enjoy the special feeling. By the time they got to the beach, the whole inside of the bus had changed, and all the people were new ones. She was the only one left from Fairfax. Then she felt like it was time to get off because someone opened a window behind her and she could smell the ocean. She pulled the cord and the bus obliged her by stopping and she got off.

Then it lurched away, and she didn't know why but it reminded her of a big puppy dog. For a moment she was scared, but then she looked around and she liked where she was. It was cooler than on Fairfax, almost chilly. The breeze tickled her hair where it was stiff from the hair spray. She could see the ocean a few blocks away. She headed toward it.

The boardwalk was filled with people strolling, enjoying the summer evening. There were roller skaters and bunches of young people. People pulled dogs, and mothers pushed toddlers in strollers. Old people picked their way cautiously. It was like a circus, or like television. Golde felt happier than she had in years. She wanted to sit for a while and look at all the people, so she found a bench that faced away from the ocean and she sat and rested and looked at all the new faces.

Just as she started to feel a little too cold, something caught her eye. She looked over to her right, on the other side of the boardwalk, and she saw a sign. It was a big Jewish star, and the sign said "King David Conva-lescent Home."

Even though the colors were starting to get soft like they do before the sun goes down, something else caught her attention. She felt eyes on her, watching her. She looked over to the porch under the sign, and she saw a few old people sitting, rocking on chairs. One of them looked familiar. Suddenly she felt a chill from the inside, because she recognized the one who was staring at her.

She picked up her purse and the shopping bag and slowly

walked toward the porch. She went over to the little figure hunched over in the chair. She held her breath, and then she spoke.

"Minnie? Is that you?"

Minnie beamed. Her front teeth were missing. She wasn't wearing her dentures. She motioned to the empty chair next to her.

"Come. Come and sit down. Sit by me for a while."

"I don't mind if I do." Golde sat herself down and got comfortable, like in the old days.

The two women rocked for a while, and then Golde turned toward her friend.

"You know, to tell you the truth, I wasn't so sure you were still alive." And then she thought that wasn't a good thing to say, so she added, "But I always thought about you."

Minnie smiled. "Well, it ain't so terrible here." She stopped rocking and looked at Golde. "So what's news?"

"A little this, a little that." Golde wouldn't have known where to begin.

"What's in the bag?"

"I got walnuts and raisins. And these cherries."

She looked carefully at Minnie. Then she confided softly, so no one else could hear. "Joseph left them for me on the bus. That's how I knew to find you."

Minnie nodded. "Ahh, Joseph. He comes by to see me once in a while. Sometimes he brings Sol."

Sol was Minnie's son, the oldest one, who got killed in the war.

Golde shivered. Minnie caught it.

"Here. Take this blanket from the back of the chair. They got plenty more."

"Thanks." Golde wrapped the thin, baby-blue thermal blanket around her shoulders. She opened the bag of cherries and offered some to Minnie.

"So does Martin come to see you?" As the words came out Golde regretted them. What kind of a son would put a mother away?

"Achhh!" Minnie spit a cherry pit down to the ground and lapsed into Yiddish. "Martin and his family, they should all take a shit in the ocean!"

It seemed like there was nothing more to talk about. It was good just to sit and rock and eat cherries and be near her friend. The sun was going down and Golde was grateful for the warmth of the blanket. Her knee was beginning to ache just a little, but she decided she didn't need to take a pill, the little bit of an ache was grounding her, keeping her anchored in time and space.

Golde let herself get lost for a minute in the sounds of birds getting ready to nest for the night. She began to miss her new bed and the smooth, lavender sheets. Had she told Minnie about the new place? About the girl Joseph sent?

She turned and was about to speak when she noticed the change, the shift in her friend. Her eyes, wise with recognition moments ago, were now blank. Minnie was gone; just the body of Minnie was left in the chair.

"Minnie?"

Minnie slowly turned toward Golde. "Pardon me, do I know you?"

Golde was about to answer when she saw an attendant, a young black man, walking toward them. He knelt by Minnie's chair.

"Are you ready for your dinner, Minnie?"

She smiled at him and nodded. He helped her up. She turned toward Golde.

"Thank you for the cherries."

"Don't mention it."

And a minute later, Minnie was gone.

Natalie was sorry she'd identified herself to Dwight Morgan. Now it was too late. She had to talk to him.

"I'll have to take a deposition," Dwight said.

"Do we have to do it over the phone?" Natalie wanted to see him. Without contact it would be like throwing words into the air. She needed to see his eyes.

"We haven't been able to locate Mrs. Moskowitz. We're going to send an investigator."

Natalie felt her heart beat a little faster. Her muscles tensed. She wished she could hang up. She started feeling sick.

"Ms. Holtzman? Are you there?"

"Yes . . . I'm sorry, I got distracted." She felt shaky. It was best to say as little as possible.

"Anyway, we need a deposition from Mrs. Moskowitz, too. So I guess I could do yours in person."

"Thank you."

Natalie was relieved. It gave her a little time to figure out what to do. She could talk to Golde, and they'd decide together how to handle it.

"I'll give you my number," Dwight offered. "I live near you. Let's do it over the weekend."

"Okay." Natalie wrote the number in her appointment book.

"I'll call you," she said and hung up.

She stared at the phone for a while. Then she walked over to the window and stretched. Her neck ached and she felt the beginnings of a headache near her left temple. Why did she feel like a criminal? She hadn't really done anything wrong. Yes, she felt terrible about the accident. And maybe she didn't use good judgment with Golde. But she hadn't meant any harm. She really just wanted to help.

Now the police might get involved, and suddenly her motives seemed suspect. She felt nervous that Golde hadn't called. What if she were lost? What if something terrible happened?

Looking down at the parking lot, she saw people from the office heading toward their cars, leaving for the day. There were two kinds of people, two kinds of cars—boxes and bullets. Box people were responsible, mental. Bullet people slid through life, they were emotional, impulsive. Christie's new boyfriend drove a bullet car, a black Camarro. Jason drove a new slate-gray BMW box.

She walked back to her office. She had barely begun her work. Distraction, immersion in the work, that's what was needed to shake off the bad feelings. Music always helped. She tuned the radio to a classical station, listened to a couple of bars of a string quartet, and then started sketching again. Soon she was lost in lines.

Before she knew it, everyone had left. She turned up the volume and kicked off her shoes. It was nearly seven o'clock when she looked at her watch. Still no word from Golde. She felt uneasy. There had to be a reason, a perfectly good reason. Golde might have run into someone she knew. Maybe she'd gone back to the apartment on Hayworth. She could have left a message on Natalie's machine at home.

But when Natalie called the apartment on Hayworth, the phone rang dozens of times. And when she called in to get her messages from the machine, there was none from Golde. She decided to wait a little longer.

At seven-thirty, the phone rang. She grabbed it, prepared to scold Golde, gently, of course, for acting irresponsibly. There would have to be an understanding between them, a contract for living, in order for their relationship to work.

"Hello?" She heard the edge in her voice. But the voice at the other end didn't belong to Golde. It was someone asking for Jason's secretary.

By eight-fifteen she simply couldn't stand it any longer. She gathered her things and put the sketches aside. She checked her machine once more, but no one had called. It was a little before eight-thirty when she clicked off the lights, turned on the alarm, and quickly left the building. There was no way for her to know that at the very moment she got into her car, just as she turned the key in the ignition, the phone in her office started ringing.

Golde was ready to come home.

Golde had plenty of change for the phone, thank God, because it cost a lot to call the number the girl had left. But then it rang and rang and nobody answered and she got worried that she wouldn't be able to get back to the place with the good bed. She knew she could always take a cab back to Fairfax, or maybe the buses were still running, but she didn't want to go to the apartment on Hayworth, and she couldn't remember how to get to the new place.

Then she thought she should call the other number, so she dug through her purse until she found it scribbled on a piece of paper and thank God she had a lot of change because this call was expensive, too. A machine picked up and it was Natalie's voice, but telephone machines frightened Golde, and she didn't want to talk into it. They were like the evil eye, they took your voice and threw away the rest. So she hung up, and then she stood there for a moment with the blue blanket wrapped around her shoulders, clutching her purse and the shopping bag with raisins and walnuts.

The sun had gone down and the air was cool and damp. Her nice hairdo was starting to sag from the moisture. She began feeling a little bit scared. Maybe the girl was on her way home. She decided she would call the number again in a few minutes. But meanwhile, she needed to sit down, her knee was starting to throb. And she could use a little something to eat. She started to walk because she didn't want to sit outside in the cold, and after a little while she heard voices and she listened more closely. It sounded like singing. It was coming from a brightly lit building, and she also smelled food—good, warm food.

As she came closer and the singing got louder, she tried to pick out the words, but they sounded strange, they weren't in Yiddish or in English. Just as she started to concentrate to figure out what was going on, a tall, thin man brushed past her and opened the door and started to go in.

He turned around and looked at her and said, "Are you coming in?"

"I wouldn't mind," she said and she followed him inside.

He was one of the strangest-looking people she had seen in a long time. She didn't figure he was very old, but he was completely bald, like a baby, and she thought, "My goodness, such a shame for a young person!"

And that wasn't all. He was wearing a long orange robe and she wanted to laugh because it reminded her of her new muumuu, the one that belonged to somebody else before the girl gave it to her. And besides that this man was wearing a dress, he had on lots of beads.

So she figured either he was crazy, or maybe he was a prophet like in the Bible. But he seemed kind, and he was taking her inside this building where it was warm and dry, so she followed him.

When she got inside she couldn't believe it! She saw lots of men, all dressed in long robes and wearing beads, dancing and singing. Lots of them were bald, and some of them had long braids, and they danced together, just like the Hassids. There were women, too, and they wore strange clothes and some of them had earrings in their noses, little gold or silver loops stuck in the sides of their nostrils. She thought it must be a problem, wouldn't it hurt when they had to sneeze?

At the end of the hall there was a table, and it had on it lots and lots of food like for a bar mitzvah. People just seemed to go up and help themselves. Golde walked closer to the table, but she wasn't sure she should eat. It wouldn't be polite unless she was invited.

She stood near the food and sighed and didn't know what to do, until finally a girl came up to her and asked her if she wanted to eat.

"I wouldn't mind," she said. "Thank you."

Golde helped herself to a heaping plateful of food—yellow stew and rice and yogurt and pieces of big, round bread. Then she found a comfortable place to sit, and ate this good, warm food and listened to the sounds of singing . . .

"Hare Krishna, Hare Krishna, Hare Rama, Hare Rama . . ."

Waves of sleepiness rolled over her, one after another, and even though she missed the new bed, this chair was big and comfortable and she felt safe and warm. She put the blanket over her and let herself drift into sleep.

The first place Natalie checked was the apartment on Hayworth. All the lights were out and no one answered when she knocked on the door. Then she drove around Fairfax, but it was nearly deserted. She felt little surges of panic. The helplessness was the worst part of it. She simply didn't know what to do. Was there anyone who might have seen Golde? She parked the car and walked for a while, into shops, behind alleys.

When she described Golde to the man at the all-night news stand, he just shrugged and said they all looked like that. She knew he was right.

She decided to go home and wait for Golde to call. Besides, she was tired and hungry and this driving around seemed pointless.

She went home by way of Coldwater, just to be certain Golde wasn't waiting at the bus stop. The sight of the empty bench gave her a feeling of nausea.

Coming home to the empty condo was even more unsettling. Golde's absence created a weight, something nearly palpable, a profound sadness. The little blinking light on the answering machine gave her hope. She assumed Golde had called. She silently berated herself for not being there to answer the phone. She listened to the messages. There was one from Caroline asking if they were still on for dinner the next night, and a hang-up, probably a wrong number.

Golde's strange little cookies, sitting on a plate on the kitchen counter, was more than she could bear, and she started to cry—deep, cleansing tears. After a while she felt a little better, so she fixed a sandwich and poured a big glass of wine and went into the living room to wait for Golde's call. She settled on the floor in front of the television and switched channels with the remote control. She found a public access program about common, everyday people, some of them downright frumpy, who frequently communicated with entities from other dimensions of being. These people thought that people who didn't have these experiences were crazy.

The program ended and she switched channels. She heard the familiar *Nightly News* music, and her heart sank. Golde should have called by now. Soon the buses would stop running. She called the apartment on Hayworth one more time, but no one answered.

How good it would be to talk to Artie. His voice would soothe her. He would know what to do. She dialed his number as she watched the news. It rang a few times. A woman answered.

"Hello . . ."

Natalie didn't recognize the voice. Could she have dialed the wrong number? She heard water running in the background.

"Hello . . . ?"

The voice was curious, innocent, a perfectly ordinary, pleasant voice.

"Who is it?" It was Artie shouting in the background, shouting above the noise of the shower.

My God, it couldn't be! She thought the others were women he met out of town, on his business trips. They weren't important, they didn't have anything to do with her. They were only for sex. *She* was the only one here, *she* was the only one who slept in that bed!

Natalie hung up. It was hard to breathe, like she had been kicked in the chest. Fury rose up in her, a rage so primitive, so powerful, it went beyond anything she had ever known.

"How could he do this to me?!! "

How could this be possible? The others were shadows, they

weren't real. She had always been able to make them insignificant, to deny them existence, to strip them of flesh and blood.

She poured another glass of wine and drank it quickly, not sipping it slowly as she usually did, not savoring the flavor, but drinking for affect. Then she poured another after that and drank that one quickly, too. She let herself sink into sadness, and then she drank a little more, this time right out of the bottle, and it felt like nothing would ever be right again. The clothes slid off her body, making a pile on the floor. Dizziness took over.

The room was spinning, pulling her down, pulling her toward the sofa, pulling her mercifully into a deep, dreamless sleep.

And out of that sleep, out of that dark hole of a place, the throbbing in her head took another form, became a noise, and gradually she realized it was the ringing of the telephone. As she woke, she remembered Golde was missing, and then she remembered the woman who answered Artie's phone, and all the work she needed to do for Jason. She reached for the phone.

"Hello . . ."

A woman's voice answered her. "Yes, I want to talk to Golde Mosko-witz . . ."

Natalie's mouth was dry, her head felt like a tin roof.

"Who is this?" She knew she sounded tentative, shaky.

"It's Myra Goldberg, Mrs. Moskowitz's landlady."

Natalie wasn't prepared for this invasion.

"She's not here," she blurted. Afraid that Myra would ask where Golde was and certain she wouldn't be able to come up with an acceptable answer, she added, "She'll call you later," and quickly hung up.

She needed to think. But first she needed relief from the physical symptoms brought on by the wine. She needed coffee, strong coffee. And a shower.

The sun streaming into the living room hurt her eyes. It was much too bright. She looked at the clock. It was nine o'clock. She felt dangerously out of control. Her hands shook as she poured coffee beans into the grinder. Some of them landed on the floor. They looked like little bugs. It terrified her to think of what might have happened to Golde. God, if only she hadn't interfered! Dr. Reynolds was right, she should have stayed out of Golde's life. She took an aspirin while the coffee brewed. She thought she had better eat something even though she wasn't hungry, so she nibbled on a slice of bread.

By the time the coffee was ready she was feeling a little stronger. It worried her that the landlady had called. That meant Golde hadn't gone back to the place on Hayworth. She might need to call all the hospitals. What about the police? They'd want to know about her, why she wanted to find Golde.

The best thing would be to wait for a while. If she didn't hear from her by, say, eleven or twelve, she'd make a plan. If only everything weren't happening at once!

She pulled the phone near the shower so she'd hear it. The rush of water was soothing. If Golde weren't missing, Natalie would probably have gone to the gym this morning. Maybe she would have taken Golde. She made the water a little hotter. She thought about the voice of the woman who answered the phone last night. She wondered if that woman knew about her. She wondered what she looked like, how she knew Artie, what she wanted from him.

Maybe she was perfectly content seeing him occasionally, not caring too much. But what if Artie loved her? She made the water colder to drive away the thought. It was simply too painful to consider that possibility.

She turned off the water, stepped out of the shower and wrapped herself in a soft bath sheet. She needed to be swaddled. In the middle of brushing her teeth, the phone rang. She grabbed it.

"Hello . . ."

"Ms. Holtzman . . . ?"

Maybe it was the police. After all, Golde had her number in her purse.

"Yes?"

"It's Dwight Morgan. I'm right around the corner. I'd like to come over now . . ."

Golde woke up early to the sound of tinkly little bells. Even though she was in a strange place and she'd slept in her clothes, she was feeling pretty good. Someone had put her feet up on a footstool and taken off her shoes, but nobody had touched her purse; it was still in her lap. She looked around. The table with all the food was empty now. Next to it was a new table, a smaller one with flowers and pictures on it. There were some people in the room, mostly men wearing those funny dresses, only they weren't dancing now, they were sitting on little carpets with their legs crossed.

She was going to get up, but then another man came in and he hit a big metal disk that made a loud, pretty, ringing sound, and the people started chanting a soft, beautiful kind of a song, and Golde figured it wouldn't be polite to interrupt. So she stayed in the chair on the side of the room, and she figured when they stopped singing she'd get up and find a bathroom and have some tea and figure out what to do.

The singing went on for a long time, but Golde didn't get impatient because the sounds were so nice, and after a while she couldn't help it, she started humming along with them, after all, it was a pretty simple tune. She added her own words, not words really, just sounds . . .

"*Yi di di . . . yi di di di . . .*"

Somehow, it was the strangest thing, this little song made her feel full, and as she sang she felt herself smiling, filling up with happiness. Then the words of their song changed, and she could understand the sound. It was "Ommmm."

She sang along with them.

"*Ommmmmmmm . . . Ommmmmmmmm . . . Ommmmmmmmm . . .*"

By the time they stopped the "Ommmm" sound, it felt to Golde like something had happened, the room lifted up, everything seemed to glow, and she didn't even think about having to go to the bathroom. No wonder everyone just sat still after that. What else could you do?

Finally, the man hit the metal disk again and the beautiful sound rippled through the room. It was so peaceful! It was like the end of a wonderful dream. People started getting up and speaking softly, and someone brought trays of breads and fruits and tea and put them on the table.

One of the women came over to Golde. She had a big red dot in the middle of her forehead. Golde resisted the temptation to spit on a piece of Kleenex and wipe it off. Maybe she would be insulted that Golde noticed what a big mistake she made putting her lipstick on in the wrong place, so she didn't say anything. Fortunately, the woman spoke first.

"Would you like some breakfast?"

"If you don't mind, " Golde said. "And maybe I could go to the bathroom."

The woman helped Golde get up and led her to the bathroom. Golde washed up and straightened her dress. Her hair didn't look so great anymore, but she combed it and did a little fussing with it and made it look better. She rinsed her mouth and washed under her arms. Then she went back out into the hall, and because the girl said it was okay, she fixed a little something to eat and sat and enjoyed the flavor of the spicy tea and the sweet breads and fruit.

It was time to take a little walk, so she folded her blanket and took her bag with the raisins and walnuts, and thanked everybody for being so nice to her and just before she left, she noticed some of the people put little gifts of fruit and flowers by the pictures and statues on the little table where there were also candles burning, so she dug into the bag and left some almonds and raisins.

"There!" she said to the picture of a wrinkled, toffee-skinned prune of a man curled up like a pretzel and smiling like crazy.

She left and walked out of the building and into the most glorious morning of her life.

Myra Goldberg had a funny feeling about all of this business with Golde Moskowitz. It just didn't add up. Why would she just take off like that? Who was this Natalie person, and why was she so anxious to get rid of Myra when she called? And why was Golde limping? The more she thought about it, the more uneasy she felt. She was in a business where you learned to follow your hunches. After all, when you managed apartment buildings you had to be careful who you rented to, you had to have a sixth sense about people. Myra definitely didn't trust Natalie.

Then there was the matter of the rent. Golde was two days late and that wasn't like her. Myra collected the rents on the fifteenth, and Golde always counted out the cash for her. Once in a great while she would be a day late if her social security check got delayed in the mail, but even then she would apologize to Myra and promise to have it the next day.

What if Golde didn't come back? What would she do with the apartment, with Golde's personal effects? As far as Myra knew, Golde had no family. Why would this Natalie person want to kidnap her? And why wasn't she with Natalie when Myra called?

Even though she didn't have anything more substantial to go on than her instinct, she nonetheless found herself dialing the police. Maybe she would file a missing person's report. Maybe she would just ask them to check on Golde to be sure she was with Natalie out of her own volition. After all, older people were so vulnerable.

"Third Precinct—Officer Davis speaking . . ."

Officer Davis usually didn't work weekends, but with the baby coming in a few weeks they needed the extra money. And he had a stack of paperwork to clear up. When the phone rang, he was just looking through the Moskowitz file, so it was a strange coincidence that the call was from Myra Goldberg.

He remembered Golde Moskowitz and Natalie Holtzman. As accidents go, it was a pretty minor one—no major injuries, no conflicts in their stories. He had much bigger cases to worry about.

He would have dropped it except for one thing. Tri-State Insurance called him because they hadn't been able to locate Golde Moskowitz. They wanted to confirm the phone number and address given on the police report.

So because it was a slow day, and because of these strange coincidences, Officer Davis agreed to take a report from Myra Goldberg.

He agreed to look into this Golde Moskowitz business himself.

Natalie just couldn't fight it anymore. Though she wanted to tell Dwight that it wouldn't be a good time for her to see him, she thought better of it. Maybe he could help. And she was feeling so frightened and confused she really didn't want to be alone.

She slipped into some shorts and a T-shirt, put a little makeup on, and started straightening up the living room. She trashed the empty wine bottle, threw her clothes in the hamper, poured another cup of coffee, and took some vitamins. The doorbell rang.

"Just a minute," she called, trying to sound natural.

She opened the door. He didn't look anything like she thought he would. He was a little bit taller than she was, just a little bit chubby, and he had enormous dark brown eyes and enviable lashes. He looked slightly rumpled, more like a writer than an insurance investigator, and he held a big, battered briefcase. His hair was dark, with a spattering of gray. It made him look vulnerable. It needed to be combed.

"Hi. I'm Dwight."

"I'm Natalie. Please come in."

"Thanks."

He followed her into the kitchen while she reheated the coffee. She saw him eyeing Golde's cookies. She put them on the table with the coffee. They sat across from one another. Her foot accidentally touched his. She pulled it away. He looked at her with his puppy-dog eyes.

"Thanks for seeing me today." He tapped the side of his cup. "I usually don't work weekends, but I got a little bit behind."

"I understand." She wanted to tell him everything. She was scared.

He sipped his coffee.

"This is great," he said. "You make great coffee." He seemed to be studying her face.

"Thanks," she said. "I grind my own beans."

"Do you live alone?" He took a cookie, looked down at it and then up at her again. "That's not really an insurance question, I just wondered . . ."

There was an awkwardness between them. She could imagine how nice he would be to hug. He had no hard edges.

"Yes." Then she thought about Golde. "Well, sort of. Do you?"

He wasn't wearing a ring.

"Yes." He took a bite of the cookie. "They need something."

"I know, " Natalie said.

"I guess we'd better get started," he said, pulling a tape recorder and pad of paper out of the briefcase.

"Oh, God. I didn't realize you were going to record this." She shifted uncomfortably.

"I'm sorry. I should've told you. It's standard procedure."

Part of her wanted to run or to trick him into leaving. She could pretend she was ill, she could ask him to come back later. She could tell him she wasn't prepared to make an official statement. But it really didn't seem to matter anymore.

What seemed to matter most was that it all needed to come out, she needed to be freed from the burden of guilt and responsibility she felt toward Golde, and even more important, toward Rose. She needed to stop running.

She looked up. She hadn't realized how intently Dwight was looking at her.

"Would you rather do this another time?"

He was giving her an out.

"No, it's okay. Let's get it over with."

He popped a cassette into the recorder and snapped the top down. He was about to turn it on.

"Listen . . . before you start recording, I need to talk to you, off the record."

He put down his coffee.

"Okay."

The distance across the table seemed enormous. She would have to leap over her own resistance. She looked down at his hands. They were good, solid hands. She could trust them. She fought an impulse to reach out to him, to make contact.

She took a deep breath and began. She spoke, haltingly at first, but then with confidence. She told him all about Golde, about her involvement, about telling the nurses she was Golde's daughter. She told him about the cookies and the little song Golde sang coming over the canyon. She told him everything. When she told him about Golde's disappearance, she started to cry.

He dug through his jeans pocket and handed her a wadded-up handkerchief.

"It's clean. I just don't iron."

"Thanks." She blew her nose.

A long moment passed. A feeling of calm came over her. She needed to know what he thought, she needed to have a marker, some way to measure the distance traveled. She looked up at him.

"Was I terrible to have gotten so involved?"

"I don't really know." He spoke slowly, carefully. "You may not have used good judgment. And of course, a lot depends on how Mrs. Moskowitz feels about all of this. But were you terrible?"

She took a sharp intake of breath and braced herself for the consequences.

He shook his head. "No, you weren't terrible." He smiled at her. "In fact, off the record, I think you were wonderful."

She suddenly felt strong, like the woman she wanted to be.

"What happens next?"

"We need to go to the police," he said.

"Oh, God . . ." she pulled back. "I'm so scared . . ."

"Don't worry." He reached out and took her hand and squeezed it, then let it go.

"I'm here," he said. "I promise I'll help you."

Golde felt better than she had in years. Why, her knee hardly hurt at all. And even though she'd slept in a strange place she felt well rested, and the breakfast they gave her sat comfortably in her stomach, pulsing, giving her strength and energy. The sounds of the singing still echoed through her head, blending with the songs of morning birds and the gently rippling ocean. The sky was so clear and bright and blue, she couldn't remember ever having seen such a sky! It was like Russia, like the skies of her childhood.

She walked along the boardwalk, stopping once in a while to look at something, a baby in a carriage, some fruit in a shop window. She passed the place where she had seen Minnie, but now the porch was empty except for a withered old man who sat staring straight ahead. She thought about returning the blanket Minnie had given her, but then she figured she might need it. Because as long as she was here, so near the ocean, she might as well go and sit and look at the waves.

She took off her shoes and put them in the bag with the raisins and nuts, and walked out onto the sand. She liked the way it felt between her toes even though it was hard to walk. The breeze made her skirt pull between her legs, like a sail. It seemed to take a very long time to get to the place she and Joseph used to sit, where she could see the shimmering waves, but finally she got to the little ridge right before the sand sloped down to meet the water.

She spread the blanket carefully, making a little blue square. Then she plopped down on it, facing the ocean. The waves rolled in, one after another, and she felt like she could watch them forever and she would never get bored. Even though they were all the same, they were all different, too. And because of the singing, the good breakfast, the salt air, because her knee didn't hurt and because she had seen Minnie and for all the reasons that made this moment so special, it seemed to her that the waves had little hands that reached out to her, and thousands of little faces.

If she listened very closely, she could hear the voices in the waves, voices that called to her. And while she couldn't really make out the words, she could tell what they meant. They meant that she was safe, that the ocean within her, the deep, watery places within that held her history, that made it possible for her to be alive, were the same as the ocean without. If she looked very closely at every face in the ocean, she knew she would know it, it would be familiar. The child and the husband and the father and all the others that had been inside of her, that had swum in her ocean, were part of the bigger ocean, too. And she didn't really understand these strange ideas, but somehow she knew she wasn't alone.

Then her face began to hurt, and she realized it was because she was smiling harder than she had ever smiled and her cheeks were wet because tears, good ones, rolled out of her eyes, and she heard a sound that was strange, and it was her, she was laughing, she was bubbling up from deep inside. Time froze and it stayed that way until slowly, bit by bit, the feeling started to fade away, and she began wondering about ordinary things again, and the faces in the ocean disappeared, and the waves rolled in and out like ordinary waves.

She began to miss Natalie, the strange, crazy daughter who seemed to love her so much. She realized that she loved this daughter, too, and she wanted to be with her.

She picked herself up and she hoped she didn't get sand inside the bag with the things for the cookies. She took the blanket and stood and looked at the ocean one more time. She let out a big sigh because she was so filled with happiness she couldn't hold it all, and walked over to a bench where she put on her shoes and folded the little blue blanket.

She dug through her purse and found lots of change for the pay phone so that she could call Natalie.

She was ready to go home.

A LITTLE HAPPINESS

Golde looked over to the phones that were stuck on poles near where the sand ended, but all of them were being used.

"So what's the hurry?" she thought to herself. "After all, a day like this, so beautiful, doesn't come along so often."

"Why, you could bathe in a sun like this, don't you think?"

Who would say such a thing?

Only a mind reader could give such an answer to a thought! Golde turned around. The voice came from a little hunched-over man with twinkly gray eyes underneath bushy gray brows thick as thumbs. Wire-rimmed glasses perched near the end on his nose. Golde hoped they wouldn't slip off, after all, they could get lost in the sand.

"I beg your pardon?" Golde said.

"Come," he said, urging her toward him, "I been watching you. Come with me, *sheyna ponem,* come and spend some time." He reached out to her with a hand as gnarled as driftwood.

And for the first time in so many years she couldn't remember, Golde felt her face get hot—not from the sun, no, from something else. She was blushing, blushing deep and rosy like a young girl, like it was the beginning and everything was new. It was like her arm lifted itself and she watched, and then she felt the cool firm hand of this man wrapping around her own and it was all the way it should be.

She smiled a big smile for him, and he did the same for her and what do you know, the two of them, Golde and Isaac, strolled off together to enjoy the glory of the day!

Nurse Taylor was just finishing her shift when the call came from Officer Davis. She might not have remembered Golde Moskowitz except that she had just reviewed her work load for the next week and saw that Golde was scheduled for a follow-up visit on Wednesday. So she talked to the officer and told him everything she could remember, including the daughter who took Golde home.

When Officer Davis told Nurse Taylor that Golde was childless, she felt a little chill go up her spine. So Nurse Taylor thought back, thought about Golde as she clocked out and walked over to the corner bus stop and sat down on the bench.

"Strange!" she thought, and she hoped the old woman was all right. But Nurse Taylor believed in the power of the Lord. She put all her faith in prayer, so she made a little positive affirmation and she tried to remember what Golde looked like so she could surround her in white light. She closed her eyes and rocked a little bit, and soon she felt peace and the Lord's goodness flow through her.

Then she heard the bus approach and she got up and smiled and climbed aboard to go all the way to Venice to visit her friend Bernice.

Dwight shoved the briefcase into the back of the faded little MG. Natalie wondered why someone who worked for an insurance company would drive a car that seemed so, well, so unsafe. Maybe it was fine mechanically, but it looked like it had been driven into the ground. The front seat sagged from his weight, and the back of it was beginning to rip. There were books on the passenger side, Nathanael West and Nathaniel Hawthorne and Philip Roth. And notebooks and a sandwich wrapper and an empty soda can. He saw her looking.

"I don't like to litter," he said. "I save it up."

Natalie suddenly felt very tired, a sleepy tired, not fatigue but rather a blend of surrender and depletion. She leaned back and closed her eyes. Her back jiggled with the bumps in the road.

She remembered the good sleepy feeling of childhood, of those very early times when night held her in the palm of its hand, like a friend.

Her father would come into her room quietly, so as not to wake her, and though she hadn't really fallen off to sleep yet, she pretended to be asleep so she could savor the tenderness with which he covered her with the warm quilt. He would kiss her lightly on the forehead and murmur good night. That was before the bad times, the fighting and tension that slowly became a part of daily life until he left.

Patches of heat danced across her face, and she thought she could feel Dwight glancing at her. She heard a click as Dwight popped a cassette into the player. Then she heard the notes, winding around and finding the place inside where tears well up.

She heard the words, the words that sang, *"Blue moon . . ."*

Golde and Isaac walked along the boardwalk and she didn't know why she was afraid to look at him, it made her feel nervous and shy, so she just snuck peeks, quick, when she thought he wouldn't see her. But she could tell even though he was bent over a little bit, he didn't have spindly legs like a chicken like most of the men her age. And the way he was bent, it was nice, like a gnarled tree, sheltering.

Maybe he didn't notice how she had all these strange, funny feelings because he just kept talking and laughing and scurrying ahead and then scurrying back, pointing out the special places, like the shul and the Senior Center. And on the side of the building was such a painting like you've never seen, with everything going on! With pushcarts and babies and angels, and such a *tzimmes,* like you wouldn't believe!

And then, she thought her jaw would drop to the ground, he told her he was a painter! Not the kind of painter Joseph was, but a regular painter, a *picture painter.*

He said, "Look, this is the part I painted! What do you think?"

It was the part with bowls of fruit and fat angels and floaty-looking things that looked like the scarves that you buy at Woolworth's.

She clucked her approval and she wanted to say how nice they looked, but she didn't know how to say it. "Very nice" didn't seem like enough to say, and if she said anything at all, all the feelings would come pouring out, so she just nodded and made a big smile.

"How about you let me paint you?" he said, and looked her up and down. She guessed her hair didn't look so bad after all. Next time she would give the girl an even bigger tip.

"Okay," she said.

He grinned, a big, crooked grin. It made her a little nervous, so she looked down at her toes, and then she smelled the pretzels from the cart.

"My, don't they smell good," she said, and what do you know, right away he bought her one and one for himself and cream sodas to wash it down and they sat on a bench and ate big, chewy hot pretzels with a lot of salt and some bright yellow mustard, maybe not so good for her blood pressure. She scraped the hard little nuggets of salt off, the ones where the mustard wasn't on them. Then her knee started to throb, and she remembered her pills, and she reached into her purse and took one.

When Isaac saw that she looked like she hurt, he asked her what happened, and she told him a little bit, what she could remember, about the crazy girl who was really okay, and the nurses who liked her, and he really seemed to listen, he really cared.

Then he said, "Come, we go to my place, you can rest a little."

So she leaned on him. She hoped he didn't think she was fresh like her dead friend Esther, who flirted with all the men from upstairs in the shul no less, even though her husband, Abe, was downstairs *davening* like a little bobbing dreidel.

Isaac led her toward a big, green box of a building that sat plopped on the middle of the sand, right by the ocean on the boardwalk. It looked like it could use a good paint job, the green was faded and even chipped. She looked up to see if Joseph was looking, he could do a great job, but for the first time in a long time, he wasn't there. That was okay because maybe he wouldn't like that she was walking with Isaac. But then a little voice chimed in. "It's okay, *maidelah,* it's okay. Go. Be happy . . ."

Was it Joseph? She couldn't tell, but she liked what the voice said. And why not? What's so terrible about a little happiness?

Nurse Taylor had seen a lot of miracles. She always said little prayers, silent of course, for all her patients and she knew they worked. But she was a realist, too, and sometimes she just prayed that the truly damaged, the souls on their way to heaven, go quietly and peacefully.

God and the angels spoke to Nurse Taylor on a regular basis, so when she looked up and saw Golde smiling and looking good and hardly limping at all, it wasn't a big surprise. And the elderly gentleman walking with Golde had a lightness about him, like a sweet little elf.

And as she looked at Golde, Golde looked back at her. She couldn't tell if Golde recognized her, but she smiled a little smile anyway.

Nurse Taylor smiled back and said to herself, "That lady's gonna be just fine."

Natalie felt a little rush of panic as they pulled up to the police station. Dwight caught it. He turned to her.

"Do we have to do this?" But she knew the answer, and thank God she wasn't alone. She wished Dwight would hug her or at least touch her hand like he did before. Instead, he led her up the stairs gently, and the way he opened the door for her was like a kiss.

"It's okay," he said. "Just tell the truth."

Even though she told it all, leaving nothing out, trying not to cry, Officer Davis didn't react. He'd heard it all. And while he asked a lot of questions, she just told the truth. She looked up at Dwight for reassurance, for support. He was there for her. She felt his pride.

When the call came from Nurse Taylor, Officer Davis excused himself and went in the other room to take it. Natalie let out a shudder of a sigh, and turned to Dwight.

"What do you think?" she asked him.

"I think you're great." he said. "I mean, I think you're doing great."

"Thanks," she said. "I'm not so scared anymore."

Dwight was glad his job with Tri-State would be ending soon. He liked this girl. She was special. He wanted to see her again.

Officer Davis came back shaking his head. This was too much, even for him. Too many coincidences. It was downright weird.

"We may have located Golde Moskowitz," he told them.

Natalie and Dwight exchanged looks.

Natalie turned back, afraid to ask but needing to know.

"Where is she? Is she all right?"

Officer Davis shook his head. "We think she's in Venice at the beach. And she's with a man."

The first thing Golde saw when Isaac ushered her into his tiny apartment were all the paintings on the walls and all of them—or nearly all of them—of fat, naked ladies. Ladies lying down, ladies standing with a hand on a hip, smiling naked ladies, naked ladies sitting so you could count the creases and folds fanning down their backs and all of them, all the naked ladies painted like colors in a dream! Purples and yellows, pinks and bright orange. Turquoise lips and bright green cheeks and blue-streaked hair!

Golde blushed when she saw them, but she couldn't stop looking, and she couldn't say, "Shame on you!" because, for one thing, she didn't feel that way. The colors, the strange, beautiful colors reminded her of the colors of the faces in the ocean. It was beginning to make sense. Looking at them made her smile. Then they made her laugh. Just a chortle at first, but then a big, fine laugh. When she was finished laughing she let out a sigh.

"Can you imagine?" she said. "Such colors, like in a dream!"

Isaac beamed. "Come. Sit at the table. I'll fix a little tea."

He led her to a little table by an open window. All the windows that lined that wall were open, and it was like the ocean and the sky poured into the room. She never saw a room so bright, why it was like being inside and outside at the same time!

And the little table. You could play canasta all day long at such a table. She felt a little ache in her knee. Then, like he could read her mind, Isaac brought over a little footstool and Golde put her foot up and gave him a nice, big smile. He scurried off to make the tea.

She looked around the room. It wasn't very big. Not like the girl's place, Natalie. Only this room didn't have to be big because it had everything you could need. In the corner, but where you could look out at the ocean, was a little counter with a tiny kitchenette. Big bright cups hung from hooks, and the cupboards had sliding doors so the hinges couldn't break like on Golde's cupboards. Against the back wall was a bed, a nice fluffy looking bed with big pillows against the wall so you could sit on the bed and look out at the blue sky and feel peaceful and good.

There was another little room and a little hallway. She tried to peer over, but she couldn't tell what was in there. She figured there would have to be a toilet.

Isaac must have seen her craning her neck, because he said to her, "First we have some tea, then I show you my studio."

Golde wasn't sure what a studio was, but she wanted to be polite so she said, "Okay."

She looked out the window, and then down to the boardwalk below. "So many sounds," Golde thought. Shrieking children, roller-skates, and radios, barking dogs and laughter and bicycles, and all of them, all of the sounds, rolling on a wave of ocean and breeze. Why, it couldn't have been any better! Here she was, right in the middle of the hustle-bustle of the boardwalk, like Atlantic City where she once went a long, long time ago with Joseph before they came to California.

Before she could think too many thoughts about long ago, she heard the blast of the teakettle and then it wound down and Isaac, this strange little man with the twinkly eyes, popped back into the room and what do you think, he had a tray with two jelly glasses of tea, just like Joseph used to make!

EPILOGUE

Natalie could hardly remember a time when it was different. Time had taken on a different meaning, not so much about her, not about deadlines and shopping and meetings for lunch, but about constructing a life out of bits and pieces.

What if she hadn't met Dwight, she sometimes wondered, but couldn't quite fathom what that would mean. Certainly losing the job at Brewer and Associates would have been doubly devastating. That weekend, with Golde missing, the frantic chase to the beach and back, the fear she felt at the police station, all the feelings of panic came rushing back, toppling the buffer of years that had passed.

She still felt the heat rising in her body, the disbelief when, having bared her soul to Jason assuming he would understand, he simply said, "That's it, Natalie. You're fired."

She was stunned, though Christie had tried to warn her. In spite of the trauma, it was all so civilized. Some of the staff even gave her a farewell lunch, as though she were going off on an adventure, a new venture rather then facing the next morning of nowhere to go, uncertainty, a blank page.

Thank God for unemployment! The weekly benefits gave her a chance to reassess, to get her thoughts in order, time to search for Golde, futile though it was.

Dwight courted her, awkwardly at first, often on the pretext of business. And indeed, there were forms to submit and additional depositions. Finally, the case was closed. No complaint had been lodged by Mrs. Moskowitz, and there was no reason to suspect foul play.

Golde had been spotted several times in the Venice area, always looking well and happy, and always elusive. Occasionally, Natalie thought she caught sight of Golde, the back of her head, her pudgy body. Her heart would pound, she'd feel a mix of anticipation and foreboding, and she would quicken her step to construct the "accidental" meeting she created in her mind. Then the disappointment, the nose the wrong shape, the face belonging to another. She wondered if she would ever get over that visceral response.

Natalie was certain she caught a glimpse of her once, just disappearing into the crowd at a farmer's market. And though she searched fervently among the tomatoes and peppers, the oranges and huge heads of lettuce, Golde was gone. Poof. Just like that.

Natalie felt better when Dwight finally left Tri-State. Their time together was no longer contrived. He loved his new work. He was a born teacher sharing his love of literature with his students at Santa Monica City College. Now the battered briefcase, the books scattered around the rent-controlled apartment they shared in Santa Monica made sense. This was the authentic Dwight, the soft, sweet man who kissed her belly, the belly holding the daughter they would share.

Golde Moskowitz sometimes thought about the girl, and she would smile thinking about the good things that happened, about the meals and the nice bed, but soon even that went away. She didn't think about the accident because she didn't hurt anymore, not like before. Only a little of the arthritis once in a while. Besides, she had so much to do these days, there was hardly any time to remember anything.

Every day Isaac would say to her, "C'mon Golde, we got a lot to do! We gotta count the sea shells!"

Out they would go, walking barefoot in the sand, she holding the bottom of the housecoat she wore so it wouldn't get wet, making big squishy footprints and watching the waves, the astonishing waves, cover them over, making them disappear. It was like all the bad times washing away.

All this walking, my goodness, why Golde could look down now and see her feet. She knew she wasn't thin like when she was a girl, but still, it felt good, now it was easier to get around, even with the arthritis.

She felt proud of her new look, but still, she wanted to know what Isaac thought. So she would point to a stranger, a lady on the beach or walking on the boardwalk, and she would say to Isaac, "Tell me something, am I as fat as that lady?"

Isaac would laugh and say to her, "No, my Golde, you're skinny like a chicken. A beautiful chicken!" And he would give her a little squeeze.

In the afternoon she would fix a little lunch, sometimes herring and boiled potatoes, sometimes a sandwich, a little fruit for dessert, and then some tea.

They would take a little snooze after lunch, and she didn't have to sleep in the middle of the bed anymore. The best part was that her dreams were sweet; the dark dreams went away.

Afternoons were always the same. Golde didn't have to go to the beauty parlor any more. Her hair was longer now, not so tight with little curls. She would wrap the ends with bright ribbons. Isaac would turn on the record player, and the sweet strands of music would float into the air. She could breathe in the sounds and they would make her feel like she was floating. Then she would put fresh flowers in the pickle jar on the small table in the studio, and Isaac would start to paint.

"Like this," he would say and he would gently move her arm or turn her chin a certain way. "Sit, my angel. I don't want you should get tired."

"Imagine," Golde would say to herself. "Imagine that, a model I should be! Who would have thought?"

She would smile to herself, but the smile would spread out and Isaac would see it and he would say, "Perfect! Don't move!"

At first she was shy, she wrapped herself with sheets, but after a while, when she learned again to be touched, when she grew into her body and knew it was good, she uncovered for him without shame. And anyway, the warmth of the sun was good, like a blessing.

The paintings of her he made were like nothing you ever saw. All the colors of the sky, like rainbows swirling around her. They didn't even look like they were real, so beautiful were they. So life went on for Golde and Isaac like a dream. In her heart she knew Joseph was happy for her, he didn't have to watch out for her any more. Now he could rest in peace and do the things that dead people do.

Then one day Isaac said to her, "I got a letter from my brother in Poland. I want to go see him."

Golde couldn't believe it. She started to cry, no sound, just a tear rolling down her cheek. And Isaac looked at her and wiped the sweet tear with his big, gentle fist.

"Why the tears, *maidelah?*" he asked.

Golde didn't know how to tell him, how to how to say all the things in her heart. And besides all the good feelings she didn't want to lose, what about the money? The old worries started to come back in a rush, whoosh! And the bad thoughts tumbled around in her head like a swarm of bumblebees. A ticket for the plane to Poland must cost more than all the social security checks she ever got!

But thank God, she didn't have to say anything because Isaac already knew, he could read her inside and out.

He laughed and said, "Don't worry, I got for both of us. We go together!"

Isaac was a very clever man, and even though he wasn't educated, he knew his paintings were good. Better than good. He hadn't told Golde because he didn't want her to feel bad or ashamed, but he had sold some of the pictures.

The night before they left for Poland, just so they would have something good to eat on the plane, Golde made a batch of cookies. This time they were perfect!

And the plane, it was like a whale, so huge Golde could hardly believe it could really fly! She was nervous and scared but sure enough it lifted them up into the sky. And so off they went, traipsing halfway around the world.

That's how it happened and that's why they couldn't be there, at the show called "Isaac and Golde: A Love Story" when it opened in Santa Monica in a fancy gallery. But when Natalie looked at all those paintings, those magical, otherworldly rainbow paintings some people called Outsider Art, she knew it was really from the inside.

Natalie smiled to herself as she held the tiny baby, Golde Rose, close to heart.

It wasn't over. In fact, it was just beginning.

The End

THE CAREGIVER

• Fran Pokras Yariv •

For my mother, "The Queen," and her
"faithful servant," Olivia Aguila Camargo.

Fran Pokras Yariv grew up in Fairfield, Connecticut, received her B.A. in creative writing and M.A. in education at Syracuse University. She was awarded a Writers Guild of America, East, Foundation Fellowship in screenwriting, and is a member of the Authors Guild, the Writers Guild of America, and P.E.N. She is the author of the novels *Leaving, The Hallowing, Last Exit,* and *Safe Haven,* and has written the screenplays for the last two titles. She and her husband, Dr. Amnon Yariv, professor of applied physics and electrical engineering at Caltech, live in Pasadena, California.

ACKNOWLEDGMENTS

I am indebted to the following people for their contributions to "The Caregiver."

The members of my writing group for their invaluable critiques: Rudd Brown, Emily Adelsohn Corngold, Rochelle Duffy, Michael Farquhar, Larry Kronish, Paul Pattengale, and Melina Price.

Felicia Aguirre, whose competence and friendship meant so much to my mother.

My old friend, Dan, and new friend, Ellen Beck, for their encouragement.

Glenn D. Wright, who kept us apprised every step of the way, Anne-lise Finegan, Lynn P. Hoppel, Mona Hamlin, and D. J. Whyte of Syracuse University Press for their enthusiasm and expertise.

Jeanne Rebillard for her efforts on our behalf.

And, finally, to my husband, Amnon, who lived vicariously through the adventures of the Sunset Hill residents.

A Bad Day for Pisces

I believe in signs and in the stars, and it must have been a bad day for Pisces the day Ms. Breur-Gordon called me, Ofelia Hernandez wrote in her journal, the one her friend Corrine gave her for her birthday, *so I should've said no when she asked me to work for her mother, but I needed the money.*

Ofelia put the pen down and took a sip of her Coke. She was sitting in the employee lounge of Sunset Hills Retirement Community while little Mrs. Breur was in the living room with the other residents watching the entertainment and snacking on wine and cheese. Ofelia could hear the singer even though the door to the lounge was closed. He came every three weeks and sang the same old songs, and all the residents seemed to know the words. She looked at her watch. She still had a good half hour before she'd have to go get Mrs. Breur and take her up to her room for a rest.

Ofelia reread the sentence she'd just written. It was true she *did* need the money if she was ever going to move out and get her own place because if she stayed at home any longer she'd really go crazy and anyway, she wasn't getting any younger.

Almost thirty! How did *that* happen!!! When she was in high school, she was sure that by the time she was twenty-six she'd be married with a couple of kids, but that wasn't the way it turned out. But better than Corrine, who'd gotten knocked up senior year and had three kids and was living with her husband in his parents' house. She wouldn't change place with Corrine for anything.

Ofelia turned the page in her journal and drew a long line down the middle to make two columns. At the top of the first column she printed the heading *Good Things about Working for Mrs. Breur*. On the other side she printed *Bad Things about Working for Mrs. Breur.* This was something her father had taught her to do. Ofelia wondered, not for the first time, if he'd made a list like that before he ran off with that slut, Ana.

In the Good Things column, she wrote *1. Pay is good.* Underneath she carefully listed the other positives. *2. I get paid on time. 3. Mrs. Breur is nice.* She wrote the number 4, but she couldn't think of anything else. How pathetic was that! So she began on the Bad Things side. That was easier. *1. Ms. Breur-Gordon. 2. Ms. Breur-Gordon. 3. Ms. Breur-Gordon.* She listed the numbers 4 through 10 and made ditto marks down the page. Ms. Breur-Gordon!

Even though Ms. Breur-Gordon had a big-deal job at an ad agency, the only thing she seemed to care about was her little old mother. She was always snooping around to make sure everybody was treating her right. One of the aides—Buddies was what they were called at Sunset Hills— warned Ofelia when she started the job that she was the fourth caregiver Ms. Breur-Gordon had hired that year. She had fired one of them and two had quit. No wonder the Buddies, the nurse, even Janice, the director, were all scared of her.

When she'd said okay to Ms. Breur-Gordon, Ofelia had been sure she could handle it. She'd been a full time aide at Pacific Villa in Santa Monica for a year and a half and had put up with all the politics. Aides were always quitting or getting fired, which meant the ones who hung in worked like donkeys. But when corporate fired the director and brought in that witch, Karla, Ofelia had had enough.

After Pacific Villa she worked for an agency, which meant that they sent her out on jobs for anywhere from a few hours to a few weeks, and she never knew what she'd get. It's not like I asked for so much, Ofelia thought, just a steady job with nice people and decent pay. She didn't understand why that was so hard. Anyway, she was really sick and tired of the agency, so when Ms. Breur-Gordon called, Ofelia was ready to take on a full-time private job.

Old Mrs. Breur wasn't in such bad shape compared to some of the others, Ofelia thought when she first met her. She was a skinny little thing, all bent over, and used a walker but she could go to the toilet herself. She wouldn't have to be changing diapers. Not yet, at least. Ofelia knew her official job would be helping her get dressed, doing her laundry, and walking her down to the dining room and to the activities. That was all she was really required to do, but Ms. Breur-Gordon made it clear that she expected much more.

"I don't want poor Mother just sitting in her room," Ms. Breur-Gordon had told Ofelia when she started the job. "I want her to have friends and to have an active lifestyle."

Well, yeah, Ofelia thought. That would be nice except that little Mrs. Breur was hard of hearing and didn't talk much and she didn't like any of the activities except bingo and nobody talked when they played bingo. Bingo was serious business because the winner got these coupons called Sunset Bucks they could use to buy things like shampoo and candy. And sometimes little Mrs. Breur just wanted to take a nap instead of going downstairs to hear a lecture on diabetes or watch a movie. What did Ms. Breur-Gordon want her to do, Ofelia wondered, drag her mother out of bed and force her to go downstairs? But if Ms. Breur-Gordon called and her mother was in her room instead of taking part in an activity, she had a fit. And she would say to Ofelia in that voice Ofelia had come to dread, "Now, Ofelia, you know I expect Mother to socialize."

No wonder Ofelia was always nervous just knowing that Ms. Breur-Gordon could show up out of nowhere and inspect the apartment and ask questions like did Mother eat all her lunch, what did she eat, did you wash her hair, were the sheets changed, and on and on. Once Ofelia forgot to sign Mrs. Breur up for an outing to the museum and you would've thought she'd poisoned her the way Ms. Breur-Gordon carried on. Ofelia felt like telling her if you're so concerned, why don't you take her to live in your big house and care for her yourself, like we do in my culture. But of course she kept her mouth shut. But Ms. Breur-Gordon must have felt bad because the next day she brought Ofelia a big box of chocolates. After that, when the weekly activity schedule came out, Ofelia made sure she was the first one down at the desk to sign Mrs. Breur up.

Money isn't everything, Ofelia wrote at the bottom of the page with the columns. Just because you were rich didn't mean you were happy or were a good person. All she had to do was look around Sunset Hills to figure that out. They didn't take any Medi-Cal people, and they charged big bucks, and on top of that they kept raising the rent and the cost of all the extras like daily housekeeping and personal laundry. She figured that the residents were rich or had rich children like Ms. Breur-Gordon, but not too many of the old people, except maybe those with Alzheimer's, looked happy. Mrs. Breur sure didn't look happy, even when she had her hair and her nails done. But then again, Ofelia knew that being poor didn't make a person happy either. Her mother was proof of that. She was a server in the cafeteria at Harding Junior High, and the little money they paid her she ended up giving to Ofelia's spoiled brother, who couldn't keep a job. She was always sighing and complaining, so you couldn't call *her* happy.

But if I had a choice I'd rather have money because then I wouldn't have to always worry that Ms. Breur-Gordon was going to fire me, Ofelia wrote.

The door opened and Connie came in balancing a small tray with a plate of fruit and cheese and a glass of wine in one hand. The Buddies weren't supposed to drink at the wine and cheese hours, but nobody except the Filipinas paid any attention to that rule.

Ofelia closed her journal. Connie was her favorite Buddy because she was friendly, and, besides, she always had all the latest gossip, which was why Ofelia wouldn't let her read anything she wrote in her journal.

Connie put the tray on the table and sat down across from Ofelia. "Want some cheese?" She pushed the plate toward her.

"Thanks." Ofelia took a little square of cheddar and a cracker.

"It is too funny out there." Connie grinned. "Mr. Grant is guzzling that cheap wine like he was in a desert and it was water! And him with diabetes!"

Ofelia giggled. Mr. Grant was a character, all right. He was always cracking dirty jokes and flirting, even worse sometimes grabbing at any female who was dumb enough to get near him. When she first started working at Sunset Hills, Mr. Grant pinched her butt when she walked by his table in the dining room. Anybody else and Ofelia would've told him off, but Mr. Grant was just like that and didn't really mean anything, so she just said, "Hey, Mr. Grant, you're way too old for me," and he said something like "but I'm young at heart." So Ofelia just laughed and said, "Well, you have to show me your portfolio before you can touch me!" and everybody at his table laughed.

Ofelia heard applause from the living room. Connie rolled her eyes, gulped down her wine, and popped a couple of pieces of cheese in her mouth. Break time was over.

People were still in the living room even though most of the food was gone. The singer was talking to Mr. Grosso, who used to play the piano for one of those big bands, and a couple of the women who had crushes on Mr. Grosso were hanging around. Mrs. Breur was sitting on the couch next to Gerri Kane, and she seemed to be having a good time, so Ofelia decided to have some cheese and crackers.

She stood in back of Debby, the activities director, and Emma Greenberg who was helping herself to some cheese from the platter.

"How about a glass of wine, Mrs. Greenberg," Debby asked in that fake cheery voice.

"No, thanks," Mrs. Greenberg said loudly. "When you spring for some decent wine, maybe I'll indulge."

Debby turned all red, and Ofelia tried not to laugh. Mrs. Greenberg always said what was on her mind, and she didn't care who heard. A couple of women gave Ms. Greenberg dirty looks, but Mr. Grant, who was standing nearby, gave one of his loud "ha-ha" laughs.

"Right on, Emma!" he said. "This stuff's rotgut. Must've got it at the 99-Cent Store."

Debby turned away from them and walked toward the piano, where the singer and Mr. Grosso were still talking. Emma made a face at her back, and Mr. Grant laughed again. Ofelia knew that was why a lot of the residents were afraid of Mr. Grant and Mrs. Greenberg—you never knew what they'd say next. But Ofelia kind of admired them. Not many people, herself included, said what they really thought. Especially not at Sunset Hills.

It was a good thing that Ms. Greenberg didn't need a full time caregiver, Ofelia thought, because with her mouth, she'd really be a handful. She put a square of cheese on a cracker and sighed. Maybe working for little Mrs. Breur wasn't so bad after all.

THE PASSWORD

Strictly speaking, Ofelia shouldn't have had a walkie-talkie because she worked for Mrs. Breur and not for Sunset Hills Retirement Community, but Connie had given her one.

"Like this way, we can help each other out," Connie had said.

They were in the laundry room, and nobody else was around. Connie shoved the walkie-talkie into Mrs. Breur's empty blue laundry bag, which was lying on top of the washing machine. "You know how to work it, right?"

"Well, duh," Ofelia said, a little offended. You had to be an idiot not to know. "Help each other how?"

Connie opened the dryer, felt the clothes inside, then slammed the door shut and pressed start. "Like if I need help with a resident I can call you. And if you need help with Mrs. Breur, you call me and I'll come."

It sounded like a good deal to Ofelia, although so far she hadn't had any problem taking care of Mrs. Breur by herself. So she told Connie yes.

Connie grinned. "So now we need, like, a password."

"What is this, some spy movie?"

"*They* listen to everything." Connie rolled her eyes in the direction of the administrative office.

Ofelia nodded knowingly. Everybody knew that Rosie on the third floor got fired because she was always gossiping on her walkie-talkie, and she'd been stupid enough to bad-mouth Janice, the director. Ofelia didn't feel too sorry for Rosie. She figured if you were that dumb, you shouldn't be taking care of old people.

"You're always writing in your notebook," Connie told her. "You think up a good code word."

Ofelia thought. There were those codes like "mayday" from the old war movies Mrs. Breur always watched on Turner Classics, but she knew what Connie meant was something that wouldn't get them in trouble or get Janice all upset.

"How about something like "room whatever needs some toilet paper."

"Too long."

Ofelia thought some more. What did you do if you had an emergency? You dialed 911, that's what you did.

"Okay," she said. "What about 119? That's 911 backwards."

"119. I like that." The buzzer on the dryer went off. Connie opened the door and pulled out a towel. "Not that we'll have to use it a lot, but you know, sometimes I could use some help like if somebody falls and if I go to one of the Filipinas, then they blab to everybody that I can't do anything by myself."

Ofelia laughed. "They're like the Mafia."

"You said it."

It seemed like a good idea at the time, Ofelia wrote in her journal after what happened, *but I wish I never said yes.* The worst part of it was that she couldn't really blame Connie, or Ms. Breur-Gordon or anybody else. She blamed herself, and she always would.

A couple of times after Connie gave her the walkie-talkie, Ofelia used the code and Connie came in and helped her get Mrs. Breur in and out of the shower. When Connie called for help with one of the residents who was acting out and wouldn't let her change his sheets, Ofelia sneaked up to the fourth floor and did what she could to settle him down. As far as Ofelia was concerned, then, it was a pretty good arrangement. And she liked having the walkie-talkie. You always knew what was going on.

But one Saturday after dinner, Ofelia and Mrs. Breur were watching an Esther Williams movie on TV when Ofelia heard Connie's voice on the walkie-talkie. "119 in 410."

Mrs. Breur looked comfortable sitting in front of the TV, so Ofelia said, "Mrs. Breur, will you be okay for a couple of minutes while I go down to get a Coke?"

"You go ahead, dear. I'm fine."

Ofelia bypassed the elevator and took the stairs up to the fourth floor. None of the Buddies were around, so she quickly went to 410. Connie was waiting for her just inside the door to Mrs. Owens's room.

"What's wrong?"

Connie pulled her into the bedroom and pointed to the sleeping Mrs. Owens. "Look at her."

"She looks kind of pale," Ofelia commented.

"Yeah, well, she's had real bad diarrhea all day, and it's like black."

"Call the nurse," Ofelia advised.

"I did. It's that new one, Jennifer, and she came up and said she was just going to give her some over-the-counter stuff like Imodium."

"It didn't work?"

"Hell, no. So after a while I called her again, and she came up and took her blood pressure, but I was watching and she didn't even do it right. I swear, she doesn't know what the hell she's doing. So I said 'I think Mrs. Owens should go to the hospital.' You know when you have that black diarrhea . . ."

"It's probably blood," Ofelia finished.

"Right. I think she's really sick."

From the looks of her, Ofelia thought so, too. "She's going to get dehydrated."

"I know."

"So what do you want me to do?"

"Go to the nurse's station and tell Jennifer to send her to the hospital."

"*Me?*"

"I can't go again, because she already came up twice and said no, Mrs. Owens would be all right. She's going to be really pissed if I go down there again."

Ofelia hadn't expected this kind of a situation. "But I don't work for Sunset Hills," she reminded Connie.

"I know. That's why *you* could go and they couldn't get back at you."

All sorts of reasons not to do what Connie asked popped into Ofelia's mind.

"Look . . ." Connie nudged Mrs. Owens' shoulder. "Mrs. Owens, Mrs. Owens, wake up."

Mrs. Owens half opened her eyes, then closed them. Connie lifted up the woman's arm, then let it drop on the bed. "See?"

Ofelia saw.

"Come on, Ofelia, do it. Just go down there."

Ofelia was really nervous. She knew she should get back down to Mrs. Breur, but she also knew that Mrs. Owens needed to go to the hospital.

"Why don't you just call Jennifer and tell her to come up again," Ofelia said to Connie.

"Because I told you she said it was just diarrhea, and she's not gonna back down."

"Well, you did what you're supposed to do. You called her. You can't get in trouble for doing your job."

"Oh no? Jennifer will think I'm saying I know more than her, and she'll write me up or something, but if *you* do it, she can't do anything."

"If she won't listen to you, why would she listen to me?"

Connie and Ofelia stood a minute looking down at poor Mrs. Owens. Her face was really pale and sweaty, and her lips had that bluish color.

"I gotta go," Ofelia said. "I told Mrs. Breur I was just going to get a Coke."

Connie didn't say anything.

Ofelia was halfway down the hall when she changed her mind. *Somebody* had to help poor Mrs. Owens. She would tell Jennifer that Mrs. Owens was really, really sick, dehydrated and out of breath, and she had to go to the hospital right away. Now that she'd made the decision, relief flooded through her.

She ran down the two flights of stairs to the second floor but decided first to quickly peek into Mrs. Breur's room and check to see that she was okay. *Please Lord don't let anything have happened* Ofelia prayed. All sorts of horrible things ran through her mind as she opened the door, like Mrs. Breur falling and breaking a hip, or having a stroke or a heart attack.

But when she stepped into the room, she saw Mrs. Breur still watching that old movie. No broken hip, no stroke, no heart attack. But there was something even worse. Mrs. Breur-Gordon was sitting in the arm chair.

"And where have *you* been?" she glared at Ofelia.

"I told you, dear, she went to get a Coke," Mrs. Breur told her daughter.

102

But Ms. Breur-Gordon ignored her. "You are paid to take care of Mother, not run out for Cokes. If you need Cokes, I will buy you a case and put it in the refrigerator."

Ofelia just stood there, her heart pounding wildly. She wanted to tell Mrs. Breur-Gordon what was going on and that she had to go to the nursing station right away to get help for Mrs. Owens. But Mrs. Breur-Gordon was still glaring at her.

"Ofelia, if you think you are not up to this job, tell me and I will find someone else. Is that understood?"

Ofelia lost her nerve. "Yes, ma'am," she said.

It was nearly midnight when she saw the blinking red lights of the ambulance outside in the driveway. Mrs. Breur was fast asleep by then, so Ofelia slipped out and took the elevator to the ground floor just in time to see Mrs. Owens being carried out on the stretcher, an oxygen mask over her face.

Connie told her the next day that Mrs. Owens died in the ambulance. Ofelia and Connie never talked about it after that, but Ofelia blamed herself for being a coward. Not saving Mrs. Owens was number one on the things she would confess when she was dying. If she had the courage.

Sunday in Purgatory

Emma Greenberg opened her eyes one Sunday morning and thought she was back in her own apartment. It was a good feeling. The Sunday paper would be lying outside her door. She would make herself some oatmeal and coffee, sit at the table with the paper, and see what had happened overnight. But the curtains on the window were the wrong color, and her large antique dresser was gone, and in its place was a small, phony, French-looking armoire.

She wasn't in her own apartment. She was in Purgatory.

Actually, it wasn't *really* Purgatory, it just felt like it. She was in Sunset Hills, thanks to Joel and Shelley. *Thanks a lot!*

Emma turned to look at the clock on the night table. It was after eight. Was it early or late? Early or late depended on your point of view. That was the funny thing about time. Back when she'd been in school, eight o'clock on a Sunday morning was early, early. In those days, she could easily sleep till ten or eleven. Later on, when Joel was a baby, she was lucky if she could sleep past seven.

You would think that by the time a person was ninety, she could sleep as long as she wanted, but no, not in Purgatory. Breakfast was supposed to be served until nine but God forbid you got down there a minute after. One of the waiters once let it slip that they actually shut down the grill at eight-thirty.

Emma took a deep breath and sighed. Being on someone else's schedule was no pleasure. She turned her body, pleased that her arthritis was not too bad this morning. She managed to sit up on the edge of the bed, reached for her cane, and slowly made her way to the bathroom.

By the time she washed and dressed, it was nearly nine. She still had to stop by the nursing station to get her meds, which meant by the time she got down to the dining room, the staff would give her the bum's rush. She hoped Louise wasn't on duty down there. She was the worst of the servers, with an attitude and a face to match. Emma was convinced Louise usually forgot half her order and served her leftovers on purpose. Sometimes Emma wondered if she should slip her a few bucks on the side like she did to Rodrigo, the van driver, even if it was against the rules, but giving anything to that sourpuss Louise went against her grain.

By the time she reached the dining room, it was five to nine. Emma made a quick survey. *Her* table, although supposedly there were no reserved tables at Sunset Hills, was empty. That was the good news. The bad news was that dirty dishes littered the surface. She bet Mr. Luskin had grabbed it. He liked that table for the same reason she did—it was in the back of the room, up against the window, and from there you could see the entire dining room and everything that was going on, like who was sitting with who, who got bumped, and who was arguing with who.

Emma stood for a moment, debating whether or not to sit there, which meant that the server would have to clean it off and reset it, which, given the fact that it was just a couple of minutes before nine, would set him or her off. Then she noticed Gerri Kane from 217 waving to her from a table near the kitchen. Although Emma preferred to eat alone, sitting with Gerri would be easier than having a hassle with the waiter.

"Good morning," Gerri said as Emma eased into the chair across from her. "How are you?"

"Not too bad. And you?"

"The same."

Thank God Alan instead of Louise materialized by Emma's chair, pad of paper in his hand.

"Hi, Ms. Greenberg," he said. "Do you know what you want?"

Emma made a pretense of studying the menu, although she ordered the same thing every morning.

"Oatmeal and coffee."

"The van's going to the 99-Cent Store at one-thirty," Gerri said when Alan left. "Did you sign up?"

"My son and his wife are coming for lunch." Just to say it made Emma feel good. God knew some people's kids never showed up.

"Oh how nice." Emma knew Gerri meant it. Since she didn't have any kids, she wasn't one to keep score. "Anyway, all they have there is junk."

"That's the truth," Emma said.

"Still, it's nice to get out."

Emma nodded in agreement as Alan set a bowl of oatmeal and a small pitcher of milk in front of her. It *was* nice to get out. There was a good chance that Joel and Shelley would take her out after lunch, maybe to Bristol Farms or The Grove by the Farmers Market. She would hint that she was out of apples and toilet paper. Then maybe after they did a little shopping, Joel would suggest they stop for coffee and a pastry. Beat the 99-Cent Store.

Back upstairs in her room, Emma went to the bathroom, brushed her teeth, spritzed herself with some Tresor her granddaughter, Lisa, had given her for some occasion, birthday or Hannukah or something. Then she settled down to wait for Joel and Shelley. To make the time go faster, she turned on the TV. CNN was full of news about some senator who had done something either illegal or unethical. Emma found it hard to concentrate. She couldn't remember which state he was from, or which party, and anyway, she really didn't care. What was the difference? It seemed to her that all of them were sleazy these days. She must have dozed off, because the next thing she knew, somebody was knocking on the door.

"Come in," she called at the same time the door opened, and Joel and Shelley came waltzing in.

"Hi, Mom." Joel bent down to kiss her cheek.

Shelley did the same but Emma saw her eyes darting around the room. Probably checking for dust or something.

"I'm glad to see you," Emma said. She reached for her cane. Joel put his hand under her arm to help her up out of the chair. "How's everything?"

"Good. Busy, busy. How's the arthritis?" Joel asked.

Emma shrugged. She noticed that Shelley was dressed up more than usual in an expensive-looking pants suit with a silk sweater.

"Lisa said she'd try to stop by," Shelley said with a smile.

Emma's heart lifted. Lisa was the only grandchild living nearby, what with Michael away at college. Emma treasured her visits, which had become less frequent since she'd started a new job in some advertising agency. Lisa was fun and lively, and Emma loved showing her off to the other residents. And why not? After all, she was far and away the best looking grandkid around.

"Good! Let's go downstairs," Emma said. She hoped it wasn't too late to claim her table.

Luck was with her. They got down to the dining room before the rush and her table was empty. Emma headed right for it and put her sweater and keys on the seat she liked.

"Where's Lisa?" she asked.

"Oh you know her," Shelley replied. "She'll be here."

"Want to wait?" Joel asked.

Before Emma could answer, Shelley shook her head. "No. Let's start. She could be stuck in traffic."

"No rush," Emma said, annoyed that Shelley had answered for her. Actually, it made her nervous to see the buffet was set up and the room was starting to fill. If they didn't start, all the good stuff would be gone. Shelley had already started toward the buffet. Joel took Emma's arm and they followed.

Emma, like the other residents, constantly complained about the food, which was boring and bland, but she had to admit that on Sundays the chef went all out. Probably because that was when most of the families came to visit. And while the staff couldn't care less if the residents complained, the last thing they wanted was to piss off the families.

Joel held the plate for her as Emma pointed out the items she wanted—sliced tomatoes, a spoonful of scrambled eggs, a bagel, cream cheese, and a couple of slices of lox. He settled her at her seat, then returned for his own plate. Emma looked across the table. As usual, Shelley was eating only fruit salad, vegetables, and an egg white omelet. God forbid she should eat a carbohydrate. To be fair, though, Emma had to admit that watching what she ate was what kept her daughter-in-law looking so good, not like Lois Brown's daughter, who looked like a whale, so maybe that was a good thing. Emma ate slowly, anxiously keeping an eye out for Lisa while they made small talk. Michael hadn't decided on a major yet, Joel told her. He loved his literature classes and hoped to get into a creative writing seminar.

"Of course that's all well and good . . . for a hobby," Shelley put in, "but that's no way to make a living."

Emma knew Joel and Shelley were pushing the boy to consider law, but she was sure whatever her grandson chose to do with his life, he'd be successful. As far as she was concerned, if he wanted to be a writer, so what? Maybe Philip Roth's parents had noodged *him* to go to law school. Who knew what *her* life might have been if her parents had encouraged her to do something other than get married to the first man who came along. It still made her mad, even though that was all water under the bridge.

"See that young man over at the big table?" Emma asked, nodding toward a round table in the center of the room. "That's Bernie Elkins's son and he's a big deal in the music industry. And see that skinny lady in the wheelchair? Her daughter's an agent."

Shelley made a face. "That's the trouble with L.A. That's the kind of men Lisa meets, wannabe writers or directors working as waiters. She should've gone to college back east."

"Nothing wrong with UCLA," Emma retorted.

"That's not the point," Shelley said like she was talking to a retard.

"Hey, speak of the devil," Joel said.

Lisa was making her way through the room. No way *she'd* have trouble meeting someone special, Emma thought with pride. She was beautiful, even wearing those tight jeans and see-through Indian type blouse with the sequins. God only knew how she could walk in those spike heel shoes. She'd have bunions before she was forty, but still Emma noticed that everyone in the room was looking at Lisa as she came right over to Emma and gave her a big kiss.

"Hi, Gran, I'm so sorry I'm late, I overslept and the traffic was horrible. Any food left?" Lisa flung her purse on the empty chair and headed to the buffet.

When she came back, her plate was heaped with food, which made Emma feel good. Now *there* was a meal worth the ten dollars, but Emma saw Shelley's eagle eyes take it all in. Shelley didn't say a word, but Emma could read her mind which was saying "if you keep eating like that you'll wind up looking like a blimp." Lisa didn't seem to notice. She ate hungrily and talked about her job. She loved everything about it except one co-worker who drove her crazy because, as Lisa put it, she was totally anal about everything.

"What exactly does that mean?" Emma asked.

Lisa waved one arm. "You know, anal. Okay, like it's freezing cold in the office, and I turn down the air conditioner and open the window just a crack, and she has a fit because all the pollution is coming in. And that's not the half of it!"

"Maybe you can change offices," Emma offered.

Lisa laughed. "Oh, right. It doesn't work that way, Granny. Anyway, my team made a big presentation last week."

And Lisa launched into a lively description of the meeting, complete with imitations of the various people who were there. Emma found herself laughing, really laughing, for the first time in ages.

But then, all too soon, Lisa looked at her watch, gulped the last of her orange juice, and got to her feet.

"Omygod! I've got to be at an art opening in fifteen minutes! I'll never make it."

She circled the table planting kisses on her parents' cheeks. When she got to Emma, she gave her a big hug, just like she used to do when she was a little girl and would spend the weekend. "Love you, Granny."

And just like that, she was gone.

That was when Emma realized that nothing had been said about the rest of the afternoon. Joel asked the waiter for more coffee and Shelley looked at her watch.

"They're going to the 99-Cent Store today," Emma said.

"That sounds like fun," Shelley responded, putting on lipstick.

"You think so? Have you ever been to one?"

"Well, not really."

"What they have is all this garbage that nobody wanted to buy in a decent store and they sell it for 99 cents. What kind of an outing is that?"

"You're right, Mom." Joel nodded. "They should go to one of the museums, or the Farmers Market or a matinee."

"Joel." Shelley pointed to her watch.

He finished his coffee and set his napkin on the table.

"I haven't been to the Farmers Market in years," Emma said hopefully. "I could use some apples. The ones they have here are no good."

Shelley put her lipstick away. Joel stood up and pulled Emma's chair back from the table.

"It's only about ten minutes away," Emma said.

"What is?" Joel asked.

"The Farmers Market."

"Oh, well. Maybe next week."

Emma got the picture. Now it made sense, why Shelley was dressed up, why she was looking at her watch all the time.

"Going out?" she asked.

"Marilyn and Ed are having an anniversary party," Shelley said. "Just cocktails, but it's all the way out in Malibu."

"Sounds like more fun than the 99-Cent Store."

Shelley blinked. Hard.

"Brunch was nice, Mom. Want to stay down here?" Joel asked.

"I'm a little tired. I'll go upstairs."

"I'll go up with you."

Emma shook her head. She felt like she was going to cry. Ridiculous, but there it was. She had never been a crier, but lately the littlest thing and she was tearing up.

"No, no. You go on. Have a good time."

The usual kisses good-bye like they couldn't wait to get out of there. *They* had a choice, which was more than she had.

The van had already left, so even if she had wanted to go on the trip to the 99-Cent Store it was too late. Emma pressed the elevator button and considered the rest of the day. There was nothing until dinner at five o'clock. Then a movie at seven. But she really was tired. She would take just a little nap, then read the paper. That's what you did in Purgatory.

THE NOTE ON THE DOOR

Emma Greenberg saw it first. Like Ofelia always said, for somebody in her nineties, Mrs. Greenberg sure didn't miss a trick. And the first person she told was Ofelia. This is how it began.

It was late on a Sunday afternoon. Ofelia was coming out of the laundry room, where she'd just put Mrs. Breur's sheets and towels in the washing machine, when she saw Mrs. Greenberg standing in front of Janice's office. As usual, the door was closed. Wouldn't you think the director of a place like Sunset Hills would keep her door open, Ofelia thought, just to make the residents feel like they could come talk to her about things, but no, not Miss High-and-Mighty Janice.

Instead of opening the door and going into Janice's office, Mrs. Greenberg turned around and beckoned Ofelia with one crooked finger.

"Come on over here, Ofelia. Look at this!" Mrs. Greenberg started to laugh.

There, pasted on Janice's door under the sign that said "Community Director" Ofelia saw a sheet of lined paper that looked like somebody tore it out of a notebook. In big black letters it read: "To: Janice. The food at Sunset Hills is SPEEDING down hill! From an Anonymous Person." Under the message, a dark arrow pointed down to the floor.

Mrs. Greenberg was still laughing.

"Did you write that?" Ofelia asked. She wouldn't put it past Mrs. Greenberg.

"Somebody beat me to it. Good for her. Or him."

Ofelia agreed with the writer of the anonymous note. The food at Sunset Hills was *definitely* going downhill, not that you could really say it had ever been uphill. No wonder. They'd had three chefs in three months. The so-called chefs were always getting into fights with the waiters, and the last one even got into it one night with Mr. Grant when he sent his fish back three times. The chef stormed into the dining room and shouted at Mr. Grant that there was nothing wrong with the fish and there was no way he was going to make him another dinner. Boy, did that cause a stir!

"You know the so-called soup they served for lunch?" Mrs. Greenberg asked Ofelia. "The so-called *vegetable* soup?"

Ofelia nodded. She hadn't ordered it for herself, but Mrs. Breur had, and she only took a couple of spoonfuls and then made a face and pushed it away.

"You know what it was? Canned corn, canned carrots, and the 'soup' was the juice from the canned corn!"

No wonder Mrs. Breur had looked nauseated.

"Maybe this is the beginning of the revolution," Mrs. Greenberg said.

"What revolution?" Ofelia asked.

But Mrs. Greenberg hobbled away, still chuckling.

What made the note on the door weird, Ofelia thought, was that there was a big suggestion box near the mailboxes and that was where people were supposed to put their remarks and complaints and what have you. Anonymous Person must have really wanted to get to Janice.

When Ofelia took Mrs. Breur down to dinner that night, the residents were talking so loudly you could hardly hear the music they always played during meals. From the bits and pieces of conversation she caught, Ofelia knew everybody had either seen the note or heard about it. There was a lot of joking going around.

Mrs. Breur had just given the waiter her order when Mr. Grant came over to their table. He was holding a piece of paper.

"We're having a pool to guess who wrote the note. A buck apiece. How about it, ladies?"

He put the paper and a pen down on the table. Ofelia saw that a dozen people had signed up. Four had written Mr. Grant's name, three put Mrs. Greenberg, and the others guessed Mr. Grosso, who was also a big kidder like Mr. Grant.

Mrs. Breur looked nervously at the paper like it was going to bite her. "I don't know. Should I do it, Ofelia?"

"Sure, Mrs. Breur." Ofelia opened her change purse and took out two dollars, which she handed to Mr. Grant.

She wrote her name, then thought a minute. She knew the writer wasn't Mrs. Greenberg. Mr. Grant was the type who'd do something like that, but Ofelia watched too many *CSI*s and *Court TV*s to know that the obvious suspect isn't always guilty. She took a wild guess. She wrote "Mrs. Kane" just because Gerri Kane was the most mild little lady in the whole place and never made a fuss about anything, even if they brought her the wrong meal.

Mr. Grant laughed loud, like Santa Claus in a department store. "Ha-ha!" He turned to Mrs. Breur. "Who do *you* think wrote it?"

Mrs. Breur backed away and shook her head. "I don't know. You vote for me, Ofelia."

Ofelia wrote Mrs. Breur's name and next to it, wrote "Mrs. Kane."

"If we win, you should keep the pot, dear, since you put in the money," Mrs. Breur said.

"No, we'll share. Okay?"

"Okay."

"So Mr. Grant, how're you going to find out who wrote the note?" Ofelia asked.

"The truth will out, sooner or later," he said and, picking up his pen and the paper, went on to the next table.

The dinner special was spaghetti and meatballs. It tasted just like that Chef Boyardee stuff they used to serve in the cafeteria when she was in junior high. Anonymous Person was right. As far as Ofelia was concerned, it should be against the law for the residents to pay the kind of money they paid and have to eat that crap. She looked around the dining room trying to figure out who Anonymous Person was.

The note was gone the next morning. Janice's door was still closed, but it was clear that she was *not* happy. The way Ofelia could tell was that instead of hiding in her office behind her door as usual, Janice made one of her rare appearances in the dining room during breakfast, and actually tried smiling at the residents. Everybody, including the waiters, watched her out of the corners of their eyes.

"And how are you today, Mrs. Breur?" Janice asked, stopping by their table.

Mrs. Breur tried to smile which was hard because her mouth was full of oatmeal.

"My, that looks good. Nice and healthy," Janice said, and without waiting for Mrs. Breur to answer, moved on.

Ofelia suppressed a laugh.

Normally, Mrs. Breur didn't like going to the weekly residents' meeting, but Ofelia was dying to hear what they had to say about the note, so after breakfast, she suggested to Mrs. Breur that she go.

Technically, the residents' meetings were just for residents, and caregivers were not supposed to be there, but Ofelia figured the rule didn't apply to her since she wasn't employed by Sunset Hills. She settled Mrs. Breur in the front row of the lounge and then took a seat in the back near the door, where she hoped nobody would notice her.

Janice, Debby, the activities director, and Jennifer, the RN, were sitting at a table in the front of the room with Mrs. Freedman, president of the Residents' Council.

Mrs. Freedman started the meeting by asking everybody to sign a sign-in sheet, and then she asked Mrs. Logan to read the minutes of the last meeting. This seemed to take a long time, and nobody was really paying attention. When that was done Mrs. Freedman asked if anybody had any changes in the minutes and nobody did, so after the minutes were approved she asked if there was any old business.

Mr. Grosso waved his hand and stood up. "Yeah, I do. Last week we were supposed to go shopping at The Grove on Saturday and I was down there right on the dot at one o'clock."

"Me, too," somebody called out and everybody started talking.

"Let's let Mr. Grosso finish," Mrs. Freedman said. You could tell Mrs. Freedman had been a teacher because she still sounded like one with her bossy, know-it-all voice.

"So," Mr. Grosso went on, "there I am all set to go, and Rodrigo comes over and says, just like that, 'no Grove today. We're going to Rite Aid.'"

Everybody started talking again.

"That's not right," Mr. Grosso said. "Hell, we can go to Rite Aid any day of the week."

"Not only can, we do!" Mrs. Greenberg put in.

"Debby?" Janice asked, looking at the activities director.

Debby turned red. "Well, I'm really sorry that happened, but, see, Rodrigo was working overtime, in the kitchen, and . . ."

Ofelia had heard Rodrigo, the van driver, was now doubling as head chef until Janice could hire a new one, but nobody had told the residents.

Before Debby could finish, people started shouting.

"Why is he working in the kitchen?"

"Hire a real chef!"

"How come the chefs keep quitting?"

"No wonder the food stinks!"

"The petit filet is getting petiter!"

Ofelia could tell that Janice was getting really pissed off. She leaned over and whispered something to Mrs. Freedman.

"Now, listen everybody, quiet down," Mrs. Freedman called out. "We're still on old business, which happens to be the Saturday outing to The Grove."

"We're going to try our best so that it doesn't happen again," Debby said, but she didn't sound so sure.

Mr. Grosso sat down, muttering.

"Any other old business?" Mrs. Freedman asked.

Mr. Grant raised his hand. A few people groaned. Once Mr. Grant started, you couldn't shut him up.

"Mr. Grant," Mrs. Freedman said.

"How about some decent wine for the wine-and-cheese hour? I'm sick of that rotgut you serve."

"You're not supposed to drink anyway with your diabetes," Mrs. Greenberg piped up.

"Mind your own beeswax," he said, but he was smiling. And so was Mrs. Greenberg.

They'd make a good sitcom team, Ofelia thought. They could call it *At Home with Grant and Greenberg.*

"I'll make a note of that," Debby said.

"What, that I have diabetes?" Mr. Grant called. "That's an invasion of privacy!"

Ofelia could tell he was having a good time.

Mrs. Freedman ignored him. "Anything else?"

Gerri Kane tentatively raised her hand. "I have something to say about the choice of movies you're showing. We're all adults here and we can handle grown-up subjects, but last week's movie was totally depressing."

A few people clapped in approval.

"What was the movie?" Janice asked, frowning.

"It was this stinkeroo about a cripple who wants to die and can't find anyone to finish him off," Mr. Grosso said.

"They should've finished off whoever made that piece of drek!" Mr. Luskin added.

"It was nominated for an Oscar," Debby protested.

"Well, all I can say," Mrs. Kane said in a soft voice, "is that I couldn't sleep all night and I was really upset. I kept wondering if I should change my living will to a DNR."

"I can understand your concern," Janice said, "and I suggest that we maybe have a review committee of the films before we schedule them. Would someone like to be in charge of reading the reviews?"

Mr. Grosso raised his hand. So did Peggy White, who used to sing cigarette commercials.

"Okay," Mrs. Freedman said. "Any other old business? If not, let's go on to new business."

Janice stood up. "I have a little new business. I would like to remind everyone that there are proper channels for suggestions. The suggestion box is where all comments should go. Yesterday, someone inappropriately taped an anonymous note on my door. I don't mind anonymity, but my door is *not* a public bulletin board."

Mrs. Greenberg gave a big snort, then tried to disguise it as a cough.

"So what *about* the food?" Mr. Grant asked.

Janice gave her fake smile. "We are in the process of interviewing new chefs, and I am sure your concerns will be met. In the meantime, we are doing our best to provide you with nutritious meals."

"Who makes up the menu?" Mrs. Kane asked.

"There is a well-qualified nutritionist at corporate headquarters in Tucson who decides on the menu."

"Yeah, well lucky for him he doesn't have to eat it," Mr. Grant grumbled.

People started talking all at once again.

"Too many fried things."

"Leftovers . . ."

"Spoiled fish . . ."

"Rotten fruit."

Ofelia was enjoying herself, mainly because she could tell Janice was getting really steamed up. She looked around at the residents and again wondered who had taped the note on the door. She was beginning to narrow it down to Mr. Luskin or Mr. Grosso, but she wouldn't have put it past anybody except Mrs. Breur or Mrs. Freedman.

"It would be a good idea if you would put your menu suggestions in the suggestion box," Janice repeated.

"Any other new business?" Mrs. Freedman asked.

Nobody was listening anymore, so she ended the meeting.

That night, after Janice had gone home, a new note appeared on her door. It read, "The Board of Health should close down the kitchen!"

By morning the note was gone, but again, the word spread. More people wanted to join Mr. Grant's pool. Ofelia decided to hedge her bet, so she put in another two dollars and voted for Mr. Grosso.

That afternoon there was a wine-and-cheese social hour, and Ofelia walked Mrs. Breur downstairs. She sat her down, then got her a glass of wine and a little plate of cheese cubes and crackers. Mr. Grosso drifted over to the piano and started playing. He was a lot better than some of the entertainers they hired. Then Peggy White rode up to the piano in her electric cart and started singing along.

Ofelia stood in the back of the room and looked around at the residents and the Buddies and thought about the two notes. Whoever wrote them picked a time when they wouldn't get caught—what that meant was that it had to be late at night.

That evening, Ofelia asked Marleny, who worked third shift, if she'd noticed anybody out in the hall near Janice's office late in the night.

"Nobody, unless you count Mr. Horn, but he's always wandering around."

Ofelia knew it couldn't have been him because he was losing his marbles fast. Ofelia asked Marleny to keep an eye out, and she promised she would. But notes were taped on Janice's door the next three nights, and Marleny said she didn't have a clue. Anonymous Person had dropped the food complaint and went on to other things like the entertainment, the waiters, and the so-called outings.

Mr. Grant's pool was really getting up there. Instead of buying her usual lottery ticket, Ofelia put in ten more dollars.

On the fourth day, a bulletin was slipped under every door. It read: "To all residents of Sunset Hills. Defacing property at this facility is against the rules. This includes posting notices on walls or doors. Anyone found violating this rule will be subject to severe penalties. Thank you for your cooperation."

A few of the residents stuck up for Janice that night in the dining room.

"It's totally juvenile," Mrs. Freedman said in her teacher's voice. "I'm not saying Anonymous Person is wrong, but that's not the way to go about things."

"Right. That's what the suggestion box is for," someone added.

"You wanna know what they do with the letters in the suggestion box?" Mr. Grosso asked. "Check the trash!"

"How about a new pool," Mr. Grant suggested. "Guess the severe penalties for violation!"

The residents, except for Mrs. Freedman and two of her pals, had a good time with that, and before the main course was even served, Mr. Grant was passing around a new piece of paper that said "Guess the Penalty!" The choices were (1) Expulsion, (2) Stoning, (3) Public humiliation (4) Grounded in your room for two weeks.

Ofelia thought it was pretty funny. But she didn't think it was so funny the next morning when Marleny pulled her aside in the hall.

"You see what management did?" she whispered.

Ofelia shook her head.

"Look up, above Janice's door."

Ofelia couldn't believe it. A security camera, just like in a bank or a liquor store!

"There's one by the nursing station and another one by the laundry room," Marleny said.

Ofelia had to hand it to Janice. She was no dummy, because the notes stopped, just like that. Ofelia decided that Anonymous Person had just wanted to stir things up. And he or she had done just that.

But the best part, as far as Ofelia was concerned, was what LeRoy, the maintenance man, told her when she ran into him by the trash bin. He was laughing so hard he could hardly get it out.

"Janice got an eyeful on that security tape! It blew her mind!"

"Like what?" Ofelia asked.

"Like Mr. Horn wandering around the hallway in his birthday suit. Like Mr. Grosso in his pajamas sneaking out of Ms. White's room in the middle of the night. Like two of the Buddies smoking weed in the laundry room!"

Putting in the cameras was pretty smart, but there was some fall-out. Mrs. Greenberg complained to the senior-care ombudsman and the ACLU. The big wheels from corporate had to come to town. They held an emergency meeting in Janice's office, and LeRoy ended up taking the cameras down as fast as he'd put them up.

Mr. Grant got up at dinner a couple of nights later and clanked a spoon against his glass. The room got quiet.

"Listen, everybody," he said. "A lot of you are asking about the pools. Since nobody's come forward to confess to being Anonymous Person and no penalties were enacted, we have . . ." he looked down at a piece of paper on his table. "We have $203.00 in the kitty! I'll be glad to hear your suggestions for what to do with the money."

"How about a refund?" Mr. Luskin called out.

"Hold on. My idea is to buy us some decent vino for our socials. Whaddya say?"

Ofelia never heard the residents of Sunset Hills clap so loudly. Even Mrs. Freedman, after a couple of seconds, joined in.

"Residents one, management zero!" Mrs. Greenberg shouted.

Although Ofelia figured it was okay the way things turned out, she couldn't help feeling cheated. Not about the money she'd put in the pool—she'd never miss the twenty bucks, she spent that much on lottery tickets and iced tea at Starbucks. More than anything, she'd wanted to be the one who figured out who wrote the notes. Now, chances were, unless she unearthed some hidden clue, she probably never would.

THE CONSERVATOR

When she looked back on everything that happened with Alex and Lily Arthur, Ofelia realized she should have been on guard. That's what her horoscope said the day Alex started working at Sunset Hills: "Be on guard. Circumstances are about to change."

Alex replaced Jackson, one of the waiters who got fired because he was always calling in sick. Alex was a real breath of fresh air. For one thing, as far as anybody could tell, he was straight. For another, he was young and really good-looking, with big dimples and a sexy smile. Most of all, he seemed actually to enjoy waiting tables, which was a welcome change from the other waiters, who walked around with sour looks on their faces. After one week, he knew everybody by name. The residents all wanted Alex to be their waiter, and the Buddies, even the old married ones, suddenly became very flirtatious.

Every time Ofelia saw him she felt like a fifteen-year-old. Just talking to him about the menu made her all nervous and giggly. When she saw that Alex was assigned to table ten, where Lily Arthur liked to sit, Ofelia started taking Mrs. Breur to her table. That wasn't a problem because Lily Arthur was pretty laid back and Mrs. Breur didn't really care where she sat, not like some people who threw a fit if the table they liked was taken.

Lily Arthur was different from the other residents. She was a Ms. and not a Mrs. and nobody knew for sure if she'd ever been married. Mrs. Freedman said she'd been married when she was young but it hadn't worked out. Peggy White claimed she'd been engaged to a soldier who died in what they called "the good war." Mr. Grant, who thought he was an expert on women, insisted she was an old maid. One thing was sure—Ms. Arthur didn't have any children and, as far as anybody knew, no other relatives. No one ever came to see her except her lawyer. But if Lily Arthur was lonesome, she never said so. She was definitely *not* a complainer.

The lawyer's name was Roger Sims. Ofelia didn't see anything unusual about him except that he always wore a bow tie. He would come by every couple of weeks carrying his briefcase and go to Ms. Arthur's room, which was next door to Mrs. Breur's. He would usually stop by Janice's office afterwards.

Lily Arthur was pretty frail. She used a walker because before she moved into Sunset Hills she'd been in a terrible car accident and had broken her back. She also had asthma, and a few times she had to go to the ER for treatment. But she had all her marbles, which made Ofelia wonder why Mr. Sims came so often.

"I like Lily," Mrs. Greenberg said once when somebody called her standoffish. "She does her own thing."

Ofelia knew what Emma Greenberg meant was that Lily Arthur didn't kiss up to anybody. Still, a few residents thought she was stuck-up.

"She thinks she's better than everybody because she went to Vassar and she reads that snooty *New Yorker*" was how one of the ladies put it.

That was one of the things Ofelia admired about Lily Arthur. She knew only educated people read magazines like *The New Yorker*, but Ms. Arthur never lorded it over anybody. Another thing Ofelia admired about Lily Arthur was that she wrote poetry. When Debby, the activities director, found out, she asked Ms. Arthur to share her poems with the residents. So every week there was a poetry session with Ms. Arthur, and she would read one or two of her poems and people would discuss them, even if they didn't understand what they meant.

"I don't get any of it, but we artists have to support each other," Peggy White said at every meeting.

After Ofelia and Mrs. Breur became regulars at Lily Arthur's table, Ofelia felt more at ease around Alex. They kidded around a lot and, even though she doubted someone like Alex would be romantically interested in someone like her—at least not until she slimmed down a little—Ofelia thought being friends was a pretty good start.

It turned out that Alex liked to read, *really* read—books, not just magazines. One night at dinner he saw a paperback book called *Zen and the Art of Motorcycle Maintenance* in the basket on Lily Arthur's walker and asked her something about it. Before you could say boo, Ms. Arthur was off and running about the book and how it was revolutionary and changed her life, and Alex seemed totally interested. All the while Mrs. Breur was practically falling asleep at the table, and Ofelia was trying her best to understand what they were talking about. She wished she'd paid more attention in her high school English class so she could be part of the conversation.

Ms. Arthur ended up insisting that Alex borrow the book. After that, the two of them had lots of talks about books. Ofelia suspected that was the reason Alex started bringing them extra helpings of everything.

"Ms. Arthur's really educated, isn't she?" Ofelia commented to Alex one day when she came downstairs to check out the lunch menu.

"She used to be a teacher."

"Like Mrs. Freedman."

Alex made a face. "Mrs. Freedman taught *second grade!* Ms. Arthur taught *literature* in junior college. She probably could've been a famous poet."

"You think?" Ofelia was impressed.

If Ms. Arthur hadn't been sixty years older than Alex, you'd have thought he had a crush on her, but Ofelia knew it was just that the two of them were special people. If Alex liked to read books who was he going to talk to about them? The Buddies? The chef? Her? No way. And if Lily Arthur had been a professor, then it was natural she would act like a mentor. If only she'd had teachers like Ms. Arthur when she was in school, but no such luck.

No sooner had Alex started reading *Zen and the Art of Motorcycle Maintenance* and talking books with Ms. Arthur, people started gossiping. Mr. Grant would kid her and say things like, "Where's your sweetheart today?" and even worse, but Ms. Arthur just chuckled and called him an old roué, whatever that was.

One day Ofelia went down to get Mrs. Breur's mail and on the way back decided to stop by the library. She thought she would see if they had that book about Zen and motorcycles. The library was empty except for Bernie Elkins dozing in a chair and Ms. Arthur, who was sitting at the table reading a notebook.

Ms. Arthur smiled up at her. "How are you, dear?"

"I'm fine. How're you, Ms. Arthur?"

"Well, the good news is I'm here."

Ofelia wanted to ask her about the motorcycle book, but she felt shy all of a sudden. Instead, she asked her if she was working on her poetry.

"I'm reading something Alex wrote."

"*Alex* wrote something? I didn't know he was going to school."

"He's not, but he's writing a short story. Come sit down, Ofelia, if you have a few minutes."

Ofelia sat down and tried not to stare at the notebook, but Ms. Arthur pushed it over to her.

"I believe Alex has real talent. Take a look at the first page and tell me what you think."

Ofelia hesitated.

"I'm sure he wouldn't mind."

Ofelia read. It was a story about a man who gets into a bad car accident and almost dies. She wondered if it was true or made up.

"That's so sad," she said.

"Yes, but the writing is compelling. He's such a lovely young man, don't you think?"

Ofelia nodded. "He's really cool."

"He's got a good heart."

"And a good body, too," Ofelia blurted out.

Ms. Arthur laughed and patted her on the arm. "Yes, indeed. Well, I'm a little past my prime, you know. But now you . . ."

Ofelia stood up. "I better get back. See you later, Ms. Arthur." She nearly ran out of the library and didn't remember about the motorcycle book until she was back in Mrs. Breur's room.

It was the next time Roger Sims came by to see Lily Arthur that Ofelia suspected something out of the ordinary was going on because he got on the elevator with her and instead of saying hello and nodding like usual, he looked straight ahead with a mean look on his face. They both got off on the second floor. Mr. Sims knocked on Ms. Arthur's door and went inside without waiting for her to let him in. Ofelia went next door into Mrs. Breur's room. She didn't have to put her ear to the wall to know Mr.

Sims was pretty mad. He was practically shouting, but she couldn't make out the words. Then Ofelia heard what sounded like Ms. Arthur crying, which made her really angry. Whatever Ms. Arthur had done wrong, there was no excuse for Mr. Sims to treat her like that. After all, she was an elderly lady and deserved some respect and besides, *he* worked for *her*. All of a sudden it got quiet. Then Ofelia heard the door slam shut.

Grabbing the plastic bag of trash from the wastebasket, she hurried out of the room in time to see Mr. Sims heading down the hallway. She watched him barge into Janice's office without even knocking. Ofelia threw the trash down the chute, wondering what had made him so mad.

She thought maybe she'd figured it out the next morning. She happened to be opening Mrs. Breur's bedroom window, which faced the street, when she saw Alex driving into the garage in a red Buick. It was the same red Buick Lily Arthur drove up until her doctor made her give up her license!

Ofelia remembered how unhappy Ms. Arthur had been when that happened. Ofelia asked her at the time if she was going to sell the car, but she just shook her head.

"I know it sounds silly, but I just can't. If I keep the car, then it's as if maybe I'll get stronger and get my license back."

Ofelia knew just how she felt. Even though they both knew she wasn't ever going to drive anymore, Ms. Arthur still hoped for a miracle. But wasn't that what everybody did? It didn't seem any different than buying a lottery ticket every week knowing you're not going to win, but hoping just maybe. Or thinking that if you stopped eating seconds of dessert, you'll look like one of those super models.

Ofelia guessed that Ms. Arthur must have lent her car to Alex, and that was what had made Mr. Sims so mad. But as far as Ofelia was concerned, the car belonged to Ms. Arthur and if she wanted to lend it to Alex, it was nobody's business.

At the weekly residents' meeting later that morning, Janice stood up when they came to new business.

"I'd like to review a standing Sunset Hills policy," she said. "Every Christmas we encourage all of you to contribute to the employee fund and your generous donations are shared by all of our very special staff.

During the rest of the year, Sunset Hills' employees, no matter how wonderful, are strictly forbidden to accept tips from residents. That goes for family members, too."

"I don't see what's wrong with a box of candy on Valentine's Day," Peggy White piped up.

"A box of candy does *seem* rather innocent," Janice answered with her phony smile, "but accepting *any* gift is looked upon as a breach of confidence. The staff is well aware of this rule. Why, I even had a very honest Buddy report to me that a resident tried to give her a little cash remembrance."

"Well, if it works," Mr. Grant cracked.

Ofelia, sitting in the back of the room with Mrs. Breur, thought the Buddy was probably Eva, the Filipina on the third floor, who was always kissing up to Janice. Everybody knew the no-tip rule, but everybody also knew that it didn't stop Rodrigo, the van driver, from taking an extra five or ten for an errand out of his way, or Connie from pocketing a few dollars for taking somebody's clothes to the cleaner. What was the harm, Ofelia thought, and anyway Sunset Hills was so cheap with the help, they deserved a little extra. And as for the Christmas bonus, all they got from the donations was a Target gift card. Like Connie complained to Ofelia when she got the Target card, "What I need is *cash* to pay my bills." No wonder people quit left and right.

Ofelia wondered if Janice knew about Alex using Ms. Arthur's car, and if that was why she was bringing up that old issue.

After lunch, Ofelia settled Mrs. Breur in the living room to play bingo, then returned to the dining room. She went to the table where they'd been sitting and pretended to search around the dirty plates and napkins. Alex was heading toward the kitchen carrying a tray with soiled dishes, but when he saw her he came over.

"Lose something?"

"I think Mrs. Breur dropped her key."

He put the tray down and looked beneath the chair cushion and under the table. "Don't see anything."

"Oh well, it's probably in her purse." Ofelia paused, then said, as casually as she could, "Hey, I saw you driving Ms. Arthur's car this morning. That was so nice of her to let you drive it."

"Actually, she gave it to me."

Ofelia was shocked. "Aren't you afraid you'll get in trouble? You know how Janice is about taking money and stuff from residents. She even brought it up again today at the meeting."

"It was *Ms. Arthur's* idea. I wanted to pay her, but she wouldn't let me."

"That's amazing," Ofelia said.

"Yeah, I know."

It was one thing for a resident to lend somebody her car, even sell it, but to just *give* it away? That was a first. That was probably what made Mr. Sims so mad.

"Nobody was ever so good to me in my whole life," Alex said. "I hope I can pay her back someday."

The flu hit Sunset Hills later that week. Ofelia blamed the outbreak on the fact that Sunset Hills screwed up the flu shots. The vaccine was supposed to be shipped to the nursing office. Residents signed up for their shots, but the shipment never arrived. Janice ended up sending those who wanted a flu shot to Rite Aid where they had to stand in line for an hour. Some of the residents, like Ms. Arthur, hadn't felt up to it, and she was one of the first to get sick.

Ofelia stopped by her room and offered to bring her meals up to her.

"That's very sweet of you," Ms. Arthur said, between hacking coughs, "but the Buddies will do it."

With so many people sick, Ofelia knew she'd have a long wait. Plus they'd charge her for room service.

"It's no problem," Ofelia assured her. And it wasn't, just so long as Mrs. Breur's daughter didn't show up unexpectedly and catch her helping Ms. Arthur.

So for the next few days Ofelia carried Lily Arthur's meals up to her, and when Mrs. Breur took her afternoon nap, she slipped next door to check on her. Ofelia had always thought of Ms. Arthur as a really private person, but she discovered that wasn't true at all. Maybe she just needed someone to listen.

Ms. Arthur told her how when she was a little girl she loved to write stories and poems. On the table next to the bed, Ofelia saw an old-fashioned-looking black-and-white photograph of Ms. Arthur when she was about eight years old. She had long blonde curls and was sitting on a swing. The photograph reminded Ofelia of drawings in the storybooks she read when she was little. Looking at the photograph, Ofelia imagined eight year old Lily Arthur sitting under a tree writing a poem.

"When I graduated from college," Ms. Arthur told her one afternoon, "I guess I was what you'd call a bohemian. I wanted to go to Paris and live with all the struggling artists and writers, but it was the Depression, so I had to go to work."

"So you never went to Paris?"

"Oh, no, I did go, but years later. I had a wonderful aunt, my Aunt Bea, who passed away and left me a generous inheritance, and after that I went to Europe every summer."

Ofelia thought that was a nice story. She wished *she* had a rich aunt who would leave her money. She knew just what she'd do. She'd get her own place ASAP, and then a new car. But it turned out the story had a sad ending because her Aunt Bea's grandson tried to cheat her. That was how Ms. Arthur met Mr. Sims.

"I'm grateful to him because he helped me when I needed help, so when I was in the hospital after my accident and he said I should have a conservator, it seemed like a good idea," Ms. Arthur told her.

"He's your *conservator?*"

Ms. Arthur nodded, and then paused. "To tell you the truth, now I regret it."

Ofelia remembered how Mr. Sims had yelled at her. "Is he mean to you?"

"Oh, no. Controlling is more like it. You know, giving up driving and managing my own affairs makes me feel helpless. I never felt helpless before. It's just not dignified, and I hate it!"

Ofelia knew what Ms. Arthur meant. She felt the same way when her mother tried to run her life and tell her what friends to have and what to wear and how to act.

"Why don't you just fire him?"

Lily Arthur sighed. "I don't have any family, so if something happens to me, I need someone to take care of things."

"You could get a caregiver," Ofelia suggested.

"In fact, I've been giving it some thought."

"If I weren't working for Mrs. Breur, I'd love to work for you."

"That would be lovely." Ms. Arthur reached out and patted her hand, then took a sip of her tea. "Actually, I've been thinking about hiring Alex."

Ofelia thought about that the rest of the day. Although management disapproved, sometimes a Buddy quit and went to work as a private caregiver for a resident. Ofelia was sure that Alex would be very good to Ms. Arthur. He would drive her around on errands and to doctors, and she would help him with his stories. It seemed a perfect arrangement for both of them.

When Ofelia brought Ms. Arthur her dinner that night, she got up her nerve and mentioned the car.

"That was so nice of you to give Alex your car."

Ms. Arthur smiled and shrugged her thin shoulders. "Well, it's of no use to me, and it makes all the difference to him."

Ofelia wanted to ask her if the car was why Mr. Sims was so mad at her that day, but that was getting too personal. Conservators were supposed to help people who were too out of it to manage their money and so forth, but she'd seen a telenovela where a really bad one ignored and cheated the old lady he was supposed to be taking care of. Maybe Mr. Sims was just as evil.

Mrs. Breur came down with the flu that night, and Ofelia was too busy taking care of her to take Ms. Arthur her meals or to think about Mr. Sims. Three of the Buddies called in sick, which made those who showed up extra busy and stressed out, so even though the waiters weren't supposed to go to the residents' rooms, nobody said anything when Alex began taking Ms. Arthur's meals up to her. Jennifer had her hands full in the nursing office, plus it wasn't part of her job. The Buddies didn't care—after all, it made their lives easier—and Janice was holed up inside her office and didn't know what was going on unless somebody snitched.

A couple of days after Alex started taking Ms. Arthur's meals to her, he knocked on Mrs. Breur's door.

"I think Ms. Arthur's really sick," he told Ofelia. "She ought to go to the doctor and get checked out."

"You better tell Jennifer," Ofelia advised.

"Hell, no. I'm not even supposed to be up here. You do it, okay?"

As soon as Ofelia gave Mrs. Breur her breakfast, she went next door to Ms. Arthur's room. Alex was right. Ofelia could hear her wheezing and her skin was pale and sweaty.

It wasn't long before the ambulance came.

Later, Jennifer told Ofelia she'd spoken to the hospital. Ms. Arthur had pneumonia, but she was doing all right.

The next day Ms. Breur-Gordon came to visit her mother, so Ofelia asked if she could take some time off to run errands. Although she really needed a haircut, she went to the hospital instead. Ms. Arthur had a real sweet tooth, so before going up to her room, Ofelia stopped in the gift shop and bought a large box of chocolates. The door to Ms. Arthur's room was closed but since there wasn't any sign saying no visitors, she went in.

The first thing she saw was Ms. Arthur with an oxygen mask covering her face and a monitor bleeping by the bed. The second thing she saw was Alex sitting in a chair near the window.

"How's she doing?" Ofelia asked him.

"Okay. No change, I mean."

Ofelia put the chocolates on the table by the bed. "It was good you told me to tell Jennifer. Who knows what would've happened."

"Yeah, well I know what would've happened. By the time somebody noticed she hadn't called for her lunch, she could've been dead."

Ofelia stood by the bed and looked down at Ms. Arthur. She couldn't tell if she was sleeping or just resting, but she took her hand and squeezed it gently.

"Hi Ms. Arthur, it's me, Ofelia."

She felt Ms. Arthur give a little squeeze back, which made her feel good.

"I just wanted to say hi. So feel better, okay? Everybody sends their love," she lied, "and I'll try to come back soon."

Ms. Arthur squeezed her hand again, and Ofelia felt like she was going to cry.

Alex went to the hospital every day after work and assured Ofelia Ms. Arthur was getting better, breathing more on her own and sitting up in a chair for long stretches. Ofelia wondered if Ms. Arthur had asked Alex to be her caregiver, or if he was going to see her just because he cared about her. Either way, she felt good that Ms. Arthur had somebody besides Mr. Sims.

Mrs. Breur's flu was lingering on, which made her unusually cranky, and she kept sending Ofelia on errands—to get her a Diet Coke from the machine, or wash her comforter even though it had just been washed two days before, or give her a manicure, which she usually had done in the beauty shop. So a few days went by before Ofelia realized she hadn't seen or heard from Alex.

"Where's Alex?" she asked Connie.

Connie looked surprised. "You didn't hear? He left. Nobody really knows what happened, but I bet Janice fired him because he was getting too friendly with the residents, especially Ms. Arthur."

"Ms. Arthur was helping him write a book."

Connie pursed her lips. "Yeah, well he was always kissing up to her."

"He cares about her," Ofelia retorted.

"Sure he does. And he cared about her car, too."

"He wanted to pay for it, but Ms. Arthur wouldn't let him."

Connie shrugged. "Whatever."

Ofelia knew there was no point discussing it with Connie. It was plain she didn't trust Alex.

The next time Ofelia was able to get back to the hospital, she found Ms. Arthur sitting up without the oxygen mask, watching CNN.

"Ofelia! How sweet of you to come," Ms. Arthur said, holding out her arms.

Ofelia bent down to kiss her cheek. "You look great, Ms. Arthur."

"Oh, I feel much better."

Ms. Arthur wanted to know all the news from Sunset Hills, so Ofelia tried to bring her up to date. There was a new resident, a lady from New York who was always complaining about everything. Mrs. Greenberg's son had moved her into a cheaper room on the second floor, and Bernie Elkins was really losing it.

"I wish I could go back right now," Ms. Arthur sighed, "but they want me to stay here a couple of more days and then go to rehab for a while. But the good news is, I hired Alex to be my caregiver."

"That's great!"

Ms. Arthur smiled. "He's a jewel. If I'd ever had a son or a grandson, I'd want him to be just like Alex."

Ofelia thought that was so sweet.

A week went by, and according to Jennifer, Lily Arthur was still in the hospital. On her next day off, Ofelia went back to visit.

"Oh, Ofelia, I'm so glad you're here!" Ms. Arthur cried as soon as she saw her. "Please help me! I can't find my glasses and I can't read the menu or anything, and I called for the nurse but nobody came." She looked ready to cry.

Ofelia looked all over the room, on the bedside table, in the closet, on the windowsill, on the bed, everywhere she could think of, but no glasses.

"I can't imagine what happened to them, but I'm lost without them. I have an extra pair at home, though."

"Why don't you get Alex to go get them?"

Ms. Arthur's eyes filled with tears.

"Janice won't let him in the building."

"What do you mean?"

"Just that. I asked him to go over yesterday to get me my address book, and Nathan wouldn't let him inside. He said it was Janice's orders."

"That's terrible! How can she do that?"

Ms. Arthur was crying. "I don't know. She just did."

Ofelia handed her a Kleenex. "Don't worry, Ms. Arthur. I'll get your extra pair for you. Just tell me where they are."

"Oh, bless you!"

When she got back to Sunset Hills, Ofelia stopped at the front desk, signed in, and waited for Nathan to get off the phone.

"What's going on with Alex?" she asked after he hung up. "Is it true that Janice won't let him in the building?"

Nathan nodded. "Yeah. I felt really shitty telling him that, but what can I do?"

"Isn't that illegal or something? I mean, he didn't break any law."

Nathan shrugged. "Hey, not my business. I just have to follow orders."

Ofelia wondered if Mr. Sims was behind it. She was beginning to believe he really was one of those dishonest conservators. Maybe he wanted to sell Ms. Arthur's car and keep the money for himself, or maybe he was afraid she'd leave everything to Alex. Ofelia was so mad she was ready to make an anonymous call to the senior-care ombudsman or the ACLU. But first she had to get Ms. Arthur her glasses.

She went right to the nursing office and told Jennifer about Ms. Arthur's glasses. Jennifer let her inside the room, and Ofelia asked her to wait while she looked around so that nobody could say later that she'd taken anything. Ofelia found the glasses in a drawer in the kitchen area.

Now the problem was getting them to Ms. Arthur. Ofelia wouldn't be able to go see her for another week, and Alex couldn't come in the building. She tried calling him to see if he could meet her at the Starbucks down the street so she could give him the glasses, but his cell wasn't working.

Ofelia worried about it while she helped Mrs. Breur get dressed for dinner. After she took her down to the dining room and got her settled at the table, she went back upstairs to Janice's office.

As usual, the door was closed, and Ofelia hoped she hadn't gone home yet. She knocked and waited until Janice called, "Come in."

Janice was alone, sitting in front of her computer. "Hello, Ofelia, what can I do for you?"

"I went to see Ms. Arthur today at the hospital, and she asked me to get her spare reading glasses." Ofelia held them up. "So I asked Jennifer to let me in her room, and she stayed with me while I looked for them."

"That was very kind."

"Well, the thing is, I don't have any time off till next week, and I don't know when Ms. Arthur's coming back, so I thought maybe you could call Alex to come get them and bring them to her."

Janice smiled her fake smile. "I'll see that she gets them." She held out her hand, and Ofelia gave her the glasses.

Ofelia knew she wasn't going to get any information, so she said thank you and turned to leave.

"Ofelia, wait a moment, please." Janice motioned to the chair facing her desk and Ofelia had no choice except to sit down.

"What you did was most considerate, but I just want to reiterate the Sunset Hills policy regarding employee-resident relations. Of course, I realize you are Mrs. Breur's private caregiver, so these rules don't apply to you in the literal sense. However, we believe that it is unethical for employees to form personal friendships with residents."

Ofelia thought that was the dumbest thing she'd ever heard. After all, if a Buddy bathed and changed a resident's diapers, escorted him or her to the dining room and back, talked to and listened to them, there was no way they *couldn't* get personally involved. It seemed to Ofelia that the help at Sunset Hills knew the residents better than their own families, who only showed up now and then, if at all. But she didn't say that to Janice.

"Personal friendships between residents and caregivers are unprofessional and can lead to unethical behavior," Janice went on. "Do you understand what I'm talking about?"

Ofelia knew exactly what Janice was getting at but she pretended otherwise. "Not really."

"Well, an unscrupulous employee could take advantage of a lonely resident. Financially, if you know what I mean."

"I don't know anybody who'd do that," Ofelia said.

"Mind you, I am not accusing Alex of that. Still, he did cross the line, and so I am forced to bar him from the premises. That should serve as an example to all employees." Janice stood up. "I will make sure that Ms. Arthur gets her glasses."

Ofelia couldn't stop thinking about Mr. Sims and Alex for the rest of the evening. That night when most of the residents were asleep, Connie stopped by as usual to talk, and the conversation turned to Alex and Ms. Arthur.

"She should be able to hire anybody she wants," Ofelia said.

Connie agreed but added, "What if Alex *is* taking advantage of her. I mean, look, he got her to give him her car."

"Who said it was his idea? Ms. Arthur was happy about it."

"Maybe."

"It's *her* life," Ofelia insisted. "And anyway, isn't it illegal to keep him out of the building? He didn't commit any crime. What right does Janice have to do that? He could probably sue her."

"You know what I think? It's that lawyer who put her up to it. He probably threatened Janice and said he'd report her to corporate because she didn't fire Alex right away when he took the car. He's looking out after Ms. Arthur's interests, and Janice is saving her own ass."

Ofelia didn't know what to believe.

It was Sunset Hills' policy for the nursing supervisor or the director to evaluate a resident who was in the hospital before he or she could come back, but Janice never went to the hospital to see Lily Arthur, and the nursing supervisor had quit five months before and hadn't been replaced. The hospital was ready to discharge Lily Arthur, and although Ms. Arthur said her doctor wanted her to go to rehab until she got her strength back, she returned to Sunset Hills instead.

Ofelia was shocked at how much older and weaker she looked, and it was clear she was still having trouble breathing. Ofelia couldn't understand why she hadn't gone to rehab, where she'd have had full-time professional care. She asked Alex about it when he called to ask her to check up on Ms. Arthur and let him know how she was doing.

"It was her conservator who decided," he told her. "He knew if she'd gone to rehab, I'd have been there with her, and he sure as hell wasn't going to let that happen."

"That sucks," Ofelia said. "Did he get you fired?"

"What do you think?" he retorted.

Ofelia couldn't get over how much power Mr. Sims had. "Why does he hate you so much? Because of the car?"

"It's the money. That's all he cares about. He's probably been ripping her off for years."

Ofelia thought that was one of the saddest things ever. Here was poor Ms. Arthur at the end of her life, and not only was she being cheated, she was being kept apart from the only person who made her happy. It wasn't fair.

Mr. Sims came by the second day Lily Arthur was back. There was no question they were having an argument, but this time Ofelia didn't hear any crying. Instead, Ms. Arthur was shouting back at him, as loud as somebody in her condition could shout. When Ofelia finally heard her door slam, she waited a few minutes, then told Mrs. Breur she was going downstairs to check the mail.

She went next door instead. Lily Arthur was sitting in the armchair staring straight ahead.

"Ms. Arthur? Are you okay?" Ofelia took a few hesitant steps forward.

Lily Arthur lifted her head. She looked like she had just woken from a bad dream. "No, Ofelia. I'm not okay. I'll never be okay."

Ofelia wanted to put her arms around her and tell her everything would be all right, just like she'd do with a baby.

"Yes, you will," she said. "You're getting stronger every day."

"What I mean," Ms. Arthur said, "is that I'll never be okay until I get out of here."

"You mean to the rehab?"

Lily Arthur shook her head, and her lips curled in a faint smile. "No, dear. This is my plan. I'm going to leave Sunset Hills and get a nice big apartment with a patio. Then Alex will come live with me and take care of me."

"That's a great idea."

"The problem is, Mr. Sims won't hear of it. He believes Alex is after my money."

"So I guess you have to fire Mr. Sims."

Ms. Arthur smiled a real smile, and for a moment she looked like the little girl in the swing. "You've read my mind."

Regardless of what Mr. Sims or Connie or Janice thought about Alex, Ofelia believed the only thing that mattered was what made Ms. Arthur happy. Even if Alex was maybe not one hundred percent unselfish, what did it matter in the long run?

Ofelia felt even more sure when she met Alex for coffee at Starbucks a couple of days later.

"I've been looking at apartments," he told her, "and there's a couple of really nice ones in Beverly Hills near her doctors and one in Santa Monica."

When she asked him about his writing, Alex told her he was working on his story. But the biggest news was that Ms. Arthur had definitely decided to fire Mr. Sims.

"She has to get another lawyer and maybe go to court," Alex said. "It's worth it to get rid of that son of a bitch."

Ofelia agreed. Once Mr. Sims was out of the picture, Ms. Arthur and Alex could start a new life.

But that very night, Ms. Arthur had a setback. At dinner, she was barely able to sit up for all her coughing and wheezing. Halfway through the meal, she asked Ofelia to get one of the Buddies to take her to her room. Later on, Ofelia could hear her coughing through the walls. Even Mrs. Breur, who was practically deaf, could hear her.

"We better get the nurse," Mrs. Breur said to Ofelia.

Ofelia went next door. One look and she knew Ms. Arthur was in trouble. The rattling in her chest was proof she needed to be suctioned like they did in the hospital. "Don't you worry. I'm going to get someone to help you," she said to Ms. Arthur.

Ofelia nearly ran down the hall to the nursing office. Jennifer was off, and her heart sank when she saw Thelma, a new substitute nurse who didn't look like she even knew how to take a temperature.

Thelma followed her to Ms. Arthur's room. Ofelia stayed and watched Thelma take her vital signs.

"Normal," she said.

"Listen to her lungs," Ofelia hissed. "You call that *normal?* Look at her! She looks like a ghost! She has to go to the hospital!"

Thelma looked nervous. "Well, I have to call her doctor first and get an order."

Crossing her arms across her chest, Ofelia stared her down. "For God's sake, it's nine o'clock! Like you're really going to get him!"

But Thelma wouldn't back down. Ofelia was tempted to pick up the phone and dial 911, but of course she couldn't. She didn't know what else she could do, so she went back to Mrs. Breur, who was waiting patiently for her bath.

Before she drifted off to sleep, Ofelia said a little prayer for Ms. Arthur, and that night she dreamed that Alex had rented them a beautiful little Spanish house with a garden.

Jennifer came back on duty in the morning, and she was the one who found Ms. Arthur.

Ofelia heard that Mr. Sims had had her cremated, which was what he said she wanted. Her door stayed closed for a week, and then one day Mr. Sims showed up carrying a bunch of cardboard cartons. He started dumping things into large plastic garbage bags and tossed them in the hall to be thrown away. Ofelia felt sad just looking at them.

She figured she didn't have anything to lose, so after a while she stepped into Ms. Arthur's room. The lawyer was going through her desk drawer, stuffing papers into a carton.

"Mr. Sims?" she said.

He looked up. "Yes?"

"I was wondering, if there isn't anybody who wants it, if I could have that picture of Ms. Arthur, the one by her bed?"

He thought a moment. "I suppose so. Why not?"

And so it happened that Ofelia took the picture of Ms. Arthur as a little girl sitting in the swing. She took it to the one-hour photo place down the street, had it enlarged, and put it in a nice silver frame. Then she went to the market, bought a few large white roses in a vase, and carefully wrote out a card in big letters that said "In Loving Memory" and she placed them all on the little table right by the elevator so that everybody could see and say good-bye to Lily Arthur.

Ofelia never saw Alex again. Nobody really knew what happened to him. One of the waiters said he thought he'd gone back to Texas, where he was from.

Ofelia liked to think that he was writing his story and that one day it would get published, maybe in *The New Yorker,* and he would dedicate it to Ms. Arthur.

As for her, Ofelia felt guilty for not defying Thelma and calling 911. She sometimes thought that in life, unlike telenovelas, there wasn't always just one villain.

GONE SHOPPING

Hannah Ostrow was waking up earlier and earlier, even with the Ambien they gave her at bedtime. It didn't make any sense, not that the pill didn't work like it should have, but now that she was old and didn't have to get up early for school or work or to make breakfast for the family and was entitled to sleep in as long as she wanted, she couldn't!

Usually, she would switch on the light by the bed and try to read a magazine or one of those university health letters she subscribed to. After a while, she'd just drift off, but that little trick wasn't working like it used to. Lately she was having trouble reading—not the words, but what they meant. She had to read the same sentence over and over until it just wasn't worth it. So, she'd toss the magazine aside and turn on the TV with the remote, not that the programs made much sense, either. She usually ended up half dozing until it was *officially* time to get up. At Sunset Hills that meant seven.

The morning of the great escape, as Mr. Grant later named it, she looked at the clock. It was five-thirty. Breakfast wasn't served before seven. She wasn't hungry, anyway. But just lying in bed for another hour and a half was a waste of time, and let's face it, how much time did she have left at eighty-six?

Hannah was fed up. She threw off the covers and slowly raised herself up and out of the bed. Everything hurt, especially her left hip, which had never felt quite right after the replacement, but what else was new? She made her way to the bathroom and sat on the toilet. When she finished, she wiped herself, flushed, and stood at the sink. She washed her hands and face, avoiding the mirror. Who needed to see that wrinkled, sagging face with the brown spots? If she didn't look, then she could go through the day thinking she was still pretty little Hannah with the flashing brown eyes and cute smile.

She didn't have a plan. All she knew was she would *not* just lie in that damn bed for an hour like an invalid, which was what they tried to turn you into at Sunset Hills. She knew that was true because if they could convince you or, more important, your family that you were out of it, they could stick you in the Alzheimer's unit and make more money. They couldn't fool her, she wasn't born yesterday.

Hannah brushed her teeth, and decided to get dressed. She put on the clothes she'd worn yesterday, navy blue pants and a navy and white striped blouse. The clothes didn't look dirty, and it was too much effort to choose something new. The shoes were easy. She wore the same ones everyday, black old-lady shoes made out of some synthetic material with the Velcro closure her podiatrist had ordered for her because of her diabetes. Who would have thought she'd come to that, she who'd subscribed to *Vogue* and always wore the latest fashions!

She combed her hair, careful not to go too hard so no more would fall out. Now that she was all dressed, Hannah thought she might as well go downstairs and wait for the kitchen to open. She took the navy sweater off the chair where she'd left it the night before, put it over her shoulders, and left her room.

Hannah walked slowly down the silent hallway. There was something she needed to do, but she couldn't remember what it was. The thought nagged at her mind like a pesky mosquito, but unlike a mosquito, she couldn't simply brush it away. What *was* it she had to do?

She reached the elevator, pushed the button, then shrugged. What the hell. She'd remember sooner or later, and anyway, what could be so important?

The elevator doors opened. Hannah stepped inside and pressed the down button. She got out on the first floor and was immediately struck by the quiet. The dining room was dark and empty. It felt like a cathedral, or a mausoleum. Creepy. Hannah made her way to the living room. It wasn't quite as dark in there because the room faced east and the sun was coming up, but still, it was eerie. Nobody playing cards, no Mr. Grosso tickling the ivories, as he always put it, nobody reading the paper or doing the crossword.

Something else was different. Nathan wasn't sitting in his usual place at the front desk by the door. Hannah stood in the empty room for a moment before she realized what that meant.

A big smile lit up her face. *Phooey!* She looked at the sign-out book on the desk, the one with sections marked for residents, guests, and caregivers. They were very strict at Sunset Hills about people signing in and out, just like when she was in college living in the dorm. Well, she wasn't a college kid anymore.

Hannah didn't think twice. Opening the front door, she stepped outside without a backward glance.

"Good-bye, you suckers!" she said out loud as the door slammed behind her. "I'm escaping!"

Jennifer, the nurse, had her hands full that morning. She had to make sure the residents got their meds. The pharmacy had not delivered Emma Greenberg's Darvocet, and she was complaining bitterly about her shoulder hurting. On top of that, Bernie Elkins refused to let Jennifer give him his insulin shot, and it took her nearly fifteen minutes to convince him he had to get it or she would call his daughter. By that time, Jennifer was desperate for her break and a cup of coffee, but as she was checking off the meds given on the chart, she saw a blank by Mrs. Ostrow's name.

"Shit," she mumbled under her breath.

Although Mrs. Ostrow was getting more forgetful, she always came by for her meds at seven-thirty on the dot. It was then that Ofelia, Mrs. Breur's private caregiver, stopped by to see if Mrs. Breur's Prevacid had come in.

"I'll check, and if it's here, I'll bring it to you," Jennifer told her. "But do me a favor, will you? Go by Mrs. Ostrow's room and remind her she didn't take her meds."

"Sure."

Ofelia went back down the hallway toward Mrs. Ostrow's room. She knocked loudly a couple of times, and when she didn't hear anything, she opened the door.

"She's not in her room," Ofelia reported back to Jennifer. "I'm taking Mrs. Breur down to the dining room. She's probably down there, and I'll tell her to come up for her meds."

But when Ofelia brought Mrs. Breur into the dining room, there were only a handful of people, and Mrs. Ostrow wasn't one of them. After settling Mrs. Breur at her table, Ofelia went to the living room. Only Mrs. Freedman was there, reading the *Times*. Ofelia walked back to the dining room and asked one of the waiters if Mrs. Ostrow had been down for breakfast, but the answer was no. She called Jennifer on her cell phone.

"I have kind of an emergency with Mrs. Dobbs or I'd look for her," Jennifer said.

"I'll go," Ofelia offered.

Mrs. Ostrow was not in the library. She wasn't in the media room. She wasn't in the computer room. She wasn't in any of the bathrooms that the help used. Ofelia even went down to the parking garage, but no Mrs. Ostrow.

She'd just disappeared! So it was that Ofelia was the one who discovered that Mrs. Ostrow was AWOL.

It felt good to be outside by herself, even with the cars whizzing down the busy street and the exhaust from the buses blowing in her face. Hannah felt freer than she had since she didn't know when. A long time. How long was it, anyway, since her son had dumped her in Sunset Hills? Four years? Five? It seemed like forever. There she'd been, living in her nice condo in Century City, driving around in her own car, going shopping every day. Then one morning she fell and knocked herself out, and when she woke up, there were the paramedics, and BOOM! Jeffrey cleaned out her condo, put her things in storage, and stuck her in Sunset Hills.

"You'll be safe, Mom," he kept saying when she protested.

Safe from what?

Hannah didn't want to think about all that now that she was outside on her own. She wanted to concentrate on the day ahead.

She didn't have a real plan. It was nice enough walking by herself. Thank God she didn't need a walker yet. Still, she was careful to avoid a large pile of garbage in a black plastic bag. The bag suddenly moved, and for an instant Hannah thought there might be rats inside, but then a shape emerged and she realized it was a person! It was hard to tell if it was a man or a woman because of the dirt and grime and wild gray hair. They exchanged a long look. Hannah felt a pang of sympathy for him or her, but only for a moment. At least *he* could come and go as he pleased!

She came to an intersection. Cars were speeding by, and she waited for the traffic light to turn green. When it changed, she stepped gingerly off the curb and fearfully started to cross the street. She'd only taken a few steps when the picture of somebody walking on the signal started blinking. What was she supposed to do now? What would happen if the light turned red while she was in the street? Everybody knew drivers were crazy these days. She held her breath and even though the light turned yellow and then red, the cars miraculously waited. Hannah made it to the other side all in one piece. Her heart was hammering in her chest, and she waited until she caught her breath.

Now that she'd crossed the street by herself, she was beginning to feel better. Almost light-headed! Another block and she was on Hollywood Boulevard. Now what?

So many cars. So many people. All ages, types, races. Where were they all going? A youngish woman in a business suit carrying a briefcase was walking purposefully toward her. She looked like she knew where she was going, and in a way she reminded Hannah of herself when she was young. Well, more like how she would've been if she'd had a career after college instead of marrying Howard and staying home all those years. Hannah decided to follow the woman.

Before she knew it, she was on an escalator riding down under the street. Then she was in a huge cavernous place that reminded her of Grand Central Station in New York. She didn't have time to think about it because the woman with the briefcase was walking faster. Hannah did her best to catch up and found herself on a train platform.

She positioned herself next to the woman. A few minutes later she felt a gust of wind, then a Metro train appeared and stopped. The doors opened and the people on the platform pushed forward.

Hannah followed the woman onto the train. Only then did she realize she didn't have a ticket. At the same time, she remembered what it was she had needed to do. She hadn't taken her meds.

Too late now. The doors closed.

Janice arrived just as Ofelia was reporting back to Jennifer. Janice immediately organized a search for Mrs. Ostrow, first dispatching LeRoy, the maintenance manager, to check out the garage and storage areas, then assigning a Buddy on each floor to go into every room. Ofelia knew the Buddies were really going to pay, not that it was anybody's fault.

Ofelia went down to the dining room and joined Mrs. Breur and Vicky Bradlee, a new resident, at the table. They'd finished eating and were exchanging medical histories. Ofelia made a bet with herself that everybody would know about Mrs. Ostrow within ten minutes—nothing could be kept secret for long at Sunset Hills. Sure enough, before the waiter could even bring Ofelia her scrambled eggs, Mrs. Freedman stopped by their table.

"Hannah Ostrow's disappeared!" She sounded almost excited. "Did any of you see her this morning?"

They didn't call her the Freedman Bureau of Information for nothing, Ofelia thought.

Mrs. Breur shook her head as though Mrs. Freedman had accused her of kidnapping.

"Has this happened before?" the new resident asked.

"Not like this. They're searching the building," Mrs. Freedman answered and marched off to spread the word to the other tables.

There was a jewelry-making class scheduled for nine-thirty, but no one was interested. Instead, the residents hung around the living room talking about Mrs. Ostrow.

"That's what I'd like to do. Pack my bags and get the hell out of here!" Mr. Grant exclaimed.

"Who said anything about bags?" Emma Greenberg challenged.

"I've noticed she's become more absent-minded lately," Peggy White commented.

Bernie Elkins said maybe she'd been kidnapped, which made everybody laugh. Ofelia didn't think that was so ridiculous. She watched *Without a Trace* and *Forensic Files*, and you'd be surprised what could happen. Mrs. Ostrow could really be in danger wandering around all by herself.

"Hey, look at that!" Mr. Grosso pointed to the front entrance.

All heads turned. Two police cars were pulling into the driveway.

"Oh, my," Mrs. Breur said.

So this was the famous Red Line. When she and Howard moved from New Jersey to L.A. back in the forties, nobody dreamed there would ever be a subway or a metro. L.A. was the city of the automobile, and Hannah had loved the clean, wide streets lined with palm trees. She loved driving on the Miracle Mile, going on to shop at Bullock's Wilshire, where she'd have lunch in the tea room and watch the fashion show. She felt sad that all the old elegant stores had disappeared and now people shopped in noisy malls.

Hannah sat down across from the woman in the suit as the train moved forward. The woman pulled out a book from her briefcase. Hannah strained to see what it was, but she didn't have her distance glasses.

She didn't pay attention to the names of the stops. She was much more interested in looking at the other passengers. Most of them were Hispanic, but by the third stop, Orientals—or Asians, as they wanted to be called now—started getting on. The Metro made Hannah think of a silent movie because nobody was talking.

Her thoughts began to drift to all the things that she grew up with that no longer existed, like silent movies, like those vacuum cylinders in department stores where the clerk put your money and it whooshed up to the credit department. But then a recorded voice called out "Union Station" and everybody stood up.

Hannah felt a moment of panic. She struggled to her feet, keeping her eyes on the woman in the suit. She was afraid if she didn't hurry up, she'd get caught in the doors, but they remained open. She found herself standing on an underground platform with stairways leading up on either side. The woman in the suit was hurrying toward one of them, and Hannah wanted to call out to her to wait, but she didn't know her name, and next thing she knew the woman was lost in the crowd.

The stairs looked steep. It would take forever to get up them, and she could easily trip and fall. But then she saw a man with a cane go to a glass enclosure and press a button. Relief swept through her as she realized it was an elevator.

Hannah hadn't been in Union Station in years, not since she and Howard used to take the train down to San Diego to visit his brother and his wife, and that had to be fifty years ago. She'd always loved the building, the high ceilings, the tiles, the old benches. As far as she could tell, it really hadn't changed, and that made her feel good.

She forgot about the woman in the suit, and she was no longer afraid to be out in the world alone. Outside, she took a deep breath and contemplated her next step. It was interesting that very often she couldn't remember what day it was, or if she'd eaten lunch, or what she had done the day before, but she remembered that Olvera Street was just a short walk away, and Chinatown not too far, either. Suddenly, she was famished.

It took her a while to walk down the driveway and cross the street, but she could smell pancakes and bacon and tortillas, so she followed the good smells up a short hill, stopping to catch her breath, until she was on Olvera Street. What was the name of that place that had the good hot roast beef sandwiches and cheap coffee? She couldn't remember, but she saw a busy Mexican restaurant, so she went inside and made her way to a small table with two chairs. A plump waitress came over with a menu.

"Coffee?"

Hannah nodded. "Okay."

She ate the same breakfast every day at Sunset Hills: oatmeal, Eggbeater omelet, and decaf. What a treat to have something else. Luckily, her reading glasses were in her sweater pocket. Hannah started to read the menu but there were so many choices. The waitress set a cup of real coffee down in front of her with a metal pitcher of cream.

"Are you ready?"

Hannah hesitated. "What do you recommend?"

"The especial," the waitress said. "It's muy bueno. Very good."

"Okay. I'll have the special."

She'd never seen so much food on one plate! Scrambled eggs mixed with green peppers and onions and bits of sausage, and heaps of warm tortillas. Hannah took a forkful. Oh, it was worth the heartburn she'd surely get.

She was amazed to see that she'd cleaned her plate except for one tortilla. And she'd had a refill of the coffee. All that coffee made her need to go to the bathroom. The waitress put the check on the table and directed Hannah to the restroom.

As she was washing her hands, she wondered how much the breakfast special was. She hadn't asked. On top of that came a terrible realization. It didn't matter what it cost. She hadn't brought her purse!

Panic set in. How could she not have brought a purse? But she reminded herself she hadn't planned to leave. The opportunity had simply presented itself, and she'd grabbed it. She felt around in her sweater pockets. Kleenex and some coins. Ninety-six cents. She stuck her hands in her pants' pockets and came up with her cardiologist's card and two single dollar bills.

The restaurant was starting to fill up when she came out of the bathroom. Nearly every table was taken. Hannah looked around but didn't see her waitress. She was afraid to look at the check on her table. She wished she had a pen so she could write a little thank-you note to the waitress. Instead, she stuck the two dollars underneath the check and walked out.

Nothing quite so exciting had happened at Sunset Hills since Connie stumbled across Jerry Brach and Lina Moldova in the storage room in their underwear. Jerry's family yanked him out the next day, and Lina landed in the Alzheimer's Unit. But this was like something out of TV.

The van was scheduled to go to Rite Aid at ten-thirty but nobody wanted to go. Instead, they all gathered around the big TV in the lounge and kept changing channels looking for news of Hannah Ostrow. Ofelia settled Mrs. Breur there with a cup of coffee, then went to see what the cops were up to.

She contacted Connie on the walkie-talkie and they met by the library.

"They're doing a room-to-room search. You should see Janice!" Connie smirked. "She's having a shit fit."

Ofelia didn't want anything bad to happen to Hannah Ostrow, but she wouldn't mind at all if Janice got into big trouble with corporate.

"What do you think happened to her?" Ofelia asked.

"She could be here someplace, dead from a stroke or a heart attack. What do you think?"

"I think she just took off," Ofelia said.

"Jeez! All the creeps in this neighborhood? Anything could happen."

Ofelia agreed, and that was what worried her. Poor old Mrs. Ostrow.

The police finished their search of the building and then spread out into the neighborhood.

Ofelia went back to the lounge, where people were watching *Judge Brown*. Just as she was about to ask if there had been anything on the news about Mrs. Ostrow, a reporter appeared on the screen.

"This just in. A search is underway in Hollywood for an elderly woman who disappeared this morning from Sunset Hills, the upscale assisted-living facility."

There was a gasp in the room as a picture of Mrs. Ostrow taken at the Valentine's Day party, flashed on the screen. It was a pretty good photo even though she was wearing a pink heart-shaped crown.

"Anyone seeing Hannah Ostrow is asked to please call the police."

A phone number flashed on the screen.

For once, everyone was quiet. Even Mr. Grant.

It was still early, and Hannah had the whole day ahead of her. The problem was, she wasn't used to planning her activities herself anymore. Debby, the activities director, planned for her and for everybody else. It was exciting, but a little intimidating, to realize she was in charge.

She knew it would be best not to linger on Olvera Street in case the waitress came looking for her, so she stopped a man on the street and asked him how to get to Chinatown.

It wasn't too far, and before long she was walking down Hill Street, peering into jewelry and gift shop windows. She liked the colored paper lanterns hanging outside the stores, and the jade, and she was sorry she hadn't taken her purse or her American Express card. But then she turned a corner and saw a sign that got her heart pumping fast. The Golden Dragon! It was still here after all these years! That had been one of Howard's favorite places, and they used to drive all the way from the Westside just for the dim sum! She could practically taste the delicious dumplings. Oh, those were the days!

Hannah chastised herself. No point in nostalgia, there was no going back. She tried instead to concentrate on the present, to make a plan. What did she really want to do?

Shopping! What else? That had always been her favorite thing. She couldn't buy anything today, but at least she could look. There were no department stores in Chinatown, none in Little Tokyo. She'd have to go to a mall like The Grove or the Beverly Center. But how was she going to get there? She hadn't brought her City Ride taxi coupons. She stood on the sidewalk feeling stupid. Then a little Chinese lady appeared in front of her.

"You need help, Mama?"

"Oh, yes, please. How do I get to a mall? Like The Grove or the Beverly Center?"

The Chinese lady thought a minute. "The bus."

"Where?"

"Not too far. Grand and Fifth."

Hannah shook her head. She had no idea how to get there."

"Look, Mama, you come with me. I take you, okay?" The Chinese lady took her arm and led her to a shiny silver car.

Hannah knew it was risky to get in a car with a stranger, but maybe that only meant men strangers. And she really wanted to ride the bus. They drove a few blocks and the lady stopped. She pointed ahead to a bus stop where a small group of people was clustered.

"There. Wait for the red-and-white bus."

"How much is it? I only have ninety-seven cents."

The Chinese lady dug in her pocket and took out a handful of change. "Here, you take this." She handed Hannah a bunch of quarters.

"Oh, thank you! You are an angel!" She felt light-headed with gratitude. What a wonderful world.

"You be careful, Mama."

And that was how Hannah Ostrow happened to find herself on a bus riding through Los Angeles.

It was clear that Mrs. Ostrow had wandered off on her own. The residents couldn't talk about anything else, and they fell into two camps as to what might have happened to her. About half of them were sure something bad had happened—or would happen—to her. Ofelia was amazed at the horrible things they came up with, including kidnapping by creatures from outer space—this from Peggy White.

The other half thought she'd just taken off, and they cheered her on. Mr. Grant wanted to take bets on when and where they'd find her. "If she's smart, she'll head for the border," he declared.

Mrs. Freedman gave him a dirty look and shook her head in disgust.

"Heads are going to roll," Mr. Grosso proclaimed gleefully, and lifted his head upward in the direction of Janice's office.

This made everybody happy.

Ofelia knew Janice was sweating it out. Whatever happened to Hannah Ostrow, it was on her watch, and this was one thing she hadn't been able to cover up.

It was the slowest day Ofelia could remember. The time was endless. No one wanted to do anything except sit in front of the TV, where every half-hour they showed that silly photograph of Hannah Ostrow with the heart-shaped crown on her head. Mrs. Breur was taking it very hard, certain that the police were going to find her in an alley with her throat cut. She called her daughter, crying, and Ms. Breur-Gordon came running over to calm her down.

"This is outrageous," she hissed at Ofelia, as though it were her fault. "The prices they charge, and they let this happen! I've a good mind to call the licensing board."

Ofelia wanted to tell her to go ahead and do it, but she kept quiet.

Ms. Breur-Gordon took her mother up to her room and put her to bed for a nap. Ofelia brought a basket of dirty clothes to the laundry room. She paused by the office, hoping to hear something, but Janice's door, as usual, was closed.

Once she was on the bus, Hannah Ostrow stopped thinking about shopping. Riding through Los Angeles was adventure enough, and besides, she was tired. Walking around would make her even more tired.

She stared out the window at the neighborhoods they drove by. Some of them had completely changed, many of the signs were in foreign languages, and there were lots of little old houses that were now churches with strange names and strange alphabets.

But other neighborhoods, like Alvarado Street and the lake, were the same as she remembered. There was a wonderful deli she and Howard used to go to for the pastrami sandwiches—what was the name? Langers! That was it!

Before long they were passing the Miracle Mile. Well, it didn't exactly look like the old Miracle Mile from the forties and fifties, but it was still standing. There had been that cafeteria, the Ontra, that she and Howard used to take Jeffrey to when he was a kid. It wasn't there anymore, but Hannah remembered exactly where it had been, and she felt a pang of nostalgia when the driver stopped the bus almost in front of the spot.

Then there was Restaurant Row, just off Wilshire on La Cienega. Lawry's for roast beef! How Howard had loved going there on special occasions. Too bad the bus didn't turn because she'd have liked to see what restaurants were there now.

Beverly Hills looked much busier than she remembered. More cars, more people, more buildings. And the same for the Westside. Huge condos everywhere. She and Howard had looked at some houses around there, just south of Wilshire, before they'd bought the one in Beverlywood.

The bus continued. People got off and on. Hannah was content to just sit and observe the city all the way into Santa Monica. Santa Monica and Venice used to be crummy places but not anymore. It would have been smart to have bought one of those broken down houses years ago, but who knew?

The bus stopped at the Santa Monica pier and the last few passengers got out. The driver stood up.

"Last stop," he said.

By the afternoon, the residents who thought something terrible had happened to Hannah Ostrow were in the majority. Only Mr. Grant and a few others predicted she'd be back when she was good and ready.

They remained in the lounge watching the big TV, and now news bulletins came every ten minutes or so. The latest showed police and dogs searching the hills and canyons near Sunset Hills.

"When they bring out the dogs, that's serious," Peggy White said.

Nobody answered. Ofelia thought people looked scared. She was getting scared, too, imagining that poor Mrs. Ostrow had gotten lost, fallen, and suffered a fatal concussion and was being eaten by coyotes.

Ms. Breur-Gordon didn't want her mother hearing any more, so she took her back home with her for the rest of the day. This gave Ofelia time off, which ordinarily she would have loved, but she was too anxious about Mrs. Ostrow to do anything except hang out with Connie and speculate about Janice.

"I hope she gets the ax," Connie said.

"That would be a bright spot," Ofelia agreed, "but it's not like it's her fault."

"Well, technically it is. Sunset Hills is responsible for the residents. Something happens to Mrs. Ostrow, her family could sue big time."

"They could lose their license."

"What a dirty rotten shame," Connie smirked.

To Hannah's relief, the bus driver changed the sign on the front of the bus and then let her back on.

"Where you going?" he asked.

"Shopping," she answered. "Saks in Beverly Hills."

"You got it."

Hannah sat back, planning the rest of her day. She hadn't counted the change the Chinese lady had given her, and she wondered if she could buy lunch with it. She was too ashamed to repeat what she'd done in the Mexican restaurant. But then she remembered that she had never cancelled her Saks credit card. Surely they had it on file, and she could have lunch in their little café and do some shopping, just like the old days.

All at once, her fatigue melted away and she was excited.

A woman got on in Santa Monica and took a seat across from Hannah. She looked right at her, and Hannah smiled in acknowledgment. But the woman kept staring at her. Hannah wondered if they knew each other from somewhere, but the woman didn't look at all familiar. Hannah was starting to feel nervous and a little uncomfortable. Maybe she had wet herself and hadn't noticed, and that was what the woman was looking at.

When they reached the area near the Federal Building, the woman stood up and Hannah was relieved, thinking she would get off. But she went up to the driver and started talking to him. Then she turned around and sat back down.

At the next stop, the driver got up and walked over to Hannah.

"What's your name, ma'am?" he asked politely.

Hannah didn't want to answer, but the driver didn't budge. He squatted down so that they were eye level with each other.

"Is your name Hannah Ostrow?"

What could she do? Not much. So she gave him her best smile and answered, "Yes, it is. And may I ask why you want to know?"

And that's how it ended. A police car pulled up in front of Sunset Hills in the late afternoon. There was a news van from KCAL and one from KNBC waiting by the entrance, and reporters jumped out and started shouting questions at Mrs. Ostrow and the policeman before they could even get out. Janice elbowed her way through the reporters, and took Mrs. Ostrow firmly by the arm.

"We're all delighted she is back, safe and sound," Janice declared, and ushered Hannah into the building before she could say a word.

The residents were crowded in the living room, and they let out a big cheer as Hannah came in. Janice tried to lead her to the elevator, but she didn't stand a chance. Everyone clustered around, and Hannah Ostrow seemed happy to be in the limelight.

"So what happened?" Mr. Grant demanded. "How'd you get out?"

Hannah pointed to the door. "Simple. Through the door."

"What did you do? Where'd you go?" Emma Greenberg asked.

Hannah Ostrow smiled widely and winked. "Shopping. I went shopping."

It was a little white lie, because she never did get to Saks, but she almost had. And next time, she'd know how to do it so she wouldn't get caught.

BAD KARMA

Emma Greenberg was bound to get into trouble sooner or later. What was surprising, Ofelia told Connie, was that it hadn't happened sooner. When Emma first moved into Sunset Hills she didn't seem any different from any of the other residents, which meant she was pissed to be there but accepted that this was the way it was and she'd have to make the best of it.

But the last few months, she'd become downright ornery. If the chef didn't cook her salmon just right, she'd send it back—sometimes with a nasty remark—and she threw a fit when Rodrigo changed the van outing from Rite Aid to Trader Joe's. Little things like that. One afternoon she got into a shouting match with Mrs. Freedman over bridge. But all that was peanuts compared to what happened the day she refused to take her med.

What happened was this. Emma Greenberg had an appointment for her teeth cleaning. No big deal, except that her doctor wanted her to take an antibiotic before any dental work. Ofelia and Mrs. Breur happened to be standing by the medicine cart across from the nursing station when she came clumping down the hall leaning on her cane.

"I'm going to the dentist," she announced to Jennifer, the nurse.

"Yes, I know, Mrs. Greenberg. I've got your pill right here."

Jennifer plucked a white envelope from the medicine cart and shook a pink tablet into a little plastic pill cup. She handed it to Mrs. Greenberg with a glass of water.

"Here you are," she said.

Emma Greenberg looked down at the cup. "That's the wrong pill."

"No it isn't," Jennifer said. "It's your antibiotic."

"It looks different."

"It's the right one."

Emma Greenberg kept staring at the little pink pill. "It was yellow last time."

Ofelia could tell Jennifer was getting annoyed by the way she sighed.

"It's the right pill," the nurse repeated.

"Let me see the envelope," Mrs. Greenberg said.

Jennifer put her hands on her hips. "Now, Mrs. Greenberg, don't be difficult. Trust me, it's the right one."

"Why should I trust you? Give me the envelope and let me read it."

Ofelia thought if she were Jennifer, she'd just give Mrs. Greenberg the envelope, but for some reason, Jennifer wasn't going to give in. She turned her back on Mrs. Greenberg.

That really got to Emma Greenberg.

"Goddammit," she sputtered and threw the cup and the pill on the floor.

Jennifer bent down to pick them up and the next thing Ofelia saw was Jennifer falling down. She didn't know if the nurse had simply lost her balance or if Mrs. Greenberg had tripped her, but whatever, there was Jennifer on the floor calling for help on her walkie-talkie.

"Oh, my," Mrs. Breur gasped.

It seemed to Emma Greenberg that she'd hardly gotten back to her room when Janice barged in without even knocking. Right behind her was a lady carrying a notebook. The stranger started asking her all kinds of questions about Jennifer and the medication, but by this time, Emma had had enough and lost her temper.

"Get out of here," she demanded.

"Now, Emma," Janice began.

"Now!" Emma shouted.

They left and she went to lie down, but it wasn't long before these two big goons wearing blue uniforms and pushing a gurney burst into her room, followed by Janice.

"This is my room! Get the hell out!" Emma yelled at them, but they ignored her.

The men picked her up and next thing she knew, Emma was lying flat on her back on the gurney.

"Call my daughter!" she cried. She tried to sit up and get off, but one of the goons grabbed her arm and tied it to the rail. Emma felt tears burning her eyes. She was more than scared—she was panicky.

"Call my daughter!" she repeated, but the man tied her other wrist.

"What is this, a jail? What the hell are you doing!"

"She attacked the nurse," Janice said to the other goon. He wrote something on a paper attached to a clipboard.

"I did no such thing!" Emma cried. "She was trying to give me the wrong meds!"

She shouted for help all the way down the hall but they acted like they didn't hear her. Then, when they wheeled her out past a bunch of residents who looked as scared as she felt, Emma suddenly thought this was how it must have felt to be rounded up by the Nazis and sent to the gas chamber.

Ofelia and Connie huddled in the back of the living room as Debby, the activities director, led the weekly group discussion of current events. For once, Connie agreed with Ofelia that Janice had overstepped her boundaries as community manager by not calling Emma Greenberg's son or daughter before having her hauled off like a cow to the slaughterhouse.

"But she did trip Jennifer, right?" Connie said.

"I'm not sure," Ofelia confessed. "I was right there, But it happened so fast I couldn't tell. It could've been she just moved her cane at the wrong time."

"Right, and Jennifer's foot just happened to be in the way."

"Whatever," Ofelia waved her hand. "But look, the rules and regulations handbook says a resident has the right to refuse medication."

Connie nodded. "I know, but then what happens if she doesn't take the med and goes to the dentist and she gets this horrible infection and dies!"

"Yeah, right. When was the last time you heard of somebody dying from a teeth cleaning?"

Connie shrugged. They did agree that Janice had over-reacted by calling in that social worker, but by that time, Emma Greenberg was so upset she wasn't making any sense, just yelling so loud everybody on the floor could hear. So the social worker signed a paper saying that Mrs. Greenberg should be taken to a psych ward under a seventy-two-hour lock-up.

"I'm telling you, bad karma for Janice!" Ofelia pronounced.

Elaine was at her Pilates class when her cell phone rang. She'd forgotten to shut it off, and she was embarrassed. With a guilty smile and a shrug of her shoulders, she went into the hallway. Her heart sank when she saw it was her brother. Joel rarely called, so she knew something was wrong. Mom had a heart attack, she thought as she pressed the speak key.

"Joel? What's wrong?"

"It's Mom."

"Is she dead?"

"Not yet, but she's in a psych ward!"

Elaine almost laughed. "Well, we always said she was a little kooky."

"Not funny, Elaine. Look, this is serious."

Elaine listened in disbelief as her brother filled her in as best he could, not that the story made sense to her. It seemed their mother had gotten into an argument with the nurse at Sunset Hills over taking a medication, and then supposedly attacked the nurse.

"Why did you let them cart her off?" Elaine demanded.

"Me? The bastards didn't call me until she was already in the place."

"What?"

"I'm going over there now to see Mom," Joel said.

Elaine knew what was coming next.

"You've got to come up."

Elaine drove home, packed an overnight bag just in case, called Stuart to tell him what had happened and that she was driving to L.A. and would call him when she knew more. She locked up, and got in the car. If only her brother weren't such a wimp, or her mother so unpredictable, if, if, if . . .

Emma knew exactly where she was. One look around at the basket cases sitting in the little recreation room said it all. The ones who weren't sleeping in their chairs were staring at the TV like they were hypnotized.

A doctor had come by and given her a so-called test, questions like "What day is it?" "What city do you live in?" "Who is the president?" "Can you count backwards from one hundred?" Emma had no choice but to play along. You'd have thought she'd earned a Ph.D. from the way he congratulated her. It was demeaning.

"So when can I get out of here?" she asked.

"We'll see," the doctor said, and left.

That *really* made her anxious. Was there any way they could keep her locked up? What had she done that was so terrible? All she'd wanted to do was make sure she was taking the right pill. Mistakes happened all the time. She was no fool. But looking around at the zombies scared her. She would have started crying, but then a nurse came in holding a telephone.

"Call for you, Mrs. Greenberg."

Emma took the portable phone and put it to her good ear.

"Hello?" she said uncertainly.

"Mom?"

Emma gasped, relief flooding through her at the sound of Elaine's voice. Thank God! Thank God!

Word spread—as it always did—and before long everyone at Sunset Hills knew that Emma Greenberg had been carted off to the loony bin, as Mr. Grant put it.

"She's no nuttier than anybody else here," he proclaimed.

The residents all agreed that she shouldn't have gotten violent with Jennifer. However, it didn't look like Jennifer was suffering any ill effects.

"No broken bones," Mr. Grosso said.

"A bruised ego is more like it," Mrs. Freedman remarked. "Emma was questioning her professionalism."

"Well, God knows we pay enough so we're allowed," Peggy White put in.

Although Mrs. Breur didn't say anything, Ofelia could tell that the whole situation upset her. She had to keep reassuring Mrs. Breur that nothing like what had happened to Mrs. Greenberg was going to happen to *her*.

Secretly, Ofelia wasn't so sure. Janice ruled, and unless she was stopped, she could do what she liked. Not for the first time, Ofelia considered writing an anonymous note to corporate, but then she saw Mrs. Greenberg's son and daughter come in the front door and ask to see Janice and they looked grim.

Ofelia smiled to herself. Maybe now Janice would get what was coming to her.

Elaine was seething as she and Joel drove toward the hospital from Sunset Hills and a less-than-satisfying meeting with Janice. *No time to call them,* Janice had told them.

"I wanted to smack that bitch in the face," Elaine said.

"Yeah, but how would that help Mom?"

Elaine sighed. Her brother was right, of course. As long as their mother was living at Sunset Hills they needed to be on the community manager's good side.

When they reached the hospital, an unassuming stucco building in the Valley, they decided to consult the doctor before going in to see their mother. They sat in his office, where he went over the various tests she'd been given.

"Is she always anxious?" he asked.

"Only when she's dragged off to a lock-up," Elaine responded, but Joel's warning look stopped her. "What I mean is, this has been a terrifying experience for a person her age."

"Right," the doctor said, apparently not offended. "But we feel she'd be appropriate for a mood stabilizer."

Elaine and Joel exchanged a look. Tell me something I don't already know, Elaine thought.

"We've, uh, talked to Mom before about it," Joel said, "but she's really against it."

"That's not unusual, but in her case it could make a big difference. In any event, we don't feel she is a danger to herself or others, so we can probably release her in the morning."

For the first time since she'd gotten Joel's call, Elaine felt some of the tension leave her.

"I suggest you talk to her about the medication," the doctor said, concluding the conference.

Elaine and Joel stood in the hallway by their mother's room.

"Who's going to tell her?" Joel asked.

Elaine backed away.

Joel made a fist, just like when they were kids.

Elaine sighed. "Odds or evens?"

Emma Greenberg would never admit it, but in truth, she was beginning to enjoy all the attention she was getting in the hellhole they'd sent her to. Doctors and nurses and social workers were giving her all kinds of tests and asking all sorts of questions and playing little games. And she wasn't scared anymore, now that Joel and Elaine were coming to rescue her.

She was already trying to shape in her mind how she'd tell the story to everybody in the dining room once she was back at Sunset Hills. She dozed off, and when she woke up, Joel and Elaine were standing by the bed. They leaned down to kiss her cheek.

"You're looking great, Mom," Joel said.

"Good news," Elaine told her. "They're going to release you. But the doctor wants to prescribe a medicine to relax you."

Emma was instantly alert. "What medicine? Like Prozac?"

Elaine shook her head. "No, just Ativan, as needed, to kind of take the edge off when you get nervous."

Emma didn't like that. What was so wrong with being nervous? Was everybody supposed to walk around like a robot? Drugged out? But she saw the expression on Elaine's face, and she figured she'd better play along. And "as needed" wasn't really so terrible.

She sighed. "Okay."

Out in the visitors lounge, Elaine and Joel waited for Mr. Carson, the admissions director, to complete the paperwork for Emma's release.

"That was easier than I thought," Elaine said.

"You know Mom. You can't predict how she'll react to anything."

"Yeah, full of surprises. She always was."

Mr. Carson came into the lounge. "As I said, your mother has a clean report," he said. "She poses no danger to herself or others. Now, do you want her released back to her facility, or to one of you?"

Elaine and Joel exchanged a wary glance.

"To the facility," they replied in unison.

"Fine. I'm just going to call the community manager."

Mr. Carson disappeared behind the nursing station.

"Whew," Joel said when he'd gone. "That was close."

Elaine laughed. "Yeah. I could just picture Shelley's reaction if you drove home with Mom."

"This whole thing's been a nightmare."

"One more story to add to the list. Anyway, it's over."

Except it wasn't.

Mr. Carson came back about fifteen minutes later, but he didn't look at all happy.

"It seems," he said, "that Sunset Hills refuses to accept your mother back."

Ofelia was in the living room checking the van schedule while Mrs. Breur was having her hair done, when Mrs. Greenberg's son and daughter came in. Nathan at the front desk gave them the sign-in book.

"Well, nice to see that Sunset Hills is such a stickler for proper procedure," Elaine, the daughter, sneered.

Her brother took the pen and signed in.

Uh oh, Ofelia thought, trouble ahead. Curious, she followed them to the elevator. "How's Mrs. Greenberg doing?" she asked once they were inside.

"Pretty good," Joel said. "Really anxious to come home."

The elevator stopped on the second floor and they all got out.

"Tell her hi," Ofelia said.

"We will," Elaine said. "Thanks for asking."

Ofelia really didn't have anything to do on the second floor, but she couldn't pass up the chance to get the scoop on what was happening with Mrs. Greenberg, so she paused in front of the nursing station. Mrs. Greenberg's room was next door, and Janice's office was just down the hall.

Jennifer was on break, and the nursing station was closed, so Ofelia pretended to study the announcements posted by the door. Mrs. Greenberg's children walked ahead and stopped in front of her room. Out of the corner of her eye, Ofelia saw Elaine take a key chain from her purse. Nathan must have called Janice, Ofelia thought, because just as Elaine started to unlock Mrs. Greenberg's door, Janice's door swung open and she strode swiftly down the hall.

Ofelia gave up all pretense of reading the bulletin about an audiologist coming to give free hearing tests to anyone who wanted one. Elaine and Joel were just about to enter Mrs. Greenberg's room, when Janice came up to them.

"How is your mother feeling?" Ofelia heard Janice ask, all fake concern.

"As you'd expect," Elaine answered. "Look, isn't there some reasonable way we can settle this thing? Our mother hasn't been a problem, and the incident with the nurse was a misunderstanding. In addition, you know my brother or I should have been called at once."

"We have our rules," Janice said.

"The hospital is ready to release her."

"I'm sorry," Janice said. "The decision is final."

Ofelia could hardly believe her ears. Management *always* kissed ass when it came to family, but it seemed like Janice was booting poor Emma Greenberg out of Sunset Hills!

"Tell me, what would you do if we just brought her back?" Elaine challenged.

That was when Ofelia saw Janice give her phoniest, coldest smile.

"We wouldn't want it to be unpleasant, now, would we?"

With that, she turned and headed back to her office.

"Unbelievable," Joel said to his sister.

She grabbed his arm and propelled him toward the elevator. "First thing, we get a lawyer."

"I'm really sorry," Ofelia blurted, as they approached her. "I mean, I heard what Janice said and all, and I was there at the medication cart when it happened and it was hard to tell whose fault it was."

Mrs. Greenberg's son and daughter just looked at her.

"We'll fight it in court," Elaine said.

"It's not really my business," Ofelia went on, "but you know there's an ombudsman who helps seniors out when they have problems like this. The number's posted by the front desk. And you don't have to pay, either."

"Really?" Elaine said.

Ofelia nodded.

She and her brother exchanged a look.

"Seems like a good way to start," Elaine said, and smiled at Ofelia.

Ofelia had a warm feeling as she watched them go toward the elevator. She hoped her suggestion would give her some good karma—God knew everybody needed all they could get.

At first, Emma didn't understand what Elaine and Joel were telling her.

"What do you mean there's a problem with my going back?" she asked them.

Joel told her again. Then she got it. Janice wasn't going to let her back because of that so-called attack on Jennifer. Never mind that she could probably sue *them* because they tried to give her the wrong meds!

"But my rent's all paid," Emma protested.

"I know, Mom," Elaine answered. "Don't you worry. We'll handle things."

But after they left, Emma did worry. She was getting a panicky feeling and felt her heart palpitating. It wasn't that she was in love with Sunset Hills, far from it, but it was her home. If Janice kicked her out, where would she go? She'd be afraid to stay alone in an apartment, not that she would ever admit it. She remembered how her neighbor in her old apartment building, Alvin Winger, had fallen down in his bathroom and lay on the floor for nearly three days until the manager noticed his mail piling up and came in to check. And then he'd had a stroke. No, living alone wasn't for her. But she'd kill herself before she'd move in with either of the kids, not that that was an option. Still, it would've been nice if they even once offered.

The worst thing about being an old person, Emma decided, was not that your body started going to hell. It was that you lost control over your *life*.

Whenever the big brass from corporate descended, as they did periodically, it always meant trouble. Nearly a week had gone by since Janice had Emma Greenberg carted off to the psych hospital, and by now everybody knew that Janice was refusing to let her back.

Most of the residents were furious.

"After all, it could happen to any of us," Peggy White declared. "It's just like the Red Scare back in the fifties"

"I don't see the connection," Mrs. Freedman responded.

"Well, you weren't in the industry," Peggy White sniffed. "Believe me, it was a real witch hunt."

"We have to stand behind Emma," Mr. Grosso said.

"How?" someone asked.

Various suggestions were offered, among them going on a hunger strike and flooding corporate with letters of protest. Mr. Grant even proposed they call Larry King and see if he would be interested in doing a segment on the situation.

As the residents were sitting around the lounge debating the pros and cons of various ways to stand up for Mrs. Greenberg, three members of corporate, dressed in suits and ties and carrying briefcases, strode by.

"What now?" Mr. Grosso exclaimed.

When Mrs. Greenberg's son and daughter followed a few minutes later, accompanied by a young black man also in a suit and tie, they had their answer.

"Who's he?" Mrs. Freedman wondered aloud.

"A lawyer, I bet," Mr. Grant said.

Ofelia, sitting to the side playing Scrabble with Mrs. Breur, knew better.

"He's the senior-care ombudsman," she announced.

Elaine had been too nervous to eat, and the three cups of coffee she'd downed with Joel and the ombudsman at Starbucks made her even more edgy. She didn't know what to expect when they walked into Janice's office and saw the array of executives seated by Janice. Even though the ombudsman—his name was Mr. Jones—had assured them that the law was on their side, Elaine, usually so sure of herself, felt totally out of her element. Their mother's fate lay in the hands of those strangers. She longed to hold her brother's hand.

Janice stood and smiled at them as she made introductions and offered them seats. Elaine was preparing herself for a heated confrontation, but instead Janice began by talking about how much they all liked Emma.

Yeah, sure, Elaine thought.

"Of course," Janice went on, "the job of the community manager is to make sure that all the residents are safe and well cared for, and a certain code of behavior is expected. In fact, it is specifically spelled out in the rental contract." She went on in that vein, while Elaine tried to ignore the growling in her empty stomach.

When she was finished, Janice asked the nurse to tell her story.

Jennifer gave Elaine and Joel an apologetic smile as she recounted the pill episode, ending with her accusation that Emma had stuck her cane out at her, causing her to fall.

Janice shook her head sadly. One of the corporate executives wrote something on a yellow legal pad. Elaine snuck a glance at the young ombudsman. He seemed unperturbed. Elaine wondered if maybe it had been a mistake to listen to that aide, Ofelia. Maybe they should have sprung for a lawyer. After all, their mother's future was at stake.

But when it was his turn, Mr. Jones was more than prepared. He went over the regulations of tenants' rights, including the right to refuse medication, the right to be given thirty days notice, and the right of appeal.

"Thank you," Janice said, when he had finished. She looked at the executives and they nodded. Then she stood up and looked at Mr. Jones, Elaine, and Joel.

"If you will give us a few minutes, we will meet you down in the lounge," she said pleasantly, and walked them to the door.

They waited until they were in the elevator before speaking.

"So what do you think?" Joel asked the ombudsman.

"It went very well. The law is clear." Mr. Jones grinned. "The real kicker, of course, is that I discovered Janice isn't even licensed in the state!"

"So what's going to happen?" Elaine asked.

"We'll just wait for them in the lounge," he said, sidestepping the question.

The meeting in Janice's office seemed to take forever. Ofelia was so nervous she couldn't concentrate on anything. She kept finding excuses to go upstairs and pass by Janice's closed door. She heard voices but was frustrated because she wasn't able to make out any of the conversation.

Finally, close to noon, when the residents were having lunch in the dining room, Mrs. Greenberg's son and daughter and the ombudsman came downstairs and went to the lounge. Elaine and Joel looked stressed out. Poor Mrs. Greenberg, Ofelia thought, they were going to throw her out for sure. About ten minutes later, the elevator doors opened, and out came Janice with the people from corporate. They went to the lounge.

Leaving Mrs. Breur at her table, Ofelia scurried to the restroom across the hall from the lounge. She went inside, but left the outer door ajar. She could hardly believe her eyes—there was Janice serving coffee to Elaine and Joel and the ombudsman, with a big, fat, fake smile on her face! That's when Ofelia knew that the ombudsman had saved the day.

"Thank you, Lord," she said out loud.

So Emma Greenberg came back that afternoon and received a tremendous welcome from the residents. Janice stood at the front door, smiling and patting her arm like they were old friends. As far as Ofelia was concerned, it was definitely weird!

But the biggest surprise was that by the end of the month, Janice was gone! There was the usual letter given to each resident saying that she was transferring to another facility out of state, and ending with how much she would miss all the residents and staff.

"Boo-hoo," Ofelia said, and tossed the letter into the wastebasket.

There was no farewell party for Janice, but the night after she left, the chef baked a huge chocolate cake and Debby served champagne after dinner.

"So they transferred Janice just like they transferred all those pervert priests," Connie said to Ofelia.

"Like I keep telling you, she had bad karma," Ofelia declared.

As for Emma Greenberg, she put the whole nasty business out of her mind, and why not? Since she'd come back, everybody treated her much better than before. Jennifer was extra nice and helpful, and Larry, the new community manager, always stopped by her table to say hello and ask how she was.

The day she came back, Elaine and Joel offered to take her out for dinner, but Emma declined.

"You kids have your own lives. You've done enough," she said.

The truth was, she was excited to tell her story. And she did, taking special care to describe the cruelty of the goons who took her away, the anecdotes of the zombies in the psych ward, and the fierce battle she and Elaine and Joel had put up to return her home.

Mr. Grosso went to the piano and started playing, and everybody sang "For she's a jolly good fellow."

It was the best time Emma Greenberg had had in a long time.

THE LOVEBIRDS

When Louise Draper moved into Sunset Hills, it was clear to Ofelia that she would be one of the "in crowd." It was weird, Ofelia often thought, how old folks were just like the kids she'd gone to high school with. There had been a popular crowd back then, and those who weren't in it would've given anything to be included.

At Sunset Hills, there was a popular crowd, too—people like Mr. Grosso, Mr. Grant, and Peggy White. They always sat together at meals and meetings and signed up for the same outings. Mrs. Freedman and her pals were like the high-schoolers who were always on student council and being voted "Most Likely to Succeed." Then there were people like Mrs. Breur, who were too shy to push themselves. And, of course, there were the losers, but in high school the losers were clueless because of their clothes and looks, while in Sunset Hills they were clueless for other reasons—mainly because they were losing their marbles.

Just by the way she dressed and walked, Ofelia knew Louise Draper had been in the popular crowd way back when. She was tall and slender, and her silver hair was just right—not too teased-out or too thin—and her shoes matched her outfits, which was why Ofelia wondered what was wrong with her. There had to be *something* because even if people looked one hundred percent, like Louise Draper, there was always a reason they were in Sunset Hills.

Louise Draper moved in on a Wednesday and by Thursday, just as Ofelia had predicted, she was sitting at Mr. Grant's table with Mr. Grosso, Peggy White, and Henry O'Neil, who everybody called The Captain because he'd been one in the war.

Mr. Grant, Mr. Grosso and Peggy White were big talkers. The Captain, on the other hand, was kind of a Gary Cooper type, quiet but a really good listener, and he laughed at all their jokes. He had moved in the year before because his kids didn't think he could manage by himself after his wife died. Ofelia was sure he'd have done just fine, but The Captain was the kind of guy who followed orders. He never made a fuss over anything.

Everybody was curious about Louise Draper. Her son had moved her in but didn't follow up right away to see how she was doing. That wasn't unusual. Lots of residents had children who lived in other cities or states or were just too busy with their own lives to drop in to check on Mom or Dad. You could say a lot of not-so-good things about *my* culture, Ofelia thought, but at least we Latinos take care of our old folks—even if we don't like them.

Louise Draper hadn't been at Sunset Hills more than a few days before Ofelia overheard Mrs. Freedman and Emma Greenberg gossiping about her clothes.

"Neiman Marcus," Mrs. Freedman said, nodding her head. "And her ring is a real emerald."

"You can't tell from a distance," Emma Greenberg retorted.

"I know stones," Mrs. Freedman insisted. "It's real."

Emma Greenberg shrugged. Mr. Grant had nicknamed her "the red-diaper baby" because she'd been a communist back in the thirties and, unlike Mrs. Freedman, Emma didn't give a hoot about jewelry or designer clothes. Sometimes Ofelia thought Emma Greenberg looked like a bag lady with those shapeless sweatpants and clunky orthopedic shoes.

Mr. Grant and Mr. Grosso immediately began showing off and flirting with Louise Draper, which annoyed Peggy White, who was used to being the center of attention. Louise, however, was so nice she quickly won Peggy over.

Moving in was always an adjustment for new residents, and sometimes they just stayed in their rooms and Debby had to make an effort to get them to activities. But from the start, Louise Draper wanted to try everything from bingo to bridge to the walking club to outings to Trader Joe's.

Ofelia liked to think she was the first one to notice the signs. About ten days after Louise moved in, Ofelia had taken Mrs. Breur down early for the wine-and-cheese hour because there was going to be entertainment and Mrs. Breur liked to sit close to the piano. Ofelia was fixing her a small plate of cheese and crackers when Louise Draper stopped at the refreshment table. She helped herself to a glass of wine and smiled at Ofelia.

"This singer's really good," Ofelia said, just to be friendly. "He sounds kind of like Frank Sinatra."

"Ol' Blue Eyes. I always liked him," Louise Draper said.

Ofelia took the plate to Mrs. Breur and watched Louise walk away with her wine. The living room was starting to fill up, but there were still lots of empty seats. Mr. Grant waved to Louise and motioned her to come sit next to him. She gave him a friendly smile, and Ofelia was sure she was going to head his way. Instead, she made her way to a chair in the back of the room next to The Captain.

Ofelia paid special attention after that and noticed that now that Louise Draper was a regular at what they all called "Mr. Grant's table," The Captain seemed to perk up. He laughed more and talked more. Ofelia just knew in her heart they were sure to become a couple.

The Captain had always been called by his Christian name, Henry, but since living in Sunset Hills he'd begun to think of himself as The Captain, since that was what everybody called him. He didn't mind. It brought back memories of when he was young and he really *was* The Captain. He was more or less in good health. He didn't need a ton of meds like some of the other residents, and he didn't even need a cane. But after Molly died, his kids went on a campaign.

"It's not good to live alone, Dad," his daughter said.

"What if you get sick?" his son added.

They pulled out all the stops. He would be lonely in the house. He could have a stroke, a heart attack. What if he fell and broke a hip and nobody was around to help? What if he lost his driver's license? Blah, blah, blah.

What if, what if. The Captain assured them he wasn't lonely. He went to the driving range and hit golf balls. He walked every day. He listened to tapes of the big bands and watched the news and baseball in the summer, basketball in the winter. What was so terrible about that? But The Captain had to acknowledge that his kids had a point. He *was* getting up there, and he had always been a practical man. A practical man had to look ahead and plan. And so he'd moved into Sunset Hills.

The Captain was a little surprised at how easy the adjustment turned out to be. He had a small but comfortable studio apartment. The food was okay although most of the people complained nonstop. Ha! They should've eaten the slop he'd had to eat back in the army. Anyway, he wasn't one of those food snobs. He could go to his room when he felt like privacy, and he was quickly befriended by Jack Grant and Artie Grosso and enjoyed listening to all their blarney. He got a kick out of the fact that Artie once played with Tommy Dorsey, and Jack Grant sure knew how to tell a good story. And Peggy White wasn't at all bad to look at, although not his type.

What was his type, anyway? The Captain didn't have a clue. He'd only had one partner—Molly—and even though you couldn't have called it a real love match like in the old movies, he was the faithful sort. No, The Captain couldn't have said what his "type" was—at least not until Louise Draper entered his life.

This was how it came about. Hildy Blum had been a regular at "Mr. Grant's table" and when she died, she left an empty seat across from The Captain. Although there were no assigned tables or reserved seating at Sunset Hills, it was an unwritten rule that a person couldn't just sit at Mr. Grant's table. You had to be invited, which a lot of residents resented, but that was the way it was. Louise hadn't been at Sunset Hills more than a day before Mr. Grant asked her to sit with them. She accepted, not knowing that this was an honor. Ofelia figured that sort of thing probably happened to her all through her life.

Louise Draper was very aware of the fact that good things just naturally came her way. It had been like that as long as she could remember. She never had to go after things or people—they just gravitated toward her. She had always had lots of friends. She had gone to college when not many women did. She'd been lucky enough to marry a good and generous husband and had a son who never got into mischief. She did sometimes feel guilty knowing that she'd never done anything to deserve her blessings, which was why when she was diagnosed with breast cancer, she didn't sit around and moan "why me?" "Why *not* me," was her reaction.

But once again, luck came to her rescue. Although she expected the worst, Louise suffered few side effects of her chemo. Her hair grew back as thick as before, and the doctors were pleased to report there was no metastasis. This time Louise couldn't quite believe her good fortune, so when her son, Charlie, suggested she sell the house and move to a retirement home, she agreed. She figured if the cancer came back, there would be one less problem for Charlie to deal with, which was why she also gave him power of attorney. She wanted to make things very easy for her boy, just as he had made things easy for her.

So Louise moved into Sunset Hills and once again, her guardian angel was looking out for her. She met The Captain.

Was there such a thing as love at first sight? Maybe when you were a teenager with raging hormones, both Louise Draper and The Captain agreed. Surely not when you were a grownup—and most definitely *not* when you were a senior citizen! Yet, how else to explain their feelings when early on they looked at each other across the dining room table?

For The Captain, it took the form of embarrassment. He would glance shyly at Louise and uncharacteristically wonder how he looked to her. Were his clothes up to snuff? Did he need a haircut? And there was this weird pang when the other men flirted with her. He felt just like an awkward teenager. But instead of crawling into a shell, his discomfort made him suddenly reckless. He joined in the conversations, even told a joke or two that didn't bomb as he'd been afraid they might.

For Louise, the recognition of her feelings for The Captain first came to her in her dreams. She liked everyone at the table, but it was The Captain she dreamed about at night. Strange, crazy dreams, even sexual dreams! And how many years since she'd had one of those! And the result of those dreams was that during the day she paid careful attention to The Captain to try and understand why this was happening. Something about him, she wasn't quite sure what, touched her. She wanted both to protect him and to be protected by him. Finally, she made the decision to stop analyzing and just to go with the flow. After all, who knew how much time she had left?

The Captain had two passions: music from the forties and golf. Turned out that Louise loved golf, too, and when she learned of this mutual interest, she asked Debby to organize weekly outings to the golf course. The trips were an instant hit because a half-dozen or so of the other residents were also golfers. The Captain lost his awkwardness on the driving range, and when Louise asked him if he would help her with her swing, he flushed with pride and readily agreed.

What followed seemed perfectly natural to both of them. The Captain took to waiting for her by the elevator at meal times, and they rode down to the dining room together. Louise checked the activity schedule every week and consulted with him about what to sign up for. And they sat next to each other during entertainment and in the van. Naturally none of this escaped the eagle eyes of the other residents, and they remarked to one another on the change in The Captain.

"He's like a new man," Gerri Kane pronounced, and everyone readily agreed.

It was Mr. Grant who started calling them "The Lovebirds" although not to their faces, and that was how everybody else began to refer to them.

"Maybe they'll get married," Ofelia said to Connie one day while the residents were playing bingo.

"Why should they?" Connie responded. "They got the perfect arrangement—living in the same place with their own rooms."

That didn't sound so perfect to Ofelia, but Connie was pretty cynical ever since her father had walked out on her mother after twenty-five years.

Ofelia didn't spend more energy focusing on the lovebirds because it was around that time corporate sent out notices to the residents and families. Ofelia first heard about it from Mrs. Breur's daughter when she came storming in waving the letter. Not only was their rent going up, but the prices for all the extra services like private laundry and medication management were also being increased

"This is outrageous!" Ms. Breur-Gordon declared.

"What, dear?" Mrs. Breur asked.

"Greedy S.O.B.s. Another damn increase!"

"Oh, my," Mrs. Breur said, looking worried.

Ofelia could tell that Mrs. Breur didn't really have a clue what was making her daughter so upset.

"But don't you worry, mother," Ms. Breur-Gordon assured her. "I'll handle it."

Ms. Breur-Gordon wasn't the only one who was angry. The residents were furious, too. Three of them gave notice a couple of days later. At the next residents' meeting nobody wanted to discuss anything except the rate increases. Mrs. Freedman circulated a petition, and everybody signed it in protest. Peggy White suggested they all go on a hunger strike until corporate backed down.

"Wouldn't be a sacrifice, with this crummy food," Mr. Grant commented.

Some of the family members, led by Ms. Breur-Gordon, demanded a meeting with Larry, the young community manager who had replaced Janice. Ofelia positioned herself outside the office door, but she could catch only snippets of conversation. When the door finally opened, everybody filed out looking madder than when they went in. To the dismay of the families, it turned out that Sunset Hills was not acting illegally.

"Just immorally," Ms. Breur-Gordon said contemptuously.

Ofelia thought Sunset Hills was expensive enough without the increases. Since they didn't take Medi-Cal, residents had to be either pretty rich or had to use up all their money and be forced to depend on their kids.

Ofelia felt lucky she didn't have to worry about her job because she worked for Ms. Breur-Gordon, who was employed full-time in a top advertising agency. Anyway, Ms. Breur-Gordon's house was way up in the hills with lots of steps. Not a good place for her to move her mother.

The lovebirds didn't pay all that much attention to the furor. They had more important things on their minds. Louise continued to dream about The Captain. She told herself that she and Henry, as she preferred to call him, were just good friends. Of course, it was clear to her from his compliments that he thought she was attractive, but there hadn't been any physical contact at all. Well, not quite true. When Henry helped her with her golf swing, he stood in back of her, their bodies touching, and she felt her heart race. And when Debby arranged an hour of dancing with live music, Henry asked her to dance. She was surprised at how graceful he was as he led her in a swing, a fox trot, and even a tango. Again, the touch of his hand, the feel of his arm around her, made her light-headed. Did he feel it, too? She had no way of knowing because that was as far as it went.

Louise found herself wondering what it would be like to kiss him, to snuggle up to him. Her face burned at the thoughts, and she chastised herself. *You are an old lady,* she told her reflection in the mirror as she put on her make-up. *This is unseemly, ridiculous.*

But she didn't feel like an old lady, and she was helpless to stop her thoughts or her dreams. In one dream, there was a fire drill in the middle of the night and she ran out of her room stark naked. She found herself in the elevator with Henry, and when he saw her, he dropped his pajama pants—but enough! She wished she had someone to confide in about all of this, but the only person she might have talked to about it—her old college roommate, Evie—had died ten years ago.

The Captain had romantic thoughts, too. He longed to embrace and kiss Louise, but he was too afraid of being rejected or of making a fool of himself to do anything. Dancing was as far as he would venture. But then Valentine's Day arrived.

Sunset Hills made a big deal out of every holiday—barbecues on the Fourth of July, formal dinners at Thanksgiving and Christmas, Irish dancers on St. Patrick's Day. Valentine's Day was no exception. Debby spent days decorating the lounge and the living and dining rooms with red and white crepe paper banners. Cupids and hearts were taped all over the walls. There was going to be a candlelight dinner with red and white roses on the tables and a singer crooning the old love songs.

Every Valentines Day Louise's husband, Allen, had dutifully brought her flowers and taken her out for dinner. It had been years since she'd celebrated the day, and Louise felt slightly silly as she had her hair done that morning and gave herself a manicure. Nevertheless, she chose her dinner outfit with extra care.

As usual, Henry was waiting for her by the elevator, looking handsome in a suit and tie. He smiled shyly at her. "You look very nice."

Louise returned his smile. "I return the compliment."

Debby's efforts paid off. The pink tablecloths and tall candles flickering on each table made the atmosphere so romantic that Louise was able to ignore the fact that the occupants of the dining room were mostly elderly women. The singer reminded her of Perry Como as he crooned songs like "April in Paris" and "There Will Never Be Another You." If she tried hard enough, she could imagine she was at the old Coconut Grove. She smiled at Henry across the table, unable to concentrate on the conversations swirling around her.

Dinner ended all too soon, and after a sumptuous dessert, the residents slowly straggled toward the elevator.

"Cappuccino in the lounge," Debby called after them.

"Sounds good to me," Peggy White said.

"Hope it's decaf," Mr. Grant grumbled.

"I'm calling it a night," Mr. Grosso said, and yawned.

Which left Louise and The Captain alone at the table.

How simple it all really was, Louise marveled later. Maybe that was life. You spent endless time worrying about things and in the end they usually took care of themselves.

When Henry walked her to her door, he pulled a card out of his pocket and handed it to her. It was a Valentine card, nothing special, but she just knew it had been carefully chosen, and it was signed "Love, Henry."

Impulsively, she reached up and kissed his cheek. "That's so sweet," she said. "Thank you."

Which was when he put his arms around her and gave her a real kiss, the kind of kiss she had been dreaming of. The rest, as she used to say, was history.

No sooner had the furor over the rent increase died down than something else happened. One night not long after Valentine's Day, Ofelia's walkie-talkie went off.

"I got a 411," Connie said excitedly, using her code for "information."

"Mrs. Breur's in bed. Come over."

Connie must have run down the stairs because only a minute went by before she knocked on the door.

"Oh my God," she said breathlessly when Ofelia let her in. "Wait till you hear this! I was on my way to check on Mrs. Haley when I heard these weird noises coming from Mrs. Draper's room. I knocked, but nobody answered. I was afraid maybe she was having a heart attack or something, so I used my key and let myself in, and there they were!"

"Who?"

"Who do you *think!* The Captain and Mrs. Draper! Buck naked, in her bed, him on top of her!"

Ofelia could hardly take it in. "What'd you do?"

"Nothing! I left. Not my business."

"Did they see you?"

"I don't think so. But you think they'll get in trouble?"

"What for?"

"Hell, I don't know. It must be against *some* rule. They got a rule for everything in this place!"

Ofelia didn't know of any specific rule against residents having sex, but she remembered the time when this oversexed resident, Mr. Glass, kept following Mrs. Lewis in the elevator and to her room. The community manager called his daughter, and next thing you knew, Mr. Glass moved out. But that was different because Mrs. Lewis was so fragile one hug and her bones would've broken, plus the fact that she really had dementia and half the time didn't know where she was. Louise Draper and The Captain knew what they were doing.

"You think I should report them to somebody?" Connie asked.

Ofelia was outraged. "No! Why should old people be treated like kindergartners?"

Connie shrugged. "I don't know. I just can't imagine some of them doing it, can you?"

Ofelia couldn't exactly picture it either, but if that was what was happening in Louise Draper's room, it wasn't hurting anybody and it sure was making The Captain happy. Now that she thought about it, lately he'd started walking around whistling, and turning down desserts.

Ofelia paid special attention to them after that and all the signs were there, not that *she'd* know since she hadn't had a boyfriend for ages and the last one was no bargain, that was for sure. But Louise and The Captain sure looked and acted like lovers to her. It wasn't like they were going at it in public or anything disgusting like that, but it was the way they looked at each other, and the way he held the chair out for her and let his hand graze her back and she would look up and give him this heavenly smile like he'd just given her a diamond. It was so romantic that Ofelia sometimes felt herself near tears. Never mind that they were old. It renewed her faith in love and romance. If Louise and The Captain could fall in love at their age, there was hope for her.

"I bet they get married," Ofelia told Connie. "Wouldn't it be fun if they had the wedding here? They could have the reception on the patio and we could all throw rice at them."

Connie snickered. "Yeah, right, and half the people would slip on the rice and break their hips."

"You are the most unromantic person I ever met."

"And guess what? I don't believe in Santa Claus, either."

But Ofelia believed there would be a happy ending, especially when The Captain's children took him for dinner and Louise went along.

"See?" Ofelia said to Connie. "The families are getting to know each other."

Connie just rolled her eyes.

Ofelia was not far off the mark. When The Captain's daughter and son-in-law told them they wanted to take him out to dinner, he wondered how it would go over if he invited Louise. The last thing he wanted was to be put through the third degree, yet Louise was part of his life now and he couldn't imagine going without her. So he gathered up his courage and told his daughter he wanted to bring a friend. He needn't have worried. She thought it was "sweet".

The dinner was a success. After a dry martini, The Captain relaxed, and just as he knew she would be, Louise was the perfect lady. He could tell that his kids and his grandkids liked her. And later that night, in her room, she let him know how much she enjoyed the evening.

Louise had been waiting for the right time to introduce Henry to her son and daughter-in-law, but their visits were sporadic and somewhat rushed. It seemed they always had a million things to do and were just fitting her in. Louise decided to take the upper hand and was about to call Charlie and invite them for dinner, when the phone rang. It was Charlie, inviting her to his daughter's school play.

Louise decided that after the play, she would tell them about Henry.

The play was *Our Town*, one of her favorites, and Louise was delighted with her granddaughter's performance. Charlie and his wife were hosting a small party for the cast at their house, and Louise went along. She was waiting for the proper time to bring up the subject of Henry. She thought it had come when Charlie took her to the family room for dessert, away from the noise on the patio. He settled her in a chair and brought her a slice of cake and a cup of tea. But Charlie had something on his mind.

"Mom, you know about the rent increase, don't you?"

"I know a letter went out a couple of months ago. Everyone was upset about it, and a few people had to leave."

Charlie nodded. "I'm not surprised."

"Well, all facilities, and apartments for that matter, raise the rents periodically," she told him. That was why she had not been particularly alarmed when the letters went out.

"That's true," Charlie agreed, "but this is a big increase. And if, in the future, you should need extra services like medication management, it'll cost even more."

Louise was beginning to get an anxious feeling. She put her cup down. "What are you trying to say, Charlie?"

"What I'm saying, Mom, is that I think it would be best to move."

Louise listened in shock, as he went on to explain how he had gone over the figures and had already found a facility that would save her a couple of thousand dollars a month.

"And it's closer to us," he had said.

It was with great effort that Louise kept from telling him that she didn't see why that mattered, since they visited so infrequently.

"I like where I am," she said instead, hoping that would be the end of it.

Charlie countered that he was sure she would adjust to the new place in time.

"You don't understand. I've made friends," she said.

Charlie stood his ground and Louise was near tears by the time he drove her back to Sunset Hills.

"Just let me take you over there so you can see it," he said at the door.

Louise reluctantly agreed. She would look at the place with him and then tell him it wasn't for her. Still, it was with a sinking heart that she made her way to the elevator.

Ofelia was shocked to learn that Louise Draper was moving out.

"Poor Captain," she said to Connie. "He's going to be heartbroken."

"Well, she should've put up a bigger fight."

Ofelia thought so, too, but then again you could never really know what went on in families.

It wasn't that Louise hadn't put up a fight, but she was no match for Charlie. Ironic, she thought. She had done far too good a job raising him.

"I wasn't brought up to be confrontational," she told Henry, "and it's hard to start at my age."

"Well, he's got no damn right," Henry retorted. "It's your life and your money."

It *was* her life, and she'd assumed it still was her money, but she realized now that since she'd given Charlie power of attorney, *he* was in charge. Pride kept her from telling Henry just how devastated she was. She didn't want him to lose all respect for her and see her as the coward she really was.

My fault, she thought. She'd always left financial matters in the hands of the men in her life, Allen and now Charlie. It had seemed so much simpler, and she'd never been a mathematical whiz. Now she berated herself over and over. If she had one piece of advice for her granddaughter it would be, "take charge." Still, she couldn't rid herself of the nagging fear that maybe Charlie was right, and if the time came that she needed all the extras her money *would* run out. Then where would she be?

"I think for the time being, I'll move over there and visit every weekend," she finally told Henry.

"Maybe I could move there, too."

How wonderful, was her first thought, immediately followed by another—what if her cancer came back? It was a fear never far from her mind. If that were to happen, she couldn't bear to think of Henry alone in a strange place.

"I don't know, sweetheart. Don't forget you've got your buddies here. If something happened to me, you'd be alone."

"We could get married," Henry said impulsively, his face turning crimson.

Louise thought her heart would break.

The Captain actually did bring up the subject of marriage to his son and daughter, but he didn't get the reaction he'd expected. While they liked Louise very much, they threw out all kinds of objections. None of them made sense to him. It wasn't as if he were a millionaire and would cut them out of his estate. Sure, he had an insurance policy and there was an investment property out in Lancaster he and Molly had bought years ago, but the kids were doing just fine on their own. He thought maybe they were afraid they'd eventually end up having to take care of both of them.

There was a marked change in The Captain after Louise moved out. Ofelia thought he looked forlorn sitting in the back of the room at the wine-and-cheese hour, and he refused to go on the golf outings or attend the entertainment when the singer he and Louise loved appeared.

"He's eating desserts again," Ofelia said to Connie. "I bet he put on five pounds at least."

A new lady moved in and made a play for him but The Captain wasn't having any of it.

But true to her word, Louise did visit on Sundays. A cab would pull up in the early afternoon, and Henry was always waiting at the door. She usually stayed until eight or so, then a cab would pick her up.

Ofelia figured a little was better than nothing. She gave Louise and The Captain credit for making the best of a bad situation. Then late one Sunday night, Ofelia got a 119 from Connie.

"Get down to the entrance right away!" she hissed.

When Ofelia got to the front desk, there was Louise sitting calmly, arms crossed. And standing by the door were her son and a uniformed cop! Charlie looked like he was about to bust a gut. The cop seemed embarrassed and kept looking around the room.

"Do you have any idea what you put us through?" Charlie demanded of his mother. "I get a call at nine-thirty telling me you signed out at one and hadn't come back. We were frantic! Hell, I called every emergency room around!"

Louise didn't reply but she didn't apologize, either.

"Don't I have enough on my mind without running all over town looking for you?" Charlie thundered.

Louise sighed and met his angry gaze. "I have my own problems," she responded.

Ofelia silently cheered her on.

The upshot was, Louise's Sunday visits abruptly stopped. There was no telling what they had done to keep her away, but whatever it was, it worked. The Captain seemed more and more lost, only perking up every evening at six o'clock when he sat by the phone waiting for her call. The regulars at Mr. Grant's table tried unsuccessfully to cheer him up.

Then one day the atmosphere at the table suddenly changed. The Captain started laughing again, and during afternoon snack times he, Mr. Grant, Mr. Grosso, and Peggy White huddled in a corner whispering.

Ofelia was beside herself with curiosity. She thought she'd figured it out when she saw the monthly list of birthdays. The Captain's name was on it, and Carlos in the kitchen told her Peggy White had reserved the card room for a private party. They were probably going to get Louise Draper there for a birthday celebration, which would explain The Captain's good mood. Ofelia asked Carlos what they had ordered, and how much. All he knew was they were bringing food in from outside.

Sure enough, on The Captain's birthday a truck from Bristol Farms pulled up in the afternoon and Peggy White signed for the platters the delivery man brought into the card room.

Louise Draper arrived around five in a taxi. Ofelia thought she had never looked better. She wore a fancy silk dress and one of those wide-brimmed garden hats they used to wear in the old movies. Mr. Grant ushered her into the card room before she could even say hello to anyone, and then he shut the door.

"This is weird," Ofelia said to Connie after forty-five minutes. "They ordered a ton of food—I counted the platters—but nobody's in there except them."

It *was* strange, Connie agreed, but then you never knew with old folks. They did nutty things sometimes.

The mystery was solved at six o'clock just as the residents were going into the dining room for dinner. Mr. Grant came into the room and banged a fork against a water glass. It took a couple of clangs before it got quiet.

"Okay, folks, give me your attention!" he ordered.

"What now," Mrs. Freedman muttered.

"Tonight's menu didn't look too appetizing, so we've arranged a buffet in the card room for everyone to celebrate The Captain's birthday . . ."

Everyone clapped.

Mr. Grant clinked the fork against the glass again and the room grew still. " . . . and the marriage of Louise Draper and The Captain!"

There was a stunned silence, and then, as Louise and The Captain walked in arm and arm, the entire room erupted in cheers.

"I might add," Mr. Grant continued when the uproar quieted down, "should anyone else be so inclined, the ceremony was performed by yours truly." He waved a document over his head like a banner. "With my one day official license—good until midnight!"

As she drifted off to sleep that night, Louise listened to Henry's reassuring, even breathing next to her and marveled once more at her incredible good fortune.

THE WALK OF FAME

The spacious two-bedroom suite on the fourth floor had been vacant since Ofelia began working at Sunset Hills. It had not one, but two patios and views of the Hollywood Hills, including the "Hollywood" sign, and it cost a fortune. Then word spread that someone was moving in.

The usual Tuesday bingo game was going on in the living room the day the new resident arrived—not driven by her son or daughter, which was what usually happened—but in a shiny, chauffeur-driven limo. A moving van pulled up behind it.

Ofelia couldn't believe her eyes. Even Debby, who was calling out the numbers, lost track of what was going on. All eyes were glued to the front entrance as the uniformed chauffeur got out of the car and opened the passenger door. A tall, lanky man with a salt-and-pepper goatee stepped out. He looked to be in his late fifties and was dressed in jeans and a black turtleneck sweater.

Ofelia knew immediately he had something to do with "The Industry," which was what people in L.A. called the entertainment business. She doubted *he* was the new resident. He looked way too young and fit. It must be his parent—more likely parents—given the size of the suite. He reached an arm into the car and a fragile-looking white-haired lady slowly emerged. The man with the goatee took her arm and led her to the entrance while the chauffeur removed two suitcases from the rear.

Nathan must have called Larry because the community manager suddenly appeared and opened the front door for them like he was a doorman.

"Welcome, Mr. Zimmer," Larry said with an ingratiating smile. And then he bowed slightly to the lady. "And Mrs. Zimmer. We are delighted to have you as a member of our community."

Ofelia nearly laughed out loud. You'd think the woman was the Queen of England or something.

"Don't want to intrude on your game," the man with the goatee said apologetically to Debby.

"Oh, no problem. We're just about done," she replied.

"*I* wasn't," Hannah Ostrow protested.

But no one paid any attention to her. The residents were far more interested in the procession as it made its way through the living room to the elevator.

Mid-morning coffee and snack in the lounge followed bingo. As the residents helped themselves to refreshments, they speculated on who the new lady was. Ofelia took it all in.

"Big bucks," Mr. Grant said. "We know that at least."

"That's a no-brainer," Mrs. Greenberg responded.

"How old do you think she is?" Mrs. Freedman wondered aloud.

"She's got to be up there, judging from the son. He's no chicken," Bernie Elkins answered.

"She's definitely had work on her face," Peggy White declared knowingly.

"Zimmer, Zimmer," Bernie Elkins mused. "Damn, that name's familiar."

"It's not exactly uncommon," Hannah Ostrow said. "I went to school with three Zimmers. It was probably Zimmerman, or Zimmerstein."

But then Peggy White broke into a big grin. "*I* know who she is! I mean I know who *he* is! He's Hank Zimmer! He just got a star on the Walk of Fame."

Mr. Grosso's face lit up. "Of course! The director! He was nominated for an Oscar." He turned to the others. "Remember, we saw his movie last month—the one about the Iraqi vet who goes nuts!"

"Oh, I hated it," Gerri Kane said. "It was so depressing."

"He's big!" Peggy White exclaimed.

Ofelia remembered an article about him in *People* not too long ago. Something about some hot starlet he was dating.

Now they understood how Mrs. Zimmer could afford the Penthouse, as they called that suite. While the residents were curious to meet her, the staff was far more interested in meeting Hank.

There was hardly a workplace in L.A. that wasn't at least partially staffed by struggling actors, writers, or aspiring filmmakers. And it was no less true for Sunset Hills. Alan, the waiter, was a writer and had a screenplay he'd been trying to sell ever since Ofelia had known him. Every once in a while he'd excitedly announce that this or that important person was reading it. He'd tried to get Bernie Elkins's son, the agent, to handle it, but it hadn't worked out. Once, he was sure he had a deal. Nothing had happened yet, but Alan was sure it would eventually. Ofelia had to admire him. She'd have given up the first time somebody passed on it.

And then there was Rodrigo, who drove the van. He had a short film he'd made and was trying to get it into a film festival. He persuaded Debby to show it to the residents, and they liked it, sort of. It was all about a convenience store owner in the barrio who has a sex change. Ofelia thought it was interesting, but she could tell it turned a lot of people off. They gave Rodrigo a big hand anyway, because everyone liked him.

But the staff member who had the most success—if you could call it that—was Jessie. Although Jessie was a Buddy, she was always quick to say that she was *really* an actress. She had actually been in a commercial for laundry detergent, and she'd had a walk-on part in a movie that was never in the theaters but went straight to video. Whenever she had time off, she was running to auditions. Ofelia didn't like her much because she thought Jessie had attitude and didn't seem to care anything about the residents she was supposed to help.

Jessie seemed the most excited about Mrs. Zimmer moving in, but Mr. Grosso and Peggy White, both having been in show business, were the first to introduce themselves to her at the wine-and-cheese hour.

"Oh, call me Dottie," Mrs. Zimmer said.

Peggy White was thrilled because Dottie remembered her commercials.

"I always loved them," Dottie told her and hummed the tune. "I think that's why I started smoking."

Peggy White didn't know how to take that since smoking was now such a no-no, but she graciously thanked her anyway. At least the lady wasn't hauling around an oxygen tank, which would have made her feel a little guilty.

"Were you in the business?" Mr. Grosso asked.

Dottie shook her head and smiled. "Oh, no. Actually, I would've liked to try my hand at acting, but it wasn't in the cards."

"So how'd your boy become a hotshot director?" Mr. Grant asked.

Dottie shrugged and held up her hands. "Who knows? We wanted him to be a professional—a doctor or lawyer—but he always loved the theater. So there you are."

Which led to a discussion of the mystery of the paths ones children took.

"My son went to Julliard, played the violin like Heifetz, and what's he doing now? Selling real estate!"

"At least he's working," Hannah Ostrow put in. "My Stanford honor student's a monk in Tibet!"

Then Mrs. Freedman had to start bragging about her perfect daughter. Emma Greenberg just rolled her eyes. They'd all heard it before.

Ofelia wondered what her mother would think if she heard all that. All people bragged about in her old neighborhood was their kid graduating high school and getting a decent job.

Dottie Zimmer was a pleasant, cheerful soul and adjusted very well to life at Sunset Hills. It didn't look like she needed any special help, but her son, the director, hired a private caregiver anyway—a Filipina named Ana.

"That's sure a waste of money," Connie said to Ofelia. "The lady can do everything for herself."

"Now," Ofelia said ominously.

"What does *that* mean?"

"It means that she might need more help than it looks like."

Indeed, Ofelia thought she detected little signs. There were times when Mrs. Zimmer seemed confused. Not big time, but two or three times she came to the dining room thinking it was dinner time when it was only lunch. Ofelia believed her son was looking ahead, which, in her opinion, was smart.

Ofelia admired Hank Zimmer not because he was a big deal director, although that was impressive, but because he was a really good son. He was the one who got Sunset Hills to have Shabbat services on Fridays because his mother wanted them. Even though about half the residents were Jewish, and they always had a Hannukah party, nobody had ever thought to have a Shabbat service.

The services turned out to be a big success. A lively lady cantor came every week with a guitar and sang a few Hebrew songs. Then they served sweet wine and challah bread. Even Mrs. Breur wanted to go.

"But you're not Jewish, Mrs. Breur," Ofelia pointed out.

"A grandfather on my mother's side was Jewish," Mrs. Breur responded. "Does that count?"

Whether it was true or not, Ofelia knew the real reason Mrs. Breur liked the Shabbat service so much was because of the wine and the challah.

Mrs. Freedman, who was always such a stickler for the rules, objected to all the non-Jews going to the Shabbat, but Peggy White justified it this way. "Well, if we go back far enough, we're all Jewish, right?"

Ofelia hadn't thought of it that way before, but she guessed Peggy White was right, except for the Buddhists and the Hindus. She wasn't quite sure where the Muslims fit.

Ofelia's intuition about Dottie Zimmer was right on the mark. After only a couple of months, it was clear she was losing it and that was why Ana was always by her side leading her into the dining room, or the lounge, or the living room. Although Dottie Zimmer still smiled a lot, she talked less and less. Ofelia had seen it before—Dottie Zimmer was in the early stages of Alzheimer's.

Her son came every week, sometimes twice, to visit, and he always brought DVDs for the residents to watch. Ofelia got a kick out of how Jessie managed to hang around him, to say nothing of Mrs. Freedman's daughter, who was trying to get her little girl into the movies. When Hank Zimmer stayed for a meal, Alan brought him larger portions of food than anyone else got, and one night Ofelia overheard him describing his screenplay to the director. Even though he was famous and had a star on the Walk of Fame, Hank Zimmer didn't look down on Alan or anybody else. He even told Alan he would read his script, which put the waiter in such a good mood that for days he brought extra desserts to everybody.

But the bad part, at least as far as the Buddies were concerned, was that Jessie really started slacking off. Connie complained to Ofelia about it one evening after Hank Zimmer left.

"Hell, she's always sucking up to Mrs. Zimmer, like she's going to give her a part in a movie or something, so when somebody needs help, they could ring and ring and forget about it. We end up doing her job. It's disgusting, not that she was so good to begin with. She doesn't even know how to change a diaper!"

Ofelia agreed with Connie that her behavior was pretty awful. She tried to put herself in Jessie's place, but she knew *she* wouldn't neglect Mrs. Breur for anything. Little Mrs. Breur depended on her, and Ofelia was proud of the good job she did for her, even though sometimes Ms. Breur-Gordon got on her case.

"She can't stay where she is," Ofelia predicted. "They'll have to move her to a nursing home or the Alzheimer unit."

Connie put her hands on her hips. "Oh, you really think management's going to give up the big bucks on the Penthouse?"

Things could—and often did—change in a minute at Sunset Hills. Dottie Zimmer developed a bad cough, and Ana became concerned. An ambulance whisked her away to the hospital, where the doctors said she had pneumonia.

"Better than lung cancer," Ofelia said to Connie when she heard.

"Maybe, maybe not," Connie replied. "Pneumonia's pretty serious at that age."

Ofelia knew she was right. She'd seen enough elderly people who seemed perfectly fine one day, caught a cold, and a week later were gone.

Dottie Zimmer was in the hospital for a little over a week, and Jessie made a point of visiting her on her day off.

"She's doing really good," Jessie reported. "They'll probably let her out any day."

"To a rehab?" Ofelia asked.

"Wherever Hank wants her to go."

"'Hank'! "Sounds like you're pretty chummy," Ofelia said.

Jessie just grinned.

As it turned out, Dottie Zimmer made good progress, but rather than transferring her to a rehab, her son decided he wanted his mother back at Sunset Hills. She returned, now in a wheelchair with an oxygen tank, looking even more fragile than before but with her usual big smile. She waved at the residents as Ana wheeled her in.

Sunset Hills was meant for people who required some assistance, and sure, some residents, like Mrs. Breur, had their own private caregivers, but Ofelia took one look at Dottie Zimmer and knew Sunset Hills was no longer appropriate. She belonged in a nursing home, plain and simple.

But surprisingly enough, Larry looked the other way, and Ofelia had to admit that Connie was right. Money talked.

When she came back from the hospital, Dottie was too weak to come to the dining room, so Ana took up her meals. Ofelia felt sad, like she always did when a resident was so clearly on the way out, but a comforting thought was that at least she was getting the best of care.

A few days after Dottie Zimmer returned, Ofelia heard the news that Jessie had quit.

"Just like that!" Connie said contemptuously. "No notice, no nothing!"

"Well, no big loss," Sonya, who was assigned to the third floor, said.

"Easy for you to say!" Connie shot back. "Fourth floor only has one Buddy now. ME! They better hire somebody fast or I'm walking, too!"

That evening, Ofelia was in the dining room with Mrs. Breur when she saw Jessie heading toward the elevator.

"Be right back, Mrs. Breur," Ofelia said and ran to the restroom with her walkie-talkie.

"Connie! Guess who's back!" she said breathlessly when she heard Connie's voice. "Jessie! I just saw her."

"No shit. And *you* guess what she's doing!"

Ofelia knew at once. "I don't believe it," she said.

It was true. Dottie Zimmer now needed lots of care. Ana had a family emergency and was taking a leave, and Jessie replaced her. It was like she had never left Sunset Hills, except that now she walked around with *real* attitude.

Ofelia noticed that she had a new hairdo and had added highlights. How could she possibly change and wash Dottie Zimmer with those new acrylic nails, Ofelia wondered. She asked Jessie about it one day when she was waiting in the dining room for Dottie's tray.

Jessie just laughed.

"So how's it going?" Ofelia asked.

She meant the job, and Dottie Zimmer, but Jessie could only talk about Hank Zimmer.

"This is the luckiest thing that ever happened to me," she said. "What are the chances I'd get to be friends with Hank *Zimmer!* It could make my career."

"What did Larry say when you quit?"

Jessie laughed again. "I could tell he was really pissed off, but what could he say? Anyway, working here is really the bottom of the barrel. I don't mean you, Ofelia, but the rest of them." She made a sweeping gesture with one hand. "Pay stinks, you got to deal with so much crap, it's unbelievable. I don't know why anybody puts up with it."

"Not a lot of choices out there, I guess," Ofelia said. "Especially if you have to support a family."

Alan brought a tray out from the kitchen. Jessie batted her eyelashes, took the tray from Alan, and sauntered off.

The residents were watching a movie one evening a few nights later, and Ofelia impulsively decided to pop into Mrs. Zimmer's room to say hi.

Jessie opened the door and let her in. The TV was on in the living room, and Ofelia could see into the bedroom, where Mrs. Zimmer was half asleep with the oxygen on.

"How is she?" Ofelia asked.

Jessie shrugged. "Hanging in there."

They chatted for a few minutes, then Jessie asked Ofelia if she would mind watching Mrs. Zimmer for a little while so that she could get some laundry done. Ofelia knew Mrs. Breur would be watching the movie for at least another hour, so she said sure.

"Thanks a lot," Jessie said. "It gets so boring all alone in here, even going to the laundry room is a treat."

After she left, Ofelia went into the bedroom, hoping she could at least say hello to Mrs. Zimmer. As soon as she got near the bed she knew by the smell that Dottie needed to be changed. It wasn't her place to do it.

"Hi, Mrs. Zimmer, it's me, Ofelia. How are you?"

Dottie stared blankly at her, then her face scrunched up and Ofelia knew something hurt her. She hoped Jessie would come back soon because the poor lady was probably miserable lying in her own poo. But Jessie had seemed in such a hurry to escape that she would probably take her own sweet time.

Ofelia looked down at Mrs. Zimmer and made a decision. She would change her. It would be doing a favor for Jessie, not to mention Dottie Zimmer.

Ofelia gently turned her to one side, and undid the thick diaper. The smell almost made her gag, but she quickly pulled the soiled diaper out from under Mrs. Zimmer and pushed it down into the plastic-lined wastebasket.

"It's going to be okay, Mrs. Zimmer," Ofelia said soothingly. "Just hold on to the rail and I'll clean you up.

Ofelia looked around for some latex gloves but didn't see any. She grabbed a wipe from the box next to the bed and looked down at the old woman's bony back. What she saw made her gasp.

The quarter-sized, festering blisters could only be bedsores.

"Oh, lord," Ofelia said out loud. She felt like crying but instead just bent to the task of cleaning up the mess.

Mrs. Zimmer was whimpering softly like a little kitten, and Ofelia made soothing noises as she looked for something to put on the sores. Finding nothing close by, she set about putting on a clean diaper.

"What do you think you're doing!"

Ofelia whirled around. Jessie was standing in the doorway holding a plastic basket of clothes.

"Look at this," Ofelia said, ignoring the question.

Jessie put the basket down and came to the bed.

"Oh, my!" she said, her eyes wide.

Fury rose up in Ofelia. "What the hell is this about?"

Jessie took a step back. "I don't know. I haven't seen them before."

Ofelia gently turned Mrs. Zimmer so that she was once more lying on her back.

"These are *not* new," Ofelia said angrily. "You know how dangerous they can be? What if they got infected? And how long has she been lying in her own shit?"

For once, Jessie seemed unsure of herself. "It's not your business. I can take care of it."

Ofelia just stared at her.

"I swear, I didn't see them."

Ofelia pushed by her and left the room. Her heart was racing. Technically, it wasn't her business. Yet in a way, it was. She thought about Mrs. Owens and that time she could have gone to the nurse and helped her and hadn't. That was a hard way to learn it was better to take the chance of getting into trouble as long as you thought you were doing the right thing. Wouldn't that be good karma? Wasn't that was life was all about?

Ofelia didn't know what would be the right thing to do. She only knew *something* had to be done. She talked it over with Connie.

"She deserves to get fired," Connie said. "She was never any good anyway. She doesn't give two cents for anybody except herself. You should report her to Jennifer."

The best thing, Ofelia finally concluded, was to kind of blackmail Jessie to go to Jennifer herself and get the right things to heal the sores. Ofelia made up her mind she'd tell Jessie that if she didn't take care of it right away, *she* would tell Hank.

By that time the movie was over, and Ofelia had to take Mrs. Breur back to her room and get her ready for bed. She resolved to talk to Jessie first thing in the morning.

The next morning, after settling Mrs. Breur in the dining room for breakfast, Ofelia took the elevator up to the Penthouse. She'd barely tapped on the door when Jessie flung it open. Her eyes were wide and she looked panicked. She seemed to have forgotten all about the previous night.

"Oh, I thought you were the paramedics!"

Ofelia pushed by her and went into the bedroom. Mrs. Zimmer was wheezing and struggling for breath.

There was nothing to say. Dottie Zimmer went back to the hospital. This time the pneumonia won.

Hank Zimmer held a "celebration of life"—which Ofelia knew was the new term for memorial service—in his mother's honor at Sunset Hills, and everyone was invited. He placed a poster-sized photograph of Dottie as a young woman at the doorway, surrounded by flowers. He brought in food from one of the best caterers. Ofelia took Mrs. Breur downstairs for the celebration, even though Mrs. Breur tended to get upset whenever a resident passed away. But Ofelia figured this was more like a party.

Some of Hank Zimmer's close friends in the business showed up, which caused a big stir. And Jessie was there, too, right in the front row, all dolled up.

Hank Zimmer, some of the family members, and an actor who had been in one of his movies gave nice little tributes to Dottie Zimmer. Then, to Ofelia's disgust, Jessie got up and gave an emotional speech about how she had come to love Dottie Zimmer and how grateful she was to have had the opportunity of caring for her at the end of her life.

Ofelia couldn't resist turning to look at Connie. Connie only shook her head.

Hank Zimmer made a big contribution to Sunset Hills, the gossip went. And every month he sent some DVDs for the residents.

"A real mensch," Bernie Elkins said.

Nearly a year after Mrs. Zimmer passed away, Ofelia was sitting with Mrs. Breur in the library watching the latest DVD Hank Zimmer had sent. It was a pretty good movie, which wasn't surprising since it was one of his. It took place in a small town in Arkansas or someplace like that, and about halfway through, the main character walked into a typical diner. He sat at the counter, and the camera focused on him as he studied the menu.

"Ready, sir?" a voice asked.

The camera moved away from him to a close-up of the waitress. Ofelia gasped. It was Jessie!

Everybody talked about it later—how great that Jessie had a part in a big movie, and wasn't she good, and on and on. Ofelia couldn't stand listening, so she walked out into the hall, angrier than she'd been in a long time. How could it be that Jessie was rewarded when she'd probably hastened Mrs. Zimmer's death?

Life wasn't fair, Ofelia thought, not for the first time. She didn't think she could go to church anymore without getting mad at God. She knew the priest would say something like we can't figure out God's ways, but Ofelia wasn't buying it anymore. The only thing that made her feel better was knowing that Jessie had some real bad karma.

I Should Worry, I Should Care

I dreamed I went to heaven in my *Maidenform bra*. Emma Greenberg could still see the magazine photograph of a curvaceous model looking like Betty Grable sexily posed in her Maidenform bra.

Emma lay in bed, letting herself wake up gradually, and wondered why in the world she was thinking of those old ads. Then, slowly, she made the connection. It wasn't the bras—it was heaven!

What a funny dream. Not funny ha ha, but funny strange. In her dream she was standing in the entrance of a tremendous cafeteria just like the one at Washington High. She saw that most of the seats were taken, which gave her a panicky feeling, just like she used to have back in high school when she wasn't sure if there would be room for her at the table where her crowd usually sat. She was thinking maybe she should just leave and go to the bathroom, when she saw her best friend, Ethel, waving to her. And just like that, all the nervousness went away and Emma felt happy.

"I saved you a seat!" Ethel called, and sure enough, there was an empty seat at the long table. But the weird part, Emma realized, was that all the people in the cafeteria, including Ethel and herself, were old. That's when Emma knew that she was in heaven. Amazingly enough, it turned out that heaven was just like a high school cafeteria!

What a comforting thought. Wouldn't it be nice if that was really how it was because then poor Ethel, who passed away five years ago, might actually be saving a seat for her.

Emma would have liked to tell somebody about her dream, but if she told her son, Joel would get uncomfortable and change the subject. As for the residents, the big "D" was not something they talked about. Most of the Buddies at Sunset Hills were religious and would either be offended or would try to convert her.

Lately, the strangest things had begun popping up in Emma's mind, things she hadn't thought of in God knew how many years. For instance, the morning after the heaven dream, she woke up, and running around in her head was that silly old refrain she and her girlfriends used to recite when they jumped rope.

I should worry, I should care, I should marry a millionaire. He should die, I should cry, I should marry another guy.

All day, the chant played in her head. At lunch, she asked a few of the ladies if they remembered it. Hannah Ostrow and Mrs. Breur said yes, they remembered, and repeated it until Mrs. Freedman rolled her eyes and changed the subject. Mrs. Breur's caregiver, Ofelia, thought it was funny and begged them for more old rhymes.

"I have one," Peggy White offered. "It goes to the tune of 'Frere Jacques.'" And she began to sing, "It's your birthday, it's your birthday, whoop de doo, whoop de doo. You're as old as cotton, better left forgotten, whoop de doo, whoop de doo."

A few people clapped, and Peggy White, who loved to be in the limelight, grinned and acknowledged them with a little curtsy.

"I never heard that one," Emma said.

"Well, you wouldn't. It's from the South," she answered.

Ofelia made Peggy sing it again while she wrote the words down on a napkin. The conversation led to reminiscences of old songs.

"Remember this one?" Mr. Grosso asked. He went to the piano and began to play.

People began singing, "The Bowery, the Bowery, we don't go there anymore."

"What's the Bowery?" Ofelia asked.

"The old theater district. You'd have to be a New Yorker to know," Bernie Elkins told her.

All that was fun, but Emma wondered just what made her dredge up that ancient jump-rope song about a ditzy gold-digger. She hoped it wasn't a sign of Alzheimer's—she couldn't think of anything worse than that. Joel and Elaine would stick her in the special wing, where she'd be led around like a circus animal. No thanks. She'd take the gas pipe before she let that happen.

But Emma had to admit that lately she'd been feeling not quite up to snuff. She was more tired than usual, and everything felt like an effort. Was that why she had that dream where heaven was a cafeteria?

Usually she hung around the living room after breakfast reading the paper or playing Scrabble, but that morning Emma went upstairs to her room and fell asleep.

When she got down to the dining room for lunch, Emma saw that unlike her dream, no one was saving a seat for her. Bernie Elkins, the old geezer, had grabbed her usual seat, and she'd be damned if she'd go over and sit with him, like it was his table and she was some guest. She threw a dirty look his way—not that he could see it from where he sat—and considered her options.

It looked like everybody had come down at the same time, and the only available seats were either with Mrs. Breur, who was hardly stimulating company, and her caregiver, Ofelia, or next to a new resident who talked with his mouth full. Emma chose the lesser of two evils and made her way over to Mrs. Breur's table.

"Hi, Mrs. Greenberg," Ofelia chirped. "Come sit with us."

Mrs. Breur looked up from her salad and nodded. Ofelia got up and pulled out the chair for Emma. Emma sat down, wondering where the two ladies who often sat with Mrs. Breur were, then she saw them at the so-called big table. Something was going on, Emma thought, but she couldn't think about it now because Alan was standing over her wanting to take her order.

But once she had her tomato soup, Emma's curiosity got the better of her. She looked over at the "big table" and started to ask Mrs. Breur why her pals weren't sitting with her, but Ofelia must've read her mind because she kind of shook her head and started talking about the afternoon trip to Vons. Mrs. Breur didn't say a word. She just kept picking at her salad.

Alan brought Emma a cheese omelet, decaf, and toast that was practically black.

"Look at this," she exclaimed, disdainfully picking up the toast. "Looks like it's been electrocuted!"

"Send it back," Ofelia advised.

Mrs. Breur looked like Ofelia had suggested she throw it at the waiter.

"I will. God knows I'm paying enough," Emma said, "and the least they can do is give us decent toast. They want to rush us through every meal."

Emma waved to Alan, who pretended he didn't see her, but Ofelia jumped up and talked to him, and next thing Emma knew, the offending item was whisked away.

The burned toast put her in a bad mood. She looked around the room, and it reminded her of the dream. It didn't seem fair that she should have to spend her so-called golden years with people she'd never have been friends with, like Mrs. Breur. They had nothing in common, although it was hard to know for sure since Mrs. Breur crept around like a little mouse and never opened her mouth except to eat. Emma wondered if she'd ever had a job. More likely she'd been one of those timid little housewives who never even learned how to balance a checkbook or drive a car.

There were a few residents she liked well enough, like Mr. Grant and Peggy White and the lovebirds, even Mrs. Freedman when she wasn't being a know-it-all, but it was nonsense to think that at this age you could make real friends. Acquaintances, yes, but not real friends like Ethel.

"Hey, guess who this is. *Everybody downstairs for karaoke!*" Ofelia chirped in a perfect imitation of Debby, the activities director.

That cheered Emma up a little.

She had signed up to go to Vons on the van at two o'clock, not that she really needed anything. She just liked to get out. But she dutifully made out a shopping list of snacks—cheese, crackers, mixed nuts. She added Tums to the list. That damn food.

When Emma got down to the living room at one forty-five, she saw Ofelia at the front desk arguing with Debby.

"I'm sorry, Ofelia, I told you the van is full," Debby said.

"I signed us up yesterday," Ofelia insisted.

"Well, her name's not on the list."

"Show it to me." Ofelia stuck out her hand.

Good for her, Emma thought. That Ofelia was nobody's fool.

Mrs. Breur looked like she was going to cry. Debby looked like she wanted to haul off and smack Ofelia—instead, she thrust the list at her.

Emma peered out the doorway and saw Mrs. Breur's "friends" boarding the van. Debby probably bumped Mrs. Breur so she could accommodate some of the more popular residents.

By the time the van returned to Sunset Hills, Emma felt so weak she could hardly make it to her room. Without bothering to take her clothes off, she got into bed and immediately fell asleep.

The next morning, Ofelia was playing Scrabble with Mrs. Breur and Bernie Elkins when the senior-care ombudsman showed up. Mr. Peters was a nice older man who stopped by every couple of weeks just to see how things were going. Ofelia knew he was a volunteer, which was probably why he was so nice. He always called the residents Mr. so and so, or Mrs. so and so, and never by their first names, unless someone said, "Oh, call me Grace," or whatever.

On this visit, he was talking about Advance Health Care Directives, which was, as Mr. Grant put it, a fancy way to say "pull the plug."

"It's a bit more complicated than that," Mr. Peters said with a smile. "We all have choices about end-of-life decisions."

"You been talking to Dr. Kevorkian," Mr. Grant said.

"He's dead," Mrs. Freedman said smugly.

"You wish!" Mr. Grant chortled.

Mr. Peters didn't let their comments throw him off track. "The advantage of an Advance Health Care Directive is that *you* make the choice while you're able, instead of leaving it to others," he went on.

Ofelia knew he was right, but the whole subject freaked her out. Maybe it was because she'd been around too many people in horrible shape, not even like people anymore. She suspected some of the residents felt the same way. She knew the men didn't like to think about those things. The women, on the other hand, were much more practical.

When he finished his explanation, Mr. Peters handed out some forms.

"I'll look at it later," Bernie Elkins mumbled, and folded his up.

But Mr. Grant made a big show of checking off the DNR box. "Hey, when I'm a vegetable, just pull the plug!"

Emma took a form and put it in her tote bag.

She mentioned always feeling tired to her daughter the next time Elaine came to visit.

"Let's get you checked out," Elaine said and made an appointment with her doctor. "I'll take you."

Emma liked her doctor's appointments because she'd been Dr. Resnick's patient for fifteen years and he always spent time with her, not like that new dermatologist, who was in and out in ten seconds. She made it a point to save some good stories for Dr. Resnick, and he always laughed, even when they were a little risqué, and then told her a couple in return. This time, Dr. Resnick told the nurse to take some blood.

As he started to leave, Emma said to him, "Dr. Resnick, did you ever hear this?" And she took a deep breath before reciting, "I should worry, I should care, I should marry a millionaire. He should die, I should cry, I should marry another guy."

He chuckled. "Don't think I have, Emma. You must have been a feminist way back when."

Elaine looked pleased and patted her hand. "I'm sure she was."

Emma wasn't quite sure how to take that.

The test results came back a few days later.

"You're anemic, Emma," Dr. Resnick told her on the phone.

That was a new one. "So should I take some vitamins?"

"Well, what I'd like you to do is go to the hospital and have some tests."

"Tests?"

"Just covering all the bases."

Emma was furious with Dr. Resnick because not only did he fax the results of the blood tests to the Sunset Hills nursing office, but he called Elaine. Emma was starting to revise her good opinion of him. He had no right calling Elaine—her health wasn't anybody's business except her own. But Elaine drove up from Orange County the next day and insisted on taking her to Cedars, as Dr. Resnick advised. Emma put up a good fight, but she was no match for her daughter.

"Mom, it's only for some tests," Elaine kept saying.

Emma didn't want to tell her that the thought of being in a hospital terrified her. She knew once you went in you didn't come out—she'd seen it happen often enough. The ambulance came, next thing you knew there was an "in loving memory" sign in the front room. Anyway, what was so terrible about being tired? So she'd take some vitamins and nap.

Elaine was frightened, too, but she would never show it in front of her mother. Dr. Resnick would not have ordered the tests if he didn't think they were necessary. While she understood her mother's fear, Elaine didn't see where she had a choice.

After what seemed like an interminable wait, an orderly sat Emma in a wheelchair and pushed her into the E.R., where a nurse took her vital signs and put her in a bed. Emma dozed off.

Elaine sat by the bed, looking at her. Her mother had always been such a force. It pained Elaine to see how fragile and vulnerable she looked as she slept with her mouth open, snoring slightly, her thinning white hair, once chestnut brown and curly, all messed up.

Dr. Resnick finally showed up and said they were going to give her a blood transfusion. "We'll probably keep her overnight," he told Elaine. "You might as well go home."

Elaine felt torn. She wanted to stay—felt a good daughter *should* stay—but on the other hand she was tired and hungry. Hospitals depressed her, and she longed to be in her own surroundings. She leaned down and kissed her mother's forehead, but Emma did not wake up.

It was the middle of the night when Elaine got the call from the hospital. She was so groggy she wasn't able to comprehend it all at first. Something about how during the blood transfusion her mother had suffered cardiac arrest and was now in the ICU.

Emma knew she'd been right—it had been a mistake to come to the hospital. Look where she was now, connected to all kinds of tubes, one even stuck in her throat so she couldn't talk! Everything seemed fuzzy. She could hear the bleep-bleep of monitors and felt a cold, tingling in her arm. She saw a needle stuck in there connected to a hanging bag of what she figured must be some kind of drug.

Slowly, her eyes focused and she saw Joel and Elaine and Dr. Resnick talking by the monitor. She could hear them but she knew they didn't know it. They were talking about Advance Health Care Directives and DNR, the same things that the ombudsman had talked about. Dr. Resnick was holding a paper in his hand.

Suddenly, the fog cleared and Emma found herself absolutely clear-headed. "Don't sign it!" she wanted to cry but she couldn't talk with that damn thing in her throat.

I should worry, I should care, I should marry a millionaire. He should die, I should cry, I should marry another guy.

Now she knew the real meaning of that old jump-rope chant! It wasn't about being a gold-digger, after all. It was about going on, no matter what.

With great effort, Emma managed to raise her hand.

"Look, she's trying to tell us something!" Elaine cried.

Dr. Resnick took a prescription pad and a pen from his white coat and handed it to Emma.

"What is it, Mom? Can you write it down?" Elaine asked.

Emma mustered all her strength and grasped the pen in her hand. Slowly, she printed in large uneven letters "Don't pull the plug!"

Joel and Elaine started to laugh. Then Dr. Resnick joined in. Emma closed her eyes. She felt peaceful and thought back to her dream. She could see the big cafeteria in the sky, and there, sitting at a long table, were Ethel and Dotty and Mary Jane, beckoning her to join them. They were waiting for her.

Sorry to disappoint you, but I still got a lot of living to do, Emma thought, certain that Ethel and Dotty and Mary Jane could read her mind. *But save me a seat anyway,* she added silently.

A CREATURE OF HABIT

I knew it was going to happen sooner or later, but not this way, *so I don't know why I feel like this,* Ofelia wrote in her journal. She put the pen down and tried to think the best way to describe how she felt. Surprised was too soft. Shocked? Sort of. She felt like when she was twelve and went to the bathroom and saw blood on her pants for the first time. Sure, she'd known since she was eight or so that that was what happened to girls, but somehow she never imagined it really happening to *her.* She'd just stared at her panties and burst into tears. Unreal! That was how she felt then, and that was how she felt when Ms. Breur-Gordon made her announcement.

Ofelia picked up the pen. *Well, it's better than the alternative,* she wrote, not even wanting to go into what the alternative was. When you worked in a place like Sunset Hills, it was there all the time, just waiting to get one of the residents. The big "D." The placards that read "In Loving Memory." *Maybe I just need time to get used to it,* she wrote, *but it won't be easy, not after spending three years with Mrs. Breur.*

"Ofelia?" Mrs. Breur's voice sounded sleepy, which was not surprising since it was after midnight.

"I'm coming," Ofelia called. She got up from the couch, which doubled as her bed, and went to the bedroom to see what Mrs. Breur wanted.

Ofelia sat on the edge of the bed. "What is it, Mrs. Breur? Are you feeling okay?"

Mrs. Breur clasped Ofelia's hand in hers. "I want to stay, Ofelia."

"I know," Ofelia said soothingly. "But won't it be nice to live with your daughter? Just think—you'll be able to see her every day."

Mrs. Breur nodded, but her eyes filled with tears. "What about my friends?"

Her words tugged at Ofelia's heart. Mrs. Breur didn't have any real friends at Sunset Hills, just a few ladies who played Scrabble with her, and that was about it.

"I won't be able to even visit or go on any of the outings if I'm up in San Francisco."

"Sure you will. Your daughter will bring you down." Ofelia hated herself for lying, but she didn't know what else to say.

Mrs. Breur knew it wasn't true. She wouldn't be visiting, but she didn't bother arguing. "You don't understand. I'm a creature of habit."

Ofelia nodded. She understood all too well. She, too, was a creature of habit, which was one reason the thought of leaving Mrs. Breur and Sunset Hills was so weird.

She sat by the bed until Mrs. Breur drifted off, then went into the little living area. She put a cup of water into the microwave and took a tea bag out of the cabinet over the sink. When her tea was ready, she took her cup back to the couch and looked at her journal.

A creature of habit, she wrote. *Mrs. Breur doesn't say much but when she does, she makes sense. She really is a smart old lady, but the other residents don't know it because she's so quiet. She's just shy, not like Mrs. Freedman or Mrs. Greenberg or some of the others with their big mouths.* And when she does leave, Ofelia thought, probably no one will miss her. That was the sad part.

Ofelia sipped her tea. She didn't feel like writing anymore so she closed the journal. What else was there to say? When Ofelia took the job as her caregiver, she knew that Mrs. Breur could get sick and die anytime—after all, she was getting close to ninety. What Ofelia hadn't anticipated was that instead of the big "D" taking her away, it would be her daughter.

And that was just what happened. Without any warning. One day last week, Ms. Breur-Gordon came by for lunch, and her mother was very happy to see her, like always. Then, after they'd eaten, Ms. Breur-Gordon suggested they all sit out on the patio since it was a nice warm day. Once they were settled she dropped the bombshell.

"I have some good news," she said to her mother.

Mrs. Breur's eyes lit up. "Tell me."

"I've gotten a promotion."

"That's wonderful, dear. I'm so happy for you," Mrs. Breur said.

"But the thing is, Mother, they're relocating me to San Francisco."

"Oh, no!" Mrs. Breur covered her mouth with her hand. And then she began to cry.

"But listen, Mother, don't cry. I haven't finished. You're coming with me."

That was when Ofelia froze. What exactly did *that* mean? How come Ms. Breur-Gordon hadn't told *her* first? Was she planning to take her along or fire her?

Mrs. Breur didn't seem to get it at first either. "How can I go with you? I live *here*," she said.

Ms. Breur-Gordon took her mother's hands in hers. "Mother, you know I wouldn't leave without you. You'll love the Bay Area. Remember when we took a trip to San Francisco and rode the cable cars and went to Fisherman's Wharf?"

"I remember."

Ofelia didn't recall the rest of the conversation, not that there was much. After a few minutes, Ms. Breur-Gordon looked at her watch and stood up.

"I have a meeting, so I've got to go," she said. "Ofelia, why don't you walk me to the car."

They left Ms. Breur sitting on the patio.

"I know this comes as a surprise," Ms. Breur-Gordon said to Ofelia when they were out on the street.

"Well, yeah."

"I want you to know that although we've sometimes had our differences, Ofelia, I'm grateful for the care you've given mother."

Not that you ever showed it, Ofelia thought. "So you mean you don't want me to go with her?"

Ms. Breur-Gordon gave a fake little laugh. "Not that it wouldn't be nice, but I'll be with mother for dinner and all night. I've looked into it, and the senior center there has wonderful daytime programs. I'm sure she'll make loads of new friends."

Right, Ofelia thought, when hell freezes over. She could just picture little Mrs. Breur introducing herself to a bunch of strangers.

"If you wanted me to still take care of your mother, I could move up there, too."

"That's sweet of you, Ofelia, but there won't be any need for that."

"But you'll be working all day," Ofelia pressed on, not even caring that she was talking back to Ms. Breur-Gordon. "What's your mother supposed to do?"

"I told you, the senior center has programs."

"But what if she doesn't like going there? She's used to me."

"I've considered all of that, Ofelia," Ms. Breur-Gordon said. "You've been a real help, but moving up with us isn't possible. Of course, I'll give you severance pay and a recommendation." Ms. Breur-Gordon pressed a button on her car key, the car lights flashed, and Ofelia heard a little click. "I've got to run."

She took off, leaving Ofelia standing on the sidewalk.

So that was it, after three years. Now what?

"Now what?" Connie asked her. They were sitting across the street in Starbucks. It was Connie's break time, and Mrs. Breur was watching a Clark Gable movie.

Ofelia shrugged.

"Hell, you can get another job like this!" Connie snapped her fingers. "Mr. Elkins's son is looking for someone for him."

"That'll be the day," Ofelia said.

"He's not that bad."

Ofelia sighed. She couldn't imagine taking care of somebody other than Mrs. Breur.

"Or you could be a Buddy here," Connie went on. "You know Carolee is leaving."

"You're always complaining how much you hate it," Ofelia reminded Connie.

"And if you don't want to move back with your mother, you could stay with me," Connie said, ignoring her comment. "The rent's really cheap and we'd have fun."

Ofelia was touched by the offer, but she didn't know what she wanted. It had all happened so fast.

Ms. Breur-Gordon's announcement reminded Ofelia of when she had graduated from high school and suddenly found herself out in the world without her routine. Like Mrs. Breur said about herself, she was also a creature of habit. After graduating, she got a part-time job at a video store and enrolled in junior college, thinking maybe if her grades were good enough, she could transfer to Cal State.

The guidance counselor at the junior college talked to her about picking a course of study and outlined all the options, but the only one that really appealed to Ofelia was the Certified Nursing Assistant program. The counselor asked her why she thought that would be a good career, and Ofelia told her about her volunteer work in a senior facility while she was in high school.

"I really liked going there," she said. "The old people were really nice, and they were so happy to see me it made me feel good. Some of them never had anybody come to visit."

The counselor thought that was a valid reason, and so Ofelia became a CNA. She interviewed at several assisted living and skilled nursing facilities, and a couple of them offered her work. She ended up accepting a job as an aide at Pacific Villa mostly because it wasn't too far from home— only one stop on the Metro.

But being an aide was hard work. It was sure different from being a volunteer. Most of the residents were nice—there were always a few mean or demanding ones—and she was surprised how quickly she became attached to them. The only real bad part was that Karla, the bitch, was the community manager. She was always on the aides' backs, pushing them to the limits, monitoring their breaks and what have you. So when Ms. Breur-Gordon asked her if she would consider working as a live-in caregiver for her mother, Ofelia jumped at it. The pay was better than the corporate cheapskates running Pacific Villa doled out. Plus, she liked little Mrs. Breur.

The main reason Ofelia took the job was that she could finally move out of her mother's house! Not that her mother was a bad person, but she was always after her to do this or do that, like get married. The few times

Ofelia had brought a guy home, her mother found all kinds of things wrong with him. Her mother was no shining example, so she didn't know why she was always on her case. You'd think she'd have learned something! Anyway, Ofelia didn't think she was ready to get married.

So she had said yes to Ms. Breur-Gordon.

And now Ms. Breur-Gordon was dumping her.

When Ofelia told her mother, her reaction was pretty much what she'd expected.

"It's a blessing in disguise," her mother said. "What kind of a life is that for a young woman? Who do you get to meet? Nobody, that's who!"

They were sitting at the kitchen table, having coffee and cake. Ms. Breur-Gordon had taken her mother shopping for the day, leaving Ofelia with time off.

Ofelia felt the old knot in her stomach at her mother's criticism. She couldn't even defend herself because she knew her mother was right.

"You used to have a life! Remember? And friends, and dates. I'll bet your school friends are all married with kids by now."

"And divorced or miserable," Ofelia countered. She felt like saying "you should know, you didn't have such a great one" but she kept her mouth shut. She knew better than to go there.

"Time flies, Ofelia!" her mother said, nervously grabbing a slice of cake and taking a bite. "There're lots of things you can do now, like go back to school. You could go to nursing school, become an RN."

"That costs money," Ofelia pointed out.

"You must've put some away. I don't see what you could've spent it on."

Ofelia had put money in a savings account. Not a fortune, but still, it was something.

"And," her mother went on, "I have some, too, and if I thought you were doing something worthwhile, I could help."

Her mother had never asked her for money, so Ofelia knew she wasn't hurting. She was still working in the school cafeteria, but Ofelia had no clue as to what she might have in the bank.

"Thank you," Ofelia said, really meaning it.

For a moment, her mother's face softened, and she smiled. But then she was back to her usual self. "You know what you've been doing in that job? Burying yourself, that's what!"

Her mother's words hurt mostly, Ofelia realized later, because they were true. She *had* buried herself in Sunset Hills. Mrs. Breur and the residents had become her whole life. Sure, she was friends with Connie, and she socialized with the Buddies and all, but they went home when their shifts ended. They went to parties, to the movies, to the beach, to whatever.

The question Ofelia had to ask herself was, why?

The answer came to her a few days later when Connie told her she had someone she wanted her to meet. Connie had started going out with Victor, a really nice guy who worked at a car dealership, and he had a friend who had broken up with his girlfriend.

"He's one of the nicest guys you could meet, and I thought of you right away," Connie told her.

Ofelia didn't know what to say.

"Come on," Connie said. "Next time Ms. Breur-Gordon takes her mother out, we can go out, the four of us."

Ofelia's heart was hammering away. And suddenly she knew why she had "buried" herself in Sunset Hills. It was safe. She was afraid to be out in the real world! The truth was, she'd been afraid ever since she graduated from high school.

Connie was waiting for her answer. Ofelia's thoughts were racing. What would she wear? She didn't have any really cool clothes. And her hair was a mess. She didn't even know how to act with guys anymore.

"So what do you say?" Connie prodded.

Ofelia tried to sound casual. "Sure. Why not?"

Connie set things up for the following Sunday. Ofelia tried not to think about it, but she was stressed out all week. She wished she had more time so she could lose ten pounds, but she gave up desserts and thought she could see a difference, even if the scale showed only two pounds lighter. Connie gave her a manicure Saturday and lent her a new sweater set.

"You look great," Connie assured her. "Anyway, it's only brunch, not the Oscars!"

Ofelia nodded. It might as well have been the Oscars for the way her stomach was turning over. But on Saturday, Mrs. Breur started coughing, and when Ofelia took her temperature, she saw that she had a slight fever. Ofelia hated herself for feeling happy, but she was.

"Hey, Connie, I'm really sorry," she said. "We'll have to do it another time. I can't leave Mrs. Breur."

Connie just looked at her. "Yeah, okay, whatever."

"At her age a cough could turn into pneumonia," Ofelia said.

"I *said* it's okay," Connie repeated.

That night Ofelia did a lot of thinking after she put Mrs. Breur to bed. She couldn't keep on postponing making plans.

Larry, the community manager, had offered her a job as a Buddy. Ofelia told him she had another offer and would get back to him. The truth was that as comfortable as she was at Sunset Hills and as much as she liked the other residents, she didn't know how much more she could take. Whenever she thought back to the old people she'd really cared about who died, about the mistakes in medications and sloppy care she'd witnessed, the money-hungry policies of corporate that came before the welfare of the old people in their care, she became depressed. Each time something happened, it took a little out of her, and she was afraid if she stayed, pretty soon there'd be nothing left!

If I were in charge, she thought, the residents would be number one. Plain and simple. Good food, fun outings, the best care possible. And that was when Ofelia knew what it was she really wanted most in the world. She wanted to run her own board and care.

She could picture it—a nice little Spanish-style house with a yard and a few bedrooms. Every room would be light and cheerful, and she would do the cooking herself. She fell asleep and dreamed of the house. She would call it Casa Ofelia.

When she woke up the next morning, Ofelia was forced to face the fact that she didn't have the money, no way, to follow her dream. But she decided she would move back home to save on rent, maybe take her mother up on whatever help she could give, and look into the rules and regulations of licensing for board-and-cares. And she would get a job maybe with a caregiving agency and save every cent she earned. One day it would happen. *I earned good karma,* she told herself.

Two weeks later, Mrs. Breur's apartment had been cleaned and her possessions packed and shipped to San Francisco. But it wasn't until the day of the actual move that Ofelia really believed it.

Everyone came to their table at breakfast to say good-bye and wish Mrs. Breur well, and Ofelia was happy to see how good that made her feel. Before they left the table, Ofelia handed her a gift box wrapped in silver paper.

"For me?" Mrs. Breur asked.

Ofelia nodded. "Open it, Mrs. Breur."

Mrs. Breur took a long time getting the ribbon untied and the paper off the white box. Then she opened it.

"Oh, my!" Mrs. Breur exclaimed, as she carefully picked up a silver picture frame. It held a color photograph of the two of them at the Valentine's Day party.

"So you won't forget me," Ofelia said.

Mrs. Breur held the frame to her chest and began to cry. "This is the nicest present I ever had!"

Ofelia was crying, too, as she leaned over and kissed Mrs. Breur's wrinkled cheek.

"I love you, Ofelia."

"And I love you, too."

And Ofelia knew it was true. That was what caregiving was all about.

GOOD KARMA

It wasn't as horrible as Ofelia had imagined. She moved back with her mother, and whenever her mother started in on her, she just tuned out. She'd learned you can't change people. And anyway she'd grown up enough to appreciate how hard her mother worked and that she only wanted the best for her, even if it wasn't her business whom she went out with or what she did when she wasn't working.

She signed up with a registry—better than an agency since you didn't have to pay the registry anything—and to her surprise, they sent her out on four interviews almost immediately. She took a job caring for an elderly man in his home. He was pleasant enough and easy to get along with, and his daughter—who was technically her boss—was also nice. Which wasn't to say that Ofelia didn't sometimes miss Sunset Hills and Mrs. Breur. She planned to go up north to visit, but somehow it never worked out. She did, however, make a point of calling Mrs. Breur every week or so for the first year just to say hi, and Mrs. Breur was always happy to hear from her.

Ofelia got up the courage to go out with Connie's friend, and they all had a good time. She didn't feel any spark like you're supposed to feel, but he was a nice guy, just like Connie said. She told herself it was okay just to go out for the fun of it.

Ofelia didn't forget about the board-and-care, and she saved as much money as she could from her paychecks. Slowly, her little savings account grew, but she knew it was going to be a long time before she even came close. Even so, she couldn't resist looking at photos of houses in the Sunday *Times* real estate section.

Connie continued to fill her in on the latest Sunset Hills news. Most of it was bad. Larry, the community manager, was suddenly fired and nobody knew why. Rumors were flying that he had embezzled or had an affair with Lily, the new receptionist who took Nathan's place when he quit. The worst news was that Mr. Grant had a stroke and was now in a nursing home. Ofelia cried when she heard that. Sunset Hills could never be the same without good old Mr. Grant. Thank God she was out of there.

It was a smoggy summer day almost two years after Mrs. Breur left that Ofelia received a registered letter. She'd never gotten one before, and the first thing she thought was that maybe she'd won the lottery. But the return address was a law firm. Was somebody suing her? Had she done something wrong? Were all her parking tickets paid? Her hands were shaking as she opened the envelope and read the letter from a lawyer.

He was writing to inform her that Mrs. Breur had passed away. Ofelia put the letter down without reading farther and began to cry. Poor Mrs. Breur. Ofelia felt terrible that she hadn't gone up to San Francisco to see her. Why had she put it off? She *should* have gone! She hoped Mrs. Breur hadn't suffered, but the lawyer didn't give any details. Ofelia wondered why Ms. Breur-Gordon hadn't called or written her herself instead of getting a lawyer to do it.

Ofelia cried some more, then blew her nose, wiped her eyes, and picked up the letter. The next paragraph answered the question of why the lawyer was writing her. Mrs. Breur had left her some money.

She couldn't believe the amount. Ofelia pressed the letter close to her heart. She had no idea Mrs. Breur had so much money, but there it was—enough for a down payment on a house for a board-and-care!

And she would call it "Mrs. Breur's Beautiful Board-and-Care."